le Islands

nushu Island

WORLD WAR II
PACIFIC THEATER

PACIFIC OCEAN

Midway Islands

Hawaiian Islands

Pearl Harbor

Honolulu

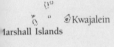

Kwajalein

Marshall Islands

Hokkaido

Makin

Gilbert Islands

Honshu

Tokyo

Hiroshima

Iwakuni

Kyoto

Nagoya

Shimonoseki

Kure

Kobe

Yokosuka

Fukuoka

Osaka

gainville

Nagasaki

Shikoku

Solomon Islands

Kagoshima

Kyushu

Citadel in Spring

Citadel in Spring

A Novel of Youth Spent at War
by Hiroyuki Agawa

Translated by Lawrence Rogers

KODANSHA INTERNATIONAL
Tokyo and New York

Originally published by Shinchosha in 1949 under the title
Haru no shiro.

Distributed in the United States by Kodansha International/
USA Ltd., 114 Fifth Avenue, New York, NY 10011. Published
by Kodansha International Ltd., 17-14, Otowa 1-chome,
Bunkyo-ku, Tokyo 112 and Kodansha International/USA.
Copyright © 1990 by Kodansha International Ltd. All rights
reserved. Printed in Japan.

ISBN 4-7700-1460-0 (Japan)
ISBN 0-87011-960-5 (U.S.)

Library of Congress Cataloging-in-Publication Data

Agawa, Hiroyuki, 1920-
[Haru no shiro. English]
Citadel in spring: a novel of youth spent at war / Hiroyuki
Agawa; translated by Lawrence Rogers.
p. cm.
Translation of: Haru no shiro.
1. World War, 1939–1945—Fiction. 2. Hiroshima-shi
(Japan)—History—Bombardment, 1945—Fiction. I. Title.
PL845.G3H313 1990
895.6'35—dc20   90-45790

Translator's Preface

A comment on the title: the phrase "citadel in spring" is taken from "Spring Prospect" by the T'ang dynasty poet Tu Fu. The poem laments the occupation of the great city of Ch'angan, capital of T'ang China, by a rebel army. It begins:

> The realm is destroyed, yet the mountains and rivers abide;
> The citadel in spring stands deep in tree and grass.

In ancient China the sinograph translated here as "citadel" meant "city," but later came to mean "castle" in Japan. Although the Japanese title *Haru no shiro* could be translated literally as "Castle in Spring," I have taken the liberty of using the word "citadel" in an attempt to encompass both senses, since the word is used in the novel specifically for Hiroshima Castle, and, in the title, becomes a metaphor for the city itself.

I would like to thank the author for explaining a number of terms, especially those related to the old Imperial Navy. I have also profited from discussions with my colleagues George Durham and Richard Howell concerning, respectively, the music festival at the Itsukushima shrine and cryptanalysis. For those readers who wish more information on the latter I recommend David Kahn's *The Code-breakers*. I would also like to thank Laura F. Jones and Shinji Ichiba of Kodansha International for their comments and suggestions. Finally, I want to express my gratitude to my wife, Kazuko Fujihira, for her constant encouragement and support.

Lawrence Rogers
Hilo, Hawaii

One

Their houses in Hiroshima were on the same river. From the Ibuki drawing room, which stood above the stone-lined riverbank, you could drop a line right into the water and fish for little goby. Koji's house was seven or eight blocks upstream, and the white riverbed behind it came alive in summer with children playing in its waters. The glistening granitic sands teemed with shellfish, and if you dove into the deep water along the opposite bank, by the woods which stood on the shrine grounds, you would see crawfish warily moving their pincers among the huge, moss-covered rocks. At flood tide the river there would be engorged bank to bank, its incoming waters laden with discarded wooden clogs and fruit peels. But when the tide ebbed, it became a limpid stream which flowed over the hiding places of crawfish, roach, shellfish, and goby, as it murmured its way toward Hiroshima Bay. When the boat rental shops began to appear along the river it was a sign that spring had come, and the closing of the shops signaled that the city was well into autumn.

Koji Obata was four years younger than Yukio Ibuki. The two of them had been good friends since middle school days, skiing and mountain climbing together, fishing, and taking trips to see plays and visit art galleries. Even now they always returned to Hiroshima during vacations and spent time together. Sometimes Ibuki's younger sister Chieko, who was one year older than Koji, would join them.

For them and those around them, at least, it was still a time of peace. Yet almost every day long columns of soldiers going off to war paraded through the city on their way to Ujina Harbor, stopping the street cars as the heavy thud of their boots kept time with the bugles. But neither Ibuki nor Koji particularly concerned themselves with this—they felt a vague distaste for the military, a distaste Chieko naturally shared. Yet from time to time the young men could not help thinking that the day when they would join those lines of men was slowly drawing nearer.

Koji was studying literature at Tokyo Imperial University, but he was not terribly enthusiastic about his studies. He hoped to become a novelist someday. Yukio Ibuki had graduated in the spring from a college in Osaka and was doing research at the Institute of Microbiological Research. Soon Ibuki was to take his pre-induction physical exam, then an examination for the navy's two-year medical course for active duty officers.

For some time now Koji had thought of Chieko as more than a friend. He liked the unpretentious way she wore her hair in braids, and several times he managed to catch the clean fragrance of her skin, a scent without a trace of make-up. He enjoyed it when she joined in animated conversation with him and her brother, and was delighted whenever she joked with him and teased him with her arch little thrusts.

Chieko, for her part, was fond of Koji, too, but her fondness seemed to grow out of her respect for her scholarly brother, and whenever she began to think of the younger Koji as a possible marriage partner, she always felt an inexplicable resistance to the idea. Koji's feelings were much the same.

Koji himself had never given any serious thought to what he ought to do about his relationship with Chieko, so he simply took pleasure in her company, and their relationship continued unclarified. His friendship with Ibuki helped to stabilize his feelings.

Yet whenever Chieko thought of the reality that her brother, and then Koji, would soon be going off to war, she felt a vague sense of irritation.

Koji's acquaintances, and Chieko's, too, had a general idea of their feelings for each other, and yet no one, not even Ibuki, made mention of it.

* * *

Just before the summer of 1941, in his second year at Tokyo Imperial University, Koji received a letter from his elder brother's home in Manchuria. It was in his sister-in-law's hand.

I suppose you are at your studies every day. No doubt you will soon return to Hiroshima for the summer vacation. We should also like to return to the home islands and visit Mother and Father, whom we have not seen for such a long time. The current situation being what it is, though, the two of us could not possibly just drop everything here to go home.

We saw Mr. Onodera, Director of the South Manchurian Railway, the day before yesterday. He stayed with us one night and then returned to Dairen. As you probably know, he is a cousin of Mrs. Ibuki in Hiroshima. It was a business visit, but we talked about Hiroshima, and then about the Ibukis' eldest daughter and about you as well. We understand that several prospective husbands were suggested to Chieko recently, but she rejected them, and this is causing her parents some concern. Mr. Onodera laughed and said that these days daughters are loath to assent to marriages arranged by their parents. We sensed—and perhaps we are over-reacting—that Mr. Onodera may have come on behalf of Miss Ibuki's parents to inquire roundabout through us what you intend to do regarding Chieko.

Not being with you, we really do not know the state of affairs, but we know that though a man can be carefree about this, a woman of marriageable age most certainly cannot. We are concerned about the fact that she is older than you, but if you intend to actively pursue this course, then Mother and Father, and ourselves as well, could reconsider this. Since we have no children we are certainly not opposed to your marrying a little early.

And so the letter went. Koji put it down with a sense of incredulity. He suddenly felt that he had somehow become an adult now, part of a family, his freedom restricted. They were asking him what he intended to do. Was it wrong, he wondered, to simply relax and enjoy the company of his friend's sister?

He did not relish having to think seriously about marriage so soon. First of all, it seemed to him that he had no reason to believe that Chieko herself was thinking along those lines. In fact, just a few days earlier he had received a casual note from her, and there was, of course, not the slightest hint of anything of the sort in it.

He left his lodgings in the afternoon, the letter in his briefcase. His friend Ishikawa was stopping off in Tokyo on his way back from Hokkaido and they had agreed to meet that evening on the Ginza. Ishikawa was a medical student at the University of Hokkaido and had been a classmate of Ibuki's in middle school, and he and Koji had been close friends since childhood.

Somehow Koji did not feel up to going to the campus before his meeting with his friend. Apart from the question of Chieko, lately he'd been in a constant state of apathy. He had entered the Department of Japanese Literature at the suggestion of Mr. Yashiro, one of his teachers at his high school in Hiroshima, but he could generate absolutely no interest in the lectures at the university. He had been attracted to a course entitled "The Literary Environment of Medieval Japan," but when he attended a lecture he found the professor earnestly belaboring the obvious.

"Hail. Defined in the ancient dictionary *Wamyosho* as frozen rain. Forest. Forest means a place having many trees. Grove. A grove refers to a place that has somewhat fewer trees than a forest." The students conscientiously took this all down.

Kurimura, a friend who was also a student in the Department of Japanese Literature, had tried to cure him of his boredom by telling him what it was like to go to the "immoral areas," as they were called.

"It's bad for your health to hang around here all the time," he had said. "Go on. You just go in like you own the place. It's as simple as going to an *oden* restaurant for the first time. And it'll clear your head."

Koji recalled his friend's advice as he passed through the great gate of the Yoshiwara prostitution district, which he knew about only from novels. He went twice. Neither time, however, did he return home feeling it was something that he could abandon himself to.

He was looking for something that he could confront openly, something—immoral or not—that could really engage his emotions, but he was utterly unable to find it.

* * *

Ishikawa was leaning against the entrance to the subway reading the evening paper. He was very nearsighted, and kept his eyes fixed on the paper until Koji had come up right under his nose and spoken to him.

It was a sunny spell during the rainy season and the streets of the Ginza were full of people out for a stroll. Joining the crowds, the two friends began walking toward Shimbashi.

Married couples loaded down with shopping bundles. University students and their girlfriends. Saucy-looking little girls. Office workers swiftly cutting their way through the columns of people. Shoulders jostling shoulders again and again. A Westerner with an Eyemo camera on a wooden-legged tripod threaded his way through the crush of people, stopping from time to time to trip his shutter at the passers-by. The lamps in the streetlights came on, clear and colorless as water.

Ishikawa looked back at the man with the camera. "He's going around taking pictures to show what wartime Tokyo is like."

"Uh-huh." Koji was wondering where they could eat. "Where'll we go?"

"Well," Ishikawa asked, "how about some Western food?"

"Okay, let's," said Koji. "Hey, it's going to be tough for you going all the way back to Hiroshima by train tonight."

"No, no," Ishikawa said, "Nothing to it. The porter will give me a third-class sleeper if I put a little money in his hand. I'll sleep all the way. You want to go back with me?"

"I'm going back in another week or so," Koji answered.

They went into Lohmeyer's, a basement restaurant. The ceiling was low, and large painted pipes ran along the wall, giving Koji the impression that they were on a steamship or man-of-war. He mentioned this to his companion.

"That reminds me," Ishikawa responded, "I hear Ibuki has gotten into the navy's short-term active duty program."

"Oh, he has? I think he made the right move. It's better than the army, at least."

"Really? Yet it seems to me that if I have to go I'd rather join the navy, but a literature major is useless in the Paymaster's Office, and there's really nothing else I can do."

"They'd probably take you as a seaman, if that's what you want," said Ishikawa, "but I hear they whack your butt with a rope."

"Well, what'll you do?" Koji asked his friend.

"I don't want to have anything to do with either of them," Ishikawa answered. "You're the kind of guy who'd rush his graduation in order to fight, so I'll tell you something right now. Try your damnedest to stay alive. If they order you to charge, make a break for the rear if you can. As for a glorious death in battle, a man who's killed is just a poor sap. You can count me out."

"You've got it all figured out," responded Koji, "but I can't quite see it your way. I really don't know what to do."

"What's to be confused about? You certainly can't tell me it's a just war. In any case, I want no part of it. I'm going to keep failing my courses and staying in school as long as I can."

The two of them continued in this vein as they ate, their voices lowered so as not to be overheard by those around them.

Koji suddenly felt a hand seize his shoulder. Startled, he turned around to see Tanii, a friend majoring in Japanese literature, standing behind him.

"Damn! Don't do that!" Koji rebuked his friend. "Can't you see you scared me to death? What is it?"

"Sorry, sorry," said Tanii hurriedly, "I was just on my way out after dinner with my family when I noticed you were here. But you're with someone, aren't you. I'll see you later."

"No. Sit down with us. We'll all leave together."

"No, I'm with my family, so I'll—"

"Oh, come on," persisted Koji, angry at having been startled. "Sit down."

"Oh, okay, then, I'll tell them to go on ahead," Tanii said, and left.

"Who's that?" asked Ishikawa, glancing up at the departing Tanii as he cut his meat.

"The most congenial friend I have at the university. He's a connoisseur of the theater and such a naive brat that everyone calls him a *botchan*."

"If *you* call him a *botchan* he must really be green," said Ishikawa, and the two young men laughed.

Tanii returned, sat down beside them, and began smoking a cigarette.

"Hey, you know Helmick?" he began. He was talking about an American, born in Japan, who was a year ahead of them in the Department of Japanese Literature at Tokyo Imperial University. "He was talking big to the owner of a second-hand bookstore in Kanda yesterday. 'If a war starts between Japan and America,' he says, 'I'm going straight back to the States to join up.'"

"He did, did he?" said Ishikawa. "So America has its share of idiots too."

Tanii stared dumbly at Ishikawa, an expression of astonishment on his face. Koji laughed and introduced the two men to each other.

*   *   *

That night, Ishikawa went back to Hiroshima on the express train. Koji decided he would return home after attending two more sessions of his Chinese class. He had taken the course more on impulse than anything else, yet now it was the only course at the university he had the slightest interest in. The students in the class,

13

each a little self-consciously, imitated the teacher's pronunciation, their mouths gaping wide like so many grammar school pupils at their lesson. Koji felt at home with this new foreign language, which was falling into place for him little by little. It was much more safisfying than the incomprehensible, purely theoretical lectures he encountered in his other courses.

The instructor, Mr. Chu, had been born in Beijing and his pronunciation of the tongue-twisting Mandarin dialect was absolutely flawless. He was a tall, spare man with a dark complexion. One day he wrote a string of words down the blackboard: "Peihai Park," "Tungtan," "cooked wheat cakes," and so on, and began to talk proudly of the city of Beijing. Then he wrote the word "Shanghai," mumbling something to himself. After that he wrote "Americanized" next to it and quickly crossed it all out. His dark face flushed red.

Mr. Chu blushed a lot. When they asked each other questions about their families in the conversation period, he would turn red as a beet when talking about his own. As Koji watched him, he thought of his high school teacher, Mr. Yashiro, who often blushed the same way.

Mr. Chu's class always ended at 4:30. He would bow farewell to his students, leave the classroom, and, with his well-worn black leather briefcase under his arm, light the inevitable cigarette. Then he would stroll alone along the road lined with ginkgo trees to the main gate of the campus. He was a strangely melancholy figure. Koji sometimes wondered to himself what the professor thought of the war that Japan and his country were bogged down in.

Koji went back to visit Hiroshima at the beginning of July. He always enjoyed watching the different scenes pass by as the train drew near the city. The train, its brakes squealing, described gigantic arcs again and again as it swung down through the long mountain pass. Then the arcs would give way to gentle curves as the train traveled along the river through a cut at the foot of a bluff. Vineyards would come into view on his right. Station signs whipped past the window facing the mountains. As the train approached the harbor, the conductor would come and lower the shades of the windows on the ocean side to hide the military transports from view. A huge building, a brewery in the middle of a field, appeared. Beyond it, Mount Gosasau, which Koji had climbed many times with Ibuki and Ishikawa. The whitish surface of the mountain. Newly planted rice paddies. A long marshaling yard on the far side of a railway bridge. A light locomotive making its steam sounds as it shunted freight cars. More locomotives. Huge crossings. The sound of bells. The train's speed would slacken. And then they would arrive at the familiar platform in the station.

The city of Hiroshima was beautiful at the end of the rainy season. Koji knew of rivers that turned into shallow streams at low tide, exposing their sandy beds. At flood tide they were transformed into deep, green pools of high water. Each of the many rivers would be full of swimming children.

* * *

That spring, Mr. Yashiro had decided that the house he was renting by the foul-smelling drainage ditch behind the high school was not a healthy place to raise his two children, so he had moved his family to a house near the heart of the city. Koji went to visit his former teacher at his new home.

Mr. Yashiro was a student of the *Man'yoshu*, the ancient Japanese poetry anthology, and books and journals on poetics stood in piles all over his study. When Koji arrived, two students from the high school were there talking with Mr. Yashiro over food and saké.

"I went to the Buttsu Temple the other day," he was saying, "and found it rather pleasant. I admire the Obaku sect too—you know the passage written on the sounding board in the temple dining hall, 'With deference we address this assembly'?" Taking pencil and paper in hand, he wrote it out for them. *Vital to salvation the cycle of life and death, impermanent and swift. Be circumspect and not wanting in restraint.* "Very well put, I'd say."

His wife brought in chopsticks and a plate of food for Koji. His son, six, and the daughter, four, followed her, circling the table again and again.

15

"Have whatever you like, if you've an appetite," he told Koji. He poured saké into his own drinking cup and poked at the vinegared bean paste with a piece of lettuce.

"Colleges these days," he went on, "make the exaggerated claim that their dormitories are just like home, but the truth is it's important for a man to live now and again where he can breathe undomesticated air, completely free of womanish influences."

"When we graduate and go into the army," said Koji, "that'll happen soon enough."

"Right you are," the teacher replied, forcing a smile. He changed the subject. "Obata, are you working on your senior thesis now?"

"No, I haven't done anything yet," Koji answered. "Somehow I've lost all interest in my lectures and seminars, although I never had that problem when I took courses from you. I tell people I'm writing a novel, but that and everything else seems like wasted effort now when I realize I'll be going straight into the service in two years."

The teacher chose not to respond to that, but continued: "Most students like to grapple with a grand theme when they write their senior thesis, but it's better to get a firm grasp on something modest, as long as it's worthwhile, and write a solid paper."

"But is it true," asked Koji, "that the students in Japanese literature at the University get better grades if they write long senior theses, the kind you have to trundle about in a wheelbarrow?"

"True or not, it's beside the point," said the teacher. "It's *your* work, after all. It's stupid just to put on a empty show."

Mr. Yashiro often went to student gatherings and listened with pleasure to the naive discussions. He was on friendly terms with Ibuki, and Chieko knew him through his outside teaching. Naturally Ibuki's decision to join the navy came up in their conversation that day.

The letter from his sister-in-law in Manchuria had made Koji reluctant to visit the Ibuki household very often. Most of the time he chose to invite Ibuki and Ishikawa out with him instead.

One day in August the three of them met at the small house on the outskirts of town that Ishikawa was renting for the summer. They were going saltwater fishing. They got their gear in order and set off.

"You know, when I had my physical exam," Ibuki said as they walked along, "I realized that even in the military guys from Osaka are a little strange. The examining officer, a lieutenant colonel, leaned toward me and said quietly in his heavy dialect: 'You'll be classified 1-B. Graduated from Osaka University, right? Are you doing some kind of research? Used to be you didn't have to go if you were 1-B, but times being what they are, reckon you'll have to go. More's the pity.' He was really comical."

The three young men laughed, then Ishikawa turned to Ibuki.

"I was telling Obata the other day. Once a man joins the navy he's there for quite a while. Why didn't you try to postpone graduation a little longer?"

"Of course I'd rather be in a lab at the Institute fiddling with a centrifuge and growing cultures than on a warship treating sailors for V.D. But what's the point? Sooner or later you have to go in."

"You know, being on a ship," interjected Koji, "that has a certain appeal."

"Sail around the world at government expense, like an American sailor, eh?" asked Ishikawa. "I doubt you'd be so lucky."

"But I'd like to be able to see the research I've started take shape before I go," continued Ibuki. "You hear that you have more free time when you're at sea and can read. Don't believe it. I asked someone who knows and he said it wasn't true. What they actually do is drink saké and read old war stories. When I come back, I'll have to start again from square one."

The three young men sat down on the stone seawall and dropped their lines into the water.

The wind blew constantly, so the sweat did not stay on their skin, and they faced a fierce sun that seemed to scorch their skin parchment dry. The tide was starting to come in and they could hear the sound of the waves slapping monotonously against the seawall. Ibuki wore a straw hat on his now-shaven head.

Koji felt a bit ill at ease when he was with Ibuki. Ibuki had decided to go into the service this winter, so it would be awkward to go on ignoring the question of Chieko. Yet the truth was, Koji was not sure of his own feelings and so had nothing in particular he wanted to say.

The huge silhouette of the island of Itsukushima was visible immediately to the west. Far to the east were shipyard buildings, and rows of houses on the south side of Hiroshima shining in the summer sun. As always, five or six ash-grey army transports sat in the harbor. One, its funnels belching black smoke, slowly turned its bow right, and right again, heading out to sea. A hectic white wake, incongruous behind the gentle movement of the hull, seethed relentlessly at the stern. Countless khaki specks, scarcely visible in the distance, clustered around the flag at the stern and on its upper decks.

Nearby a train passed by on tracks that skirted the water's edge, shaking the ground under them for some time.

Now and again Ibuki caught gilthead fry, but Koji had no luck at all. All he had in his creel was a single goby three inches long. He was using small crabs for bait. He would feel a tug at his line and jerk his pole up, but each time all that would be left on the end of his hook was a thin crab shell. They had placed the bait box in the shade, but even so a lot of the crabs, which they had sprinkled with sand, had died from the heat, and lay white underside up.

Koji had resigned himself to not catching anything. His eyes vacantly followed the progress of the transport steaming out of the harbor, but his mind was on other things. He was feeling vaguely depressed.

"We're not doing so well," said Ibuki.

"Best forget it," said a voice behind them. They turned to see a fisherman, his wrinkled face sea-burned and ruddy. He was carrying a large sea bream.

"Red tide's in, so you aren't gonna catch nothing."

"Let's quit and go home," said Ishikawa, who hadn't been doing any better.

* * *

Koji visited Mr. Yashiro's home often during the summer vacation, partly because he felt uneasy about visiting the Ibuki house.

His former teacher talked about the *Okagami*, an old historical tale, suggested he read the historical novels of Ogai Mori, and chatted about Cézanne and the poems of Han Shan. And now and again he would say something disparaging about the army.

Whenever Koji's face betrayed his listlessness, the teacher would matter-of-factly tell his wife to prepare some food for them and he himself would bring a small amount of saké into the study. If Koji were in high spirits and prattling on in a shallow vein, Mr. Yashiro, stammering slightly, would reproach him diffidently. Walking back home through the ever-cloudless summer evening, Koji would somehow sense in himself a new-found courage. Of course, this courage never lasted long.

Koji always went to a news theater when he was downtown. Among the grey and gloomy images, he saw the bearded face of a soldier laboriously hiking up a mountain road deep in the mountains of Shansi, a disassembled weapon on his back, and a sailor busily waving his signal flags on a destroyer buffeted by the waves of the South China Sea. These scenes would bring tears to his eyes. Countless Japanese were doing their utmost in the face of great adversity. If all this were really benefiting the nation, he thought, then obviously he could not stand aloof in the self-serving way that Ishikawa had suggested. He would simply have to set his mind to it, go into the service and become an outstanding soldier. And yet sometimes he found himself wondering if what was happening was right, if it was really best for the country. Above all, the thought of dying made his blood run cold.

From time to time he would stand and watch the columns of soldiers in full battle dress march through Hiroshima to Ujina Harbor, thinking to himself that a good percentage of them would die soon. Which of these men will be killed, he wondered.

And he knew that regardless of what happened to them, he, too, would be going off in two years, and this left him with a curious lack of interest in attending the university or studying literature. He could only look upon his life now as something equivocal and half-baked.

Koji's father had formally withdrawn from his business in Manchuria and now stayed at home playing *go* or working in his vegetable garden. Koji spent his idle summer days going out with his parents to eat sweetfish and swimming in the rivers of Hiroshima and in the bay.

Hiroshima was beautiful that summer. The sun shining or hiding behind clouds, the water sparkling, the sound of the waves, evening showers suddenly sweeping down a mountainside and obscuring its peak. He was in good spirits when his mind could free itself of the army and of Chieko. He received a letter from his elder brother in Manchuria inviting him for a visit, but he put that off until next year. As it turned out, he saw practically nothing of Chieko that summer and in September went back to his lodgings in Tokyo.

* * *

One could now sense, even from the censored stories in the newspapers, that relations between Japan and the U.S. were evolving toward a difficult stage. Near the end of August Koji read a report that Ambassador Nomura, who was in America, had delivered a message to President Roosevelt from Prime Minister Konoe regarding the problems in the Pacific. Later Koji frequently heard rumors that Konoe was holding secret talks with Roosevelt on a warship somewhere, or that he would hold them soon.

An Air Defense Agency and a Territorial Agency were created in the Ministry of Home Affairs, and a unit known as the Defense Command was also established. One could sense a nebulous unease beginning to spread over Japan like a storm cloud, a dilatory, ill-defined force which at any moment could begin its terrifying, ever-accelerating descent.

Would there be a new World War? Where would the Japanese fleet attack? What sort of action might the American fleet take? Would B-17s bomb Tokyo immediately? Did Japan, which seemed to be short of just about everything in its long conflict with China, really have the necessary resources? In the end, Koji's ruminations never rose above the level of an adventure story.

As though a reflection of this unease, it was suddenly announced that the graduation dates of all students in Japan had been moved up.

Koji and his friends learned of it in October while they were at military barracks at Narashino, where they had gone for field training. A student ran officiously from barracks to barracks spreading the news. Those who were scheduled to graduate next spring would be graduated this year in December. Koji and those who were supposed to graduate in the spring of 1943, the year after next, would be graduated the summer or fall of next year, 1942. Pandemonium reigned briefly, but gradually the students quieted down.

The student in the bunk next to Koji's, a junior majoring in French literature, grimaced as though he had been informed he had stomach cancer. Wordlessly, he kicked under his blanket, then pulled it up over his head. But the news was not that much of a shock to Koji.

It was from about this time that he began to receive an occasional letter from Chieko. Her letters reproached him for not visiting the Ibuki home during the summer vacation. It seemed to Koji now that if he were to indicate even the slightest suggestion of pursuit, Chieko would most certainly react negatively, and this depressed him. When he was in high school Koji heard through the grapevine that one of his friends had ridiculed their relationship, saying that Koji and Chieko were playing a game of rejecting and being rejected. Koji now felt that they could no longer play the game. If the two of them did not intend to marry, they would have to have a serious talk about their heretofore easygoing relationship and come to a decision by the time Ibuki, who served as the bridge for their feelings, went into the service. Having read his sister-in-law's letter, he could well imagine the concern of Ibuki and Ibuki's parents.

Another letter arrived from Chieko in the middle of October. She wrote that her brother's induction had finally been set for early November and would be at the Naval Medical College in Tokyo's

Tsukiji district. Because he would work in his lab up to the last moment, however, he would not return to Hiroshima, but go straight on to Tokyo after tying up loose ends and making the necessary arrangements at his uncle's place in Osaka's Sumiyoshi district. Since it appeared that once he went in they would have no chance to see him for some time, she and her father would soon go to Osaka to see her brother off. Chieko wondered if Koji wouldn't mind coming to Osaka, too, if he could. Her father wanted very much to see him. If he were able to come, she would send him a telegram as soon as a date was decided on.

This seemed to Koji an excellent opportunity. He sent her a reply agreeing to come. A telegram arrived saying they would be waiting at Osaka Station the morning of the 17th. Koji immediately sent off a telegram informing her of his arrival time, and departed Tokyo for Osaka on the 16th.

Koji stood in the vestibule between cars as the train left the station platform. As the train passed through the Yurakucho area of the capital, he could see the yellow lights of the illuminated news sign blinking a message leftward around the face of the Asahi News building. It informed him that the second Konoe cabinet had resigned en masse.

The train was relatively uncrowded. He pictured Chieko's face. She would be riding toward Osaka on the Sanyo line about now. Over and over again Koji thought to himself, not without a sense of pathos, that come tomorrow he would be parting from both Chieko and his old and good friend Ibuki.

He woke from a light sleep at Maibara. At daybreak he washed his face, went into the dining car and ate breakfast, staring outside at the scenery, wet with the mists of morning. Koji's express arrived in Osaka at 8:30.

* * *

Chieko was waiting for him at the west exit, standing on tiptoe, as tall as her small frame would allow. Their eyes met at once.

Chieko smiled at him, but her body was tense. Koji's face stiffened in response. The tip of one white *tabi* was soiled. Someone had apparently stepped on her foot.

Ibuki's father was at the other exit scrutinizing the waves of people leaving the train. Once together, the three of them walked to a nearby hotel where Chieko and her father had left their luggage.

"My brother and niece are also arriving tonight," said Chieko's father, "and we're having a farewell party for Yukio. Why don't you join us?"

Ibuki had met Chieko and his father at the station early that morning, then gone off to attend to some business.

When they entered the hotel room, Chieko's father sat down without taking off his overcoat.

"Thanks for coming. Make yourself at home," he said, motioning toward a chair. "You've had breakfast?" He lighted a cigar.

The three of them were silent for a while, then Chieko's father spoke.

"As a matter of fact, I want to talk to you about her." He indicated Chieko with a thrust of his chin.

"Your relationship with her seems to have gotten—how shall I put it—progressively more involved. She refuses to consider any of the eligible men I suggest and so I'm going to have to ask you to decide once and for all just what you intend to do."

"Yes, I . . . ," Koji began, but the strangeness of it all left him speechless.

Chieko looked embarrassed. "Father, please!" she interjected, but he hushed her and she said no more.

The three of them proceeded to have a somewhat meandering conversation for about an hour, then went out together. Chieko's father left, promising to meet them again at six in the evening in the waiting room at Osaka Station. Now they were alone.

"Let me carry that," said Chieko. It bothered her that Koji was carrying his briefcase and she offered to take it several times. It struck Koji as odd that Chieko, who had always played the role of the spirited elder sister, was acting quite differently now.

23

To pass the time they walked along the river to Yodoyabashi, then took the subway to the zoo. It was not very crowded, but they could find no place where they could talk.

"I like that one," said Chieko, stopping Koji at the cage of a snow-white snake that was deathly still.

"I think there's something sinister about it," Koji said. "I don't like it." In fact it struck him as unearthly.

They had been waiting for lunch-time. They went to Kitahama by streetcar, entered a restaurant serving Western-style food, took seats in a corner of the room, and were finally able to relax a bit.

"You must have hated it when Father talked to you like that."

Koji gave their order to the waiter.

"It didn't bother me, but I couldn't give him an answer. Actually, I came down here because I thought that your brother's going into the service was a good opportunity for us to clarify our relationship."

Chieko nodded.

"I'm not sure where I should begin," said Koji. "First of all, you have no intention of marrying either, do you?"

Chieko put down the spoon she was holding and looked at him.

"If I did not, I would not have come to Osaka today."

Koji was stunned. He realized instantly he had been stupid. He felt his mind whirling.

* * *

In the afternoon they strolled through the pines at Ashiya and returned to Osaka's Umeda district before the agreed-upon time.

Chieko told him uneasily, in an uncharacteristically feminine tone, how she had arrived at the decision to marry, about the situation at home, and how her feelings for him had evolved. Koji felt within himself a confused mixture of exhilaration and an oppressive sense of responsibility. He promised Chieko that he would think things over once more and meet her again tomorrow in Kyoto, where he planned to spend the night.

Her father came by before long, and on his heels came her uncle, who sat on the Osaka Stock Exchange. The uncle brandished several evening newspapers at them.

"Well, this settles it," he began in his Osaka patois. "General Tojo has received the Imperial mandate to form a cabinet. This is really awful. Everyone says it finally means war."

They looked at one another in amazement.

Just then Ibuki arrived, late. His uncle took them to an oyster boat restaurant on the river. An air-raid drill was going on and the city was pitch black.

The talk of war did not abate even after they were seated.

"The question is," began Chieko's uncle again, "how long can we fight America on even terms? How soon will they out-produce us? If we bungle it, I tell you there'll be hell to pay."

"But will there really be a war?" Ibuki asked. "They say that the navy is against it."

"And we're having all sorts of shortages because of the fighting in China," said Koji. "Are we really up to the awesome demands of such an encounter?"

"That's exactly what I mean," Chieko's uncle answered. "But our stockpiles of war munitions now are really something. The navy is secretly building the biggest damned ship in the world. Even blabbing about it could get me this," he said, putting his hands together behind him as though manacled. "And there's going to be a round-up of Reds pretty soon, too."

It was a little early in the season for oysters. They had *sashimi* and some side dishes. Chieko said nothing, occasionally sipping her saké.

They left the oyster boat a little before nine.

The uncle departed immediately for Sumiyoshi, and Chieko and her father went back to the hotel. Koji walked toward Osaka Station with Ibuki, who would return to his room in Nishinomiya. The sky was overcast and the streets were dark and cold.

"They say once you go into the Naval Medical College you're forbidden to go out or have visitors for some time," said Ibuki.

Koji nodded. They walked along saying little. When they came to the gate for the Hanshin trains, Ibuki broke the silence.

"Well, take it easy." He was trying to make the parting a casual one.

Koji quickened his pace briefly and called to his friend to stop. Ibuki looked back over his shoulder as he walked on.

"It's okay. Don't worry," Ibuki said. "Just make sure there're no loose ends."

He waved his thin magazine at Koji, took out his railway pass, and walked briskly toward the ticket-taker's gate.

*　*　*

Koji returned to Tokyo three days later.

He had met Chieko in Kyoto and turned down her proposal.

In his room the night before in Kyoto his thinking had been uncertain, but a voice within him sounded again and again like the beat of a drum: *Don't! Don't! Don't! Your youth lies yet ahead of you. There are plenty of beautiful women and there is so much to enjoy. Don't! Don't! Don't!* beat the drum.

Chieko had closed her eyes for a moment.

"I understand. Thank you. Well then, I'll be going back to Hiroshima."

Koji had suddenly pulled her to him and kissed her hard on the lips. A sweet sensation, as fragrant as a flower, had spread throughout his body.

Koji went back to Tokyo, only to be tormented by the affection he still felt for her. He felt as though he had made a damnable mess of everything, as though he were filled with all sorts of vague, conflicting impulses. He hated the feeling.

He received a special-delivery letter from Chieko saying she was coming to Tokyo and wanted to meet him just one more time. Koji remembered what Ibuki had said about no loose ends and forced himself to write a letter declining to meet with her.

By now it was late November, 1941.

Koji went out drinking a good deal with two college friends, Tanii and Kurimura. One night when they had had a few too many, strolling along the moat surrounding the Imperial Palace, they were jostled by two young army officers.

"Hey, you! Student!" said one of them as he grabbed hold of Koji's shoulder. The officers were drunk too. "We, all of us, have dedicated our lives to His Imperial Majesty. There is no difference between us when it comes to that. Am I right?"

The students said nothing.

"Hey! Can't you answer me?" His sword, caught by his boot, clanked noisily.

"To His Imperial Majesty!"

"Right," said Koji, "let's dedicate our lives. We shall not lose!"

"Good! Shake!"

The young officer gave Koji's hand a painful squeeze with his hardened, huge hand. The two officers then went off humming a martial tune.

Eight days later, the war in the Pacific began with the surprise attack on Hawaii.

The main force of both America's Pacific Fleet and England's Eastern Fleet were annihilated in a matter of days. The American air force in the Philippines, which had been prepared to attack the home islands of Japan, was dealt a crushing blow before it could get off the ground. News of astounding triumphs was endless. All Japan seemed to seethe with excitement and high emotion.

Even Koji's confused state of mind became crystal clear once the war started. He began to feel that he was really capable of giving up his life, at least in this struggle. He looked upon it as both a duty and an honor for young men like himself.

A sailor with a moustache, a big man, strutted proudly along the Ginza, his cap at a rakish tilt. The Japanese Imperial Navy, which until now had been quietly devoting itself to exercises, was now beginning to be thought of as a force to be reckoned with.

Koji and his friends were always gathering at one another's houses and talking endlessly about the war.

Singapore fell at the beginning of the year, and while Koji was home in Hiroshima during the spring vacation he read in the newspaper a story told by an English sailor who had survived the sinking of the *Prince of Wales*. Fleet Admiral Sir Thomas Phillips, commander in chief of Britain's Eastern Fleet, stayed on the bridge all the while the *Prince of Wales* was under attack, and as the ship was about to go down a destroyer drew alongside signaling that it wished to take him aboard. His response: "No, thank you." He raised his hand in salute and, together with the ship's captain, accepted the ship's destiny as his own. Koji was exhilarated and inspired by the story.

He brought this mood of martial excitement into Mr. Yashiro's house as well. His teacher, however, urged him to concentrate on his studies.

"What a disaster if you ended up abandoning your senior thesis because you became distracted by the war."

Mr. Yashiro told him the story of when Shoin Yoshida, the 19th-century scholar-patriot, was in jail. Yoshida had begun lecturing his cellmates on the *Analects of Confucius*. Saying that they were to be executed the next day, the cellmates demanded he stop. But Yoshida pointed out that in spite of their scheduled execution the next day they were still eating. Ethics, he told them, were more precious than food, and he continued his lecture.

Nevertheless, the war completely occupied Koji's thoughts. Since his and his friends' graduation had been moved up, after the summer vacation they would immediately be transformed from students into soldiers.

Koji passed his pre-induction physical examination and was given the highest classification. The student reserves had been established and so the way was now open for those in literature to become naval midshipmen. He gave up thinking about his depressing, soon-to-be-cut-short student routine and fantasized about life in the navy, which he imagined as a surfeit of dazzling sunlight, sparkling waters, rigorous precepts, and singleminded self-sacrifice.

His friend Ibuki had completed his two months of training at the Medical College and been commissioned a lieutenant junior grade. He had been assigned to an aircraft carrier and was said to be sailing outside of home waters, but Koji had no concrete information.

For Koji, the restless days bridging spring and summer went by with the flow of war.

Two

Koji spent the last two weeks of summer that year at his elder brother's home in Antung, Manchuria. It was his last vacation as a student. He would be going into the military soon, so he was able to enjoy those two weeks in luxurious idleness, being fussed over by his brother, his sister-in-law, his father, who had come with him, and everyone else there.

When he and his elderly father left Manchuria, his sister-in-law and her children, whom he had gotten to know during his stay, all came to the station to see him off. The Pusan-bound express, already dirty from its long journey from Changchun, had been held up for some time in the station on the Korea-Manchurian border for customs inspection. Well-wishers crowded around the compartment window. Koji's father sat in his seat smoking a cigarette. Koji hurriedly ran about getting a porter to take the luggage, greeting those who had come to see him off, and conversing with his brother and sister-in-law.

Customs officials and train conductors went back and forth along the platform. Chinese vendors walked from window to window hawking their wares. A tall girl nicknamed O-Chu, daughter of the local branch manager of a large trading company, gave a gift-wrapped package to Koji.

"Here you are. A farewell present."

As he took the present from her, she threw her shoulders back and asked familiarly, "Who is really taller, I wonder, Koji or me?"

"I'll grant you you're on the lanky side, O-Chu, but I'm still taller than you." He stood next to her for a moment so they could all see. Everyone burst into good-natured laughter.

"You're probably right," said O-Chu, nodding. "I'll bet you'll look fine in a navy uniform."

Things were done here as befitted a colony, the "current situation," as it was called, notwithstanding. Even married women, by and large, were dressed in florid, gay attire. The social scene for the small elite of this small town consisted of welcoming parties for people arriving from the home islands and send-offs for those going away. Koji had been introduced to O-Chu at the golf course and had seen her several times during his stay.

The departure bell rang. Once again people briefly bustled about on the station platform.

"Well, let's shake." O-Chu held out her hand to Koji. Koji's brother and his wife were smiling. As the train began to move everyone waved their handkerchiefs. Gradually they receded into the distance.

The train left the station behind, crossed the railway bridge over the Yalu River, and began its run southward. Koji's compartment was full: a military man, a continental adventurer, and a woman who looked like she might be a bar girl or a geisha. Huge pieces of luggage were piled up in the aisle. The place was filthy with tobacco smoke and scraps of food. From time to time Koji visited his father, who was in a first-class compartment. They would eat the sandwiches his sister-in-law had made for them and drink whiskey.

"You enjoyed yourself this time and were finally able to do whatever you wanted to, which must have been satisfying," said his father. "I don't suppose you'll leave with any regrets now."

"I guess not. . . . Will you come to Tokyo for my graduation?"

"I will. And I'll bring your mother along, too."

The express ran on through the night, passing through Pyongyang, Seoul, and Taejon.

The sky was clear over Pusan, but a day earlier a typhoon had come across from Kyushu through Yamaguchi prefecture in southern Japan and caused the cancellation of the last night's connecting ferry, so there was a terrible crush of people at the dock. Since Koji's father was getting on in years and could not move quickly, they found themselves quite far back in line. As boarding started the line of people would move, then stop, move a little, then stop again. Enough passengers to fill three boats were eventually sent onto the one ferry. The military police manning the gate finally shut it when Koji was about tenth in line from the boat.

Military police, regular police, and men in civilian clothes who were obviously detectives were watching everyone very carefully. From time to time a Korean or a student who didn't have his hair close-cropped was called out of line and made to open his trunk, or have his fruit basket poked into.

Koji and his father were forced to rest at an inn until evening and finally boarded the *Koan Maru* that night.

The boat left the dock and Koji waited for the restricted period to end. As an anti-espionage precaution, passengers were not permitted on deck during that time. When the signal was given, he worked his way through the people who were lying almost on top of one another amid the luggage, and went up on deck to enjoy the cool evening air. His father had become exhausted and was fast asleep below deck.

On deck, he could see that the ship's lights had all been turned off. It was deserted and quiet. Thick black smoke, visible in the darkness of this beautiful, starry night, the sort that follows a storm, billowed up out of the ship's funnel and trailed off into wisps hanging low over the arrow-straight, faintly whitish wake. Tiny flecks of cinder dappled Koji's hair and shoulders. The meager lights of Pusan blinked far behind.

High atop the ship's mast a single light swayed lazily as the boat itself swayed. Koji imagined himself as he would doubtless be one year later, standing on deck at night, a naval officer attending to his pressing duties. It was a pleasing act of the imagination, and he clearly saw himself playing a part in saving his country in its time of crisis.

The *Koan Maru* continued to pitch slowly and deeply in the darkness. It was absolutely still on deck, with only the soughing of the wind to be heard. Koji gradually felt himself getting chilled.

They sailed in the wake of the typhoon and the waves were large, yet the ferry pulled into the slip at Shimonoseki at 6:40 the next morning, right on schedule. Cool breezes blew back in Antung now, but in Shimonoseki the mid-summer morning sun was shining. A small navy boat knifed its white way through the water, its large naval flag, dingy and soiled, rippling in the wind. A pilot boat passed by. A tug let out a volley of piercing blasts on its whistle. A ship of the 10,000-ton class, camouflaged in a light, irregular pattern, drew near them.

Koji disembarked with his father. After the long crossing they found themselves swaying unsteadily as they walked.

The Sanyo train line, which would have taken them back to Hiroshima, was not in operation. The damage from the typhoon in Fukuoka, Oita, Yamaguchi, and Hiroshima prefectures had been heavier than they had expected. The platforms in Shimonoseki Station, surprisingly, were deserted, but here and there they could see clusters of people eating their lunches as they waited patiently in the trains, even though no one knew when they would start moving. The inns across from the station, on the other hand, were all full.

Koji, burdened with his exhausted father and all their luggage, had become testy. Suddenly the days that remained to him were all the more dear, all the more precious.

He heard from someone about a boat landing with passenger service through the Inland Sea and went to investigate. He found that a boat stopping at ports east of Shimonoseki would leave for Hiroshima's Ujina Harbor that evening. He returned to his father in a better frame of mind.

The boat was a small steamer a little over 200 tons, but it was jammed to the gunwales with passengers. Nonetheless, the two of them were at last able to leave Shimonoseki at 5:30 that night.

Koji's father had been born in the Shimonoseki area and pointed out those places of interest that could be seen from the vessel. Two small islands, their red clay soil gnawed at by the sea, were called Kanju and Manju. They could see fishing boats riding the tide back to shore, hillsides dyed a deep purple by the hues of evening, and an outbound train snaking its way through the foothills from Mitajiri under a plume of white smoke. A gentle surf broke against the stone seawall that ran along the shore.

A group of young men who were going into the naval barracks at Otake had gathered on the upper deck to sing. They were delighted that they were not going to be late for their scheduled enlistment, having had the good fortune to find this boat.

The summer sun, casting its light lushly upon the sea and coloring the placid evening water golden yellow, slowly set amidst the monotonous, hurried throbbing of the engines.

While Koji and his father were in Manchuria, Chieko Ibuki had been called up in the semi-compulsory civilian draft for women. She put on her work uniform every day and left for her job at an army clothing depot. Ishikawa had taken his pre-induction physical up in Hokkaido and succeeded, at least for the present, in escaping military duty, having importuned the medical officer, a former schoolmate, who conveniently diagnosed his extreme nearsightedness as a detached retina.

Koji, ignorant of both of these developments, returned immediately to Tokyo from Hiroshima for his examinations and graduation.

*   *   *

They were already giving the final lectures at the University, followed immediately by the examinations. Koji's instructor in the course on Sung-dynasty Confucianism read the concluding paragraph of his lecture, then, looking directly at his students, spoke to them in formal Japanese.

"I hereby complete my lectures on Confucianism in the Sung Period, which have lasted approximately one and a half years. I now part with you, gentlemen, as you finish your third year of study. You are bringing to a close your lives as students, which have lasted for 16 or 17 years. At this juncture you are setting forth into the world. The situation of the State may not permit you splendid prospects and most of you, I believe, will forthwith enter the service and go off to war. As I bid you farewell I find that I, myself, do not know the proper words to say at this time. I will recommend to you at this point a passage from *The Account of Yoyang Tower* by Fan Chung-yen, who was in the vanguard of Neo-Confucianism during the Northern Sung dynasty. I should like these to be my words of parting, however insignificant, with which you can face a future that doubtless harbors abundant hardships for you."

The instructor then spun around and wrote the following on the blackboard in literary Chinese:

> When he occupies the heights of Royal service he is anxious for the people, and when he retires to country rivers and lakes far distant he is anxious for the Sovereign. He takes office and is anxious. He withdraws from office and is anxious. If this is so, when does he rejoice? There is a simple answer. He is anxious before the world is anxious and rejoices after the world rejoices.

He read the passage out loud in his sonorous voice, then repeated it again. He bowed, turned smartly, and went out of the classroom.

Mr. Chu, in his last hour, wrote two T'ang dynasty poems on the blackboard and recited them to the students. The first was by Wang Chi, the second by Wang Po.

> In the eastern hills I face the evening dusk;
> I pause on my journey, yet where shall I stay?
> Tree after tree is autumn hued,
> on mount after mount the setting sun's radiant display.
> The herdsman chases home his calves,
> the hunter's horse bears home his prey;
> I look about, yet see no friends around me,
> a long song sung, I yearn to pick bracken and loyalty portray.

> The Palace gave succor to the three of Ch'in,
> through the winded haze I view the five fjords of Shu;

separation from you touches me,
both of us are far journeyers for the State;
be there within this realm a dear friend
then the ends of the earth are as next door;
let us not at this fork in the road,
as would woman or babe, wet our kerchiefs with tears.

Mr. Chu then erased the verse he had written. He slapped at the chalk dust that clung to his black sleeves and took a step backward.

"Farewell. Until we meet again," he said in Chinese and bowed his head to his students.

Later Koji checked an annotated edition of T'ang dynasty poetry. He was startled to find the following comment in the introduction to the first poem, which was entitled "Prospect of the Wilds": *Because this describes a soon-to-wither landscape on an autumn eve, it would seem to lament the fall of the Sui dynasty.*

The date had been set for Koji's entry into the navy. He would be mustered in on September 30 at the naval barracks in Sasebo, after which it appeared he would be sent somewhere outside of the Japanese islands for training. Koji and Tanii and another student named Hirokawa, all from the Department of Japanese Literature, had been accepted into the Student Reserves.

Koji's mother and father came up to Tokyo from Hiroshima for the graduation ceremony, bringing a formal kimono with the family crest for Koji to wear. The two thousand graduating students of Tokyo Imperial University and their parents, the latter dressed in their finest, swarmed about outside Yasuda Hall, where the ceremony would be held. Koji introduced his parents to Kurimura's mother and to Tanii's parents and they exchanged cordial greetings.

"Hey, you guys," said Kurimura, "we're gonna come back alive." He had dragged Tanii and Koji over to Sanshiro's Pond, his face flushed with emotion. Kurimura would be going into Sendai's East 22nd.

"Always be sure to keep your wits about you, come what may, and you'll return to tell about it."

"I'd certainly like that to be the case, if possible," Koji said.

"'If possible,' nothing! We're coming back alive. Listen, it's a question of will."

"But you can't say that!" protested Koji. "*I* intend to give it all I've got. Anyway, today let's part in good spirits."

Tanii groaned nostalgically. "Remember how we used to drill on the parade grounds, then go to the restaurant *U.S.* for a beer?"

"No matter what happens," implored Kurimura, "don't do anything impulsive. If the order 'Suicide squad, one step forward!' is given, I will serenely take one step backward. We all have to."

"Well, let's go. They're going in," said Koji, pointing toward the entrance to the hall, where students were starting to file in. Prime Minister Tojo sat on the platform as a special guest. Wearing his heavily medaled soldier's uniform, he spoke his words of farewell to the 2,000 early graduates before him.

"In terms of a lifetime, the shortening of one's schooling by roughly half a year is no impediment whatsoever, and I, here, an important . . ." The Premier was at a loss for words for a moment, then continued. "Perhaps, I should say, I provide a good example."

When the graduates realized the Prime Minister was referring to his own experience, a gentle wave of laughter rippled through the audience, then quickly subsided. His graduation from the military academy had come just at the time of the Russo-Japanese War and he had also been graduated ahead of schedule, in spite of which he now stood before them as Prime Minister. This was the main point of his speech.

After the ceremony there was a farewell party in the basement cafeteria sponsored by the student literary club. The students, their hair close-cropped, and the faculty, in formal dress, stood about eating sushi and drinking beer.

Koji and his friends quickly drained their mugs and left.

"What'll we do?" Tanii asked. "Shall we go somewhere one last time and get something to eat?"

"Why not go our separate ways now?" suggested Kurimura.

"Right you are. Well, then, goodbye."

And with that they waved cheerfully at each other and parted.

Koji still had the feeling somehow that they would be getting together again tomorrow to talk over beer.

That night Koji left Tokyo with his mother and father on the 8:20 to Shimonoseki. He wondered when he would return to the city again. And yet he felt full of life. Standing alone in the vestibule at the end of the car, he suddenly noticed the illuminated news sign, the same one that had told him of the resignation of the Konoe Cabinet, flashing its message around the Asahi building: "Imperial Navy Submarine Advances into Atlantic."

* * *

As soon as he returned to his home in Hiroshima the maid came to him with some news.

"Uh . . . while you were away, sir, Mr. Ibuki's daughter came by." Koji felt his cheeks instantly redden.

"Uh . . . she wondered if your date of induction had been decided."

"What did you tell her?"

"I told her I wasn't sure. When I told her you were expected back from Tokyo on the 26th or 27th, she said goodbye and left."

He thought about Chieko as he put away the books he would be leaving behind and finished up some letters and his diary.

"I hope I haven't left anybody out." Koji's mother came in, a piece of paper in her hand with names listed on it. These were the guests who would be coming to the farewell dinner the next day.

He glanced at the list and grunted noncommittally.

"Neither Ishikawa nor Ibuki will be here this time," he said casually, "but I wonder if Ibuki's younger sister and the others could come. I was thinking we might invite them, if you wouldn't mind."

"I wonder." His mother tilted her head to one side, suggesting her reluctance. "I have my doubts about that. Wouldn't it be better if we didn't ask them?"

"I suppose you're right. Yes, that's best. Let's forget about it." Koji's reply came easily.

The next evening a dozen or so relatives, old friends, and chums from elementary school gathered at the house. Mr. Yashiro also came over, dressed in the traditional Japanese style.

When the guests had taken their places, Koji's father, sitting at the other end of the room, addressed the group formally:

"My son Koji, having been called upon to serve his country, is to depart for Sasebo the day after tomorrow, a navy man. It is to bid him farewell that I have invited you here this evening. I am delighted that all of you to whom we have become indebted over the years, including Koji's esteemed teacher, Mr. Yashiro, have deigned to favor us with your presence, your busy schedules notwithstanding. Given the times, we have nothing worthy of your palates, but do please make yourselves at ease."

His father had a tendency to slip now and again into the dialect of his hometown when he spoke on formal occasions. After his father finished, Koji bowed courteously to the guests.

The exchange of drinking cups began.

His sister-in-law's younger brother, Mizuki, thrust his cup at Koji.

"Well, in any case, we can't beat America without you, eh?" he said in his broad dialect. "But it's such a waste, when you stop and think about it."

Mizuki sang an amusing song that had the women of the family tittering in shared delight.

Koji's friends from primary school began telling stories about Koji when he was a child, affecting a somewhat knowing tone.

The occasion was enjoyable enough, yet as the evening wore on Koji became more and more restless. It was pointless, he felt, to continue to sit here out of a sense of duty and waste the scarcely more than forty hours of freedom left to him.

He met his mother in the hall as he was returning from the bathroom.

"I'm going to go pick up my express ticket now," he said, to his mother's astonishment.

"What? Can't you get the ticket tomorrow? You could send someone to pick it up."

"No. It's better to be on the safe side. In any case, I'm going out for a bit."

"Why? All of a sudden like this? Don't you think you'll offend Mr. Yashiro, not to mention the others?"

"I'll talk to Mr. Yashiro myself." He went immediately to his guests, offered his apologies and left the house, just as a fish dealer who had been selling to the family for years began a Noh chant behind him.

Ah! How imposing!
We knew well our abilities;
I remember the battle of Dannoura.

Koji broke into a run and headed for the Ibuki house.

The Ibuki household was startled by Koji's sudden late evening visit. He told them he was going to the train station to buy a ticket for the special express *Fuji* and wanted Chieko to accompany him.

"You seem to have drunk quite a bit, haven't you?" Chieko's mother laughed, but there was anxiety in her voice. "What will you do, Chie, dear?"

"I shall go," Chieko answered, her tone brusque, then went back into the house.

"If your sister's going," the mother suggested to the younger girl, "why don't you go along too, Ikuko."

"Okay," responded the girl half-heartedly.

"You'll soon be a navy man, won't you," said Chieko's mother. "You might find yourself together with Yukio someplace."

Ikuko waited until her mother's attention was elsewhere, then whispered into Koji's ear.

"I won't go. I think I'd just be in the way."

"Don't be silly!" Koji's face flushed.

Chieko had gotten ready, put on her shoes on the stepping stone beneath the veranda, and come around to the entryway. The two of them hurried out through the gate, as if to evade a summons that might call them back into the house.

The city was asleep. The smell of wood shavings was in the air. They hurried on silently, Koji feeling restless and having no idea why he was hurrying. From time to time Chieko had to run to keep up with him.

"I wear a factory worker's uniform to work now." Chieko made the statement as though it was something she had just remembered.

"Called up?"

"Yes."

"Hard for you?"

Chieko shook her head. Suddenly Koji picked up the small woman and carried her in his arms.

"I knew you would come," she said, pressing her face against him.

Koji stumbled over a tree root and they fell together onto the grassy embankment that ran along the train tracks. A freight train heading south ground its way ponderously toward where they lay. As the fireman stoked the boiler, crimson flames shot out into the surrounding darkness, dyeing the steam red and throwing their light on Chieko. Heavily, slowly, the freight train, red flames flashing, crawled by above their heads at a measured pace.

They lay enchanted in each other's arms, but after 10 or 15 minutes they stood up and began once again to hurry along the road, as though they had suddenly realized they could no longer stay where they were.

Three days later, on a ship out of Sasebo, Koji's by-the-book, double-time navy routine, every bit of which was absolutely new to him, began in earnest.

As she sorted the clothing delivered to the depot where she worked, Chieko knew that she would wait for Koji to return, come what may. And at that precise moment the grey *Argentine Maru*, 500 student reservists aboard, ran a zig-zag course southward at 16 knots, rolling on huge swells, the main island of Okinawa to starboard.

Three

Two old Western-style red brick buildings stood on the east side of the boulevard that ran from Sakuradamon to Toranomon in downtown Tokyo. The one to the north was the Ministry of Justice, the one to the south the Navy Ministry. At the south end of the Navy Ministry grounds rose the antenna towers of the Tokyo Communications Corps. At some point during the war, a nondescript barracks had been built across the road from these, on land facing the unfinished grey Finance Ministry building. On it was posted a sign reading *Navy Ministry, Annex Five*. Certainly no one who passed by gave it a second glance. On those rare occasions when someone took note of the sign, no doubt he simply thought that with a war going on even the navy, growing by leaps and bounds, was forced to do its business in such an unprepossessing place. But a rather special sort of activity was going on there.

Several thousand intercepted messages—overheard enemy radio communications—were funneled into the building daily. This was the Special Services Group of the Naval General Staff and its mission was to break enemy codes and ciphers and to determine, by analyzing these communications, the enemy's situation and intentions. The unit was linked to a communications unit in Owada in nearby Saitama Prefecture by telephone and three mail deliveries a day.

One year after it was established, Koji Obata was assigned to duty there. He had been taken from the naval base at Sasebo to a training area in southern Taiwan, where for half a year he was whipped into shape, as they said in the navy. When asked to choose a technical specialty, he decided to go into communications. Since he had gone to the trouble of joining the navy, he certainly did not want to end up in the Marine Service, nor did he relish the idea of being put in the Shore Defense Corps to search and sweep for mines. He chose communications because it seemed to be the kind of work he was most suited for, and he also thought it might get him assigned to a battleship or aircraft carrier. Fifty men of similar intent had had their requests granted. They were not transferred to the fleet, however, but were sent instead to the Naval Communications School at Yokosuka for another half year, where they received training in special techniques, after which—it was now the fall of 1943—they found themselves living in Tokyo like ordinary office workers. Koji, wearing his ensign's uniform, commuted every day between the annex building and his lodgings.

At over 100 typewriters, typists, all women, worked all day banging out rows of apparently meaningless numbers and letters of the alphabet, sounding like so many machine guns. The Special Services Group was made up of a directorate and five sections. The first section was called A Section and was responsible for American intelligence; the second section, B, for British; the third, D, German, Italian, French, Swiss, Thai and others; the fourth, C, Chinese; the fifth, S, Soviet intelligence.

The code and cipher technology that the major powers used for military and diplomatic communication had made remarkable—albeit secret—advances during the 20 years between the two World Wars. The major powers had been attempting to read each other's codes and ciphers, and when they had trouble cracking a system, they would even go so far as to break into the embassy of the country in question and open the safe. This was the dirty work that went on behind the scenes. Breaking a code or cipher could, under the right circumstances, be worth more than an army division or naval flotilla. Like America's legendary Black Chamber and Britain's Room 40, the Special Services Group was the Imperial Navy's secret chamber.

America's cryptography was the most advanced. They enciphered messages using a duralumin plate that looked something like a portable chessboard incorporating 26 strips, upon each of which the English alphabet was inscribed in random distribution. Its messages were absolutely undecipherable. The next best, after the Americans, were the British, followed by Germany, Japan, and the Soviet Union.

The codes and ciphers used by the Nationalist Chinese government in Chungking, regardless of type, were a good four or five years behind those of the major powers, and the Chinese forces were continually compromising them, so many had been decrypted. Koji was assigned to the China section, C Section. He found it an odd quirk of fate that the Chinese he had studied in college on a whim should have led him to this.

He had also made some friends, men he felt at home with. Besides Tanii and Hirokawa, who had both come with him to the Special Services Group from the same department at the university, there was Kuki, who was officially with the Foreign Ministry (and who believed Japan would lose the war), Wada, who had studied anthropology in college, and Tsutsumi, a laid-back gourmand who had never gone to a professor's lecture if he could buy the notes. When they were off duty the collegiate atmosphere made service life seem like an extension of the university. As a student Koji had grown thoroughly disaffected with the college environment, but now he looked back on it with fondness and relished getting together with his companions.

They had all mastered the occult techniques drilled into them at the communications school. By now they could solve in one or two hours ciphers that were made by substituting the letters of an English text one by one for different letters or by transposing letters. When you got the hang of it the exercises were simple enough. Of course, the cipher systems the various countries were currently using were not so easy to deal with.

And while they really had no complaints about the collegiate ambience in the office, on the outside they were required to maintain absolute secrecy about what they did.

*   *   *

Koji was responsible for the Chungking military-attaché code known as Blue Secret, used for communication between the Chungking Naval General Staff and attachés stationed abroad in Washington, London, Moscow, Tehran, New Delhi, and Sydney. Koji's predecessor had already broken the code to the point where there was ordinarily little difficulty in coming up with intelligence, so Koji simply selected the more important messages and copied down the information. At the same time, however, he would try to identify the codewords that remained unknown. Even though he knew the five-letter group EHKPT, for example, meant enemy, he had no idea what the next one, EHKPU, signified.

One day he was working on a 30-word cryptogram sent from "Navisino, Washington" (the Chinese Nationalist naval attaché stationed in Washington) to General Headquarters, Chungking. He wrote in the letter groups, found the transposition key and pieced the text together.

> Acknowledge your earlier message. Went to the mat with U.S. Navy authorities, but they say our cryptosystems are vulnerable and they strongly suspect they are being broken by the enemy; thus they say that, regretfully, they cannot provide us with any more intelligence than we are receiving now.

A good intercept had been made just the week before of the message referred to, and Koji had decrypted and read it. It had been a directive from General Headquarters, Chungking, to the attaché in Washington telling him to try to get the Americans to send them more information relative to operations in the Pacific area. For the most part, the thrust of C Section's work in the Special Services Group was to break the codes of the Chungking government, not the difficult American and British ciphers, and seek out the secrets of the Allied Powers through the back door. Koji saw now this meant they could expect little in the way of good intelligence.

He was nonetheless pleased. He pulled out one of the blank

worksheets from a desk drawer, wrote out a clean copy of the message in translation, and went and put it on the desk of Lieutenant Iwamoto, head of C Section. As he returned to his own desk, a petty officer from General Affairs came in and handed him a slip of paper.

"Ensign Obata," he said imperiously, "a visitor."

Koji looked at the name scrawled in pencil and started. *Yukio Ibuki, Lieutenant, Medical Corps.*

He asked his section chief for permission to leave, then hurried out of the office. Outside the door stood Ibuki in his lieutenant's uniform. They had not seen each other for two full years. Ibuki had apparently been to the south. His face wore a magnificent dark tan.

"Can I come in?"

"Just a minute," said Koji. Those who were not connected with Special Services, even other navy personnel, were restricted to the reception room.

"What brings you here out of the blue?" he asked as he knocked on the door of the reception room next to the office.

"Coming." A woman's voice, easy-going, responded to his knock. A typist, a tall girl, stuck her head out. When she saw it was Koji she said, "You want to use this room? Okay, we'll be out in a second." She ducked back into the room, then emerged with another girl, carrying bundles of documents. They seemed to have been doing some sort of filing.

"Sorry to keep you waiting," said the tall girl.

"It's okay," Koji replied brusquely.

He felt as though he had seen the woman somewhere before. She had joined Special Services recently. He didn't know her name yet and couldn't recall where he might have seen her.

Ibuki and Koji entered the empty reception room.

"This is a surprise. What brings you here?" Koji asked again. "From out of nowhere. It's a wonder you were able to find me."

"I read in the *National Register* that you were attached to the Naval General Staff. I had the Personnel Bureau look for you a while back and they found you right away."

"I found out you were on the *Zuikaku* in the *Register*, too," said Koji. "Is the *Zuikaku* in port?"

"No."

"You transferred to another ship?"

"Uh, no, that's not what happened," said Ibuki. "The First was wiped out."

That was it. Koji was more or less aware that the First Carrier Division had suffered heavy losses in an air battle off Bougainville some time back, but he did not yet know the circumstances surrounding Ibuki's return.

"I'll tell you all about it later. Are you off this evening?"

"Yes. How about coming to my place?" suggested Koji. "You can stay over."

"No, I have to go back to the Ministry now, then return to Yokosuka tonight. Can you come back with me to Yokosuka?"

"I should be able to," Koji replied. They agreed to meet again in front of the annex at five when the office closed.

Koji saw Ibuki to the door. When he returned Lieutenant Iwamoto called him over.

"About that message you worked on just now," he began. "I'll be going to Sasebo in a few days and will be there a while, so keep a watch out for the reply to it while I'm gone."

As Koji was taking care of the remaining intercept traffic, he thought about Ibuki and, once again, Chieko. He was sure his late-night encounter with Chieko last year just before he was inducted had left her with ambiguous feelings, and this made him all the more insecure with Ibuki.

He waited until five, put his papers away in the safe, put on his short sword, picked up his hat, and stepped outside Special Services. Ibuki had not come yet. The wind was a bit cold, so he went back inside the doorway. His fellow officers in the British and American sections, Hirokawa, Kuki, Tanii, and Tsutsumi, and the women typists, putting on their coats as they walked, were coming down from the second floor in a babel of voices. Koji spotted the tall typist he had seen earlier. She looked at him as she put on her shoes. She came out, buttoned up her overcoat, and pulled her hair out from under her collar.

Suddenly she spoke to him.

"Have you forgotten me, Ensign Obata?"

Koji flushed slightly.

"Oh, I, let's see, you're—"

"I'm Kawai."

"Oh." Now he remembered who she was. "From Manchuria. Right! I knew I'd seen you someplace before. O-Chu. I remember. You've moved to Tokyo?"

"I certainly have, Ko-*chan*," said O-Chu, familiarly using the diminutive *chan*. "You seemed to have forgotten me entirely, so I couldn't have said anything to you, now could I?"

O-Chu nodded to the typist with her, a girl wearing a blue sweater, turned on her heel, and hurried off toward the street.

"What's this? You're Ko-chan now?" asked Kuki in a bantering tone. "She's tall and then some. The one in the blue sweater with her works for Wada. Everyone talks about how gorgeous she is. Boy, you sure know all kinds."

"Yeah, the other day I was pretty sure I'd seen her somewhere before. Her father is head of the Antung office of a trading company, and my brother lives in Antung and . . ." Koji went on with his explanation, somewhat embarrassed.

"Everyone's going over to the Officers' Club for a drink," said Tanii. "Want to go?"

Koji saw Ibuki hurrying along the tree-lined sidewalk as he walked toward them from the Ministry, slightly round-shouldered, as always. Koji said goodbye to his co-workers.

"Are you hungry, Koji?" Ibuki asked.

"I am, but I can wait until we get to Yokosuka."

"Well, I hope you don't mind, but I'd like to stop off for a while in Kamakura. Let's eat someplace around here."

"Okay, then we could go to the Officers' Club or the Officers' Mess. My buddies are out in full force at the Officers' Club now, so I doubt we'd be able to talk there."

The two of them walked toward the Diet building, up the hill where the sycamore trees that lined the street were already shedding their leaves. Two army cars with low license numbers—obviously top brass—were parked in front of the mess hall. They were new and had apparently been captured in Southeast Asia or the South Pacific.

"You've got yourself a nice, uncrowded mess hall," said Ibuki, sitting down and looking around the room. "It reminds me of the lodge on Mt. Dogo." He was referring to a mountain ski resort they had often gone to. "It's great to be back in Japan! This morning, as I was coming up from Yokosuka, the scenery from the train almost made me shiver with joy."

"I had that feeling, too, when I came back from Taiwan."

Koji told his friend how he had returned in the spring after his training program from Kaohsiung to Kure on the converted cruiser *Aikoku Maru*. As soon as they passed through the Kanmon Straits they met the aircraft carrier *Zuikaku*. The captains of both ships had exchanged signals of greeting. Koji knew that Ibuki must be on the carrier. He could see seamen on deck as the two ships passed each other.

"How is sea duty?"

Ibuki shook his head. "It's really rough. It's obvious now we're feeling pressure everywhere we turn in the southeast."

The withdrawal from Guadalcanal in February 1943 had been the turning point. The American forces mounted a tenacious counterattack in the Solomon Islands, pushing north, and by early November the enemy had landed on Torokina Point on the west coast of Bougainville. The planes assigned to the *Zuikaku*, the *Shokaku*, and the *Zuiho*, the First Carrier Division on standby at the Harushima anchorage at Truk, had been ordered out, the bombers and fighters to Rabaul and the attack planes to Kavieng. The medical unit had likewise been split into two groups. Ibuki had been sent by destroyer after the planes that went to Kavieng, where he stayed for some ten days. There were three big air battles while he was there. The first two were lopsided Japanese victories, but in the third, which was fought off Bougainville during the daytime but in stormy weather, almost all the planes from the First Carrier Division were lost. The surviving units were ordered back to Truk and then at the end of November it was decided that they would return to Japan again to regroup and retrain at Iwakuni and Kanoya.

Ibuki had been billeted with a Lieutenant Katsuta, also a doctor, all through these operations, and was scheduled to return to Yokosuka with him when their ship came back with the other converted carrier. However, they were informed by the adjutant that one man would be assigned to the carrier *Unyo*, the other to the carrier *Chuyo*. The two men talked it over and decided to toss a ten-*sen* coin to decide who would be assigned where. Katsuta tossed tails, so he went aboard the *Chuyo*. Late at night on December 3, the day before his ship was to arrive at the naval base at Yokosuka, Ibuki, sleeping in the wardroom of the *Unyo*, was startled awake by the sudden sounding of the General Quarters bugle call. At the time the two carriers were being escorted by a cruiser and three destroyers. The *Chuyo* had already been hit by one torpedo from an enemy submarine when Ibuki awoke. The night was dark, the sea heavy. Visibility was zero. Moments later the *Chuyo* took another torpedo and apparently went down in a few minutes. Almost all of its crew and air complement perished. The *Unyo* returned to the safety of Yokosuka.

Nothing was known about the circumstances of Lieutenant Katsuta's death. He had been with the Department of Internal Medicine at Tokyo Imperial University and his family lived in Kamakura. This was why Ibuki was stopping off there.

"If it had been heads," Ibuki said, eating his salad and cold cuts, "I would be a dead man."

Koji was fascinated by his friend's story. He recalled talking with Tsutsumi and Kuki at a briefing on the war situation two days before and one of them saying the *Chuyo* had gone down south of Tokyo Bay.

"So now I'm going to Iwakuni." Ibuki changed the subject. "How's that joker Ishikawa doing?"

"I don't know. I've heard nothing at all from him."

"I heard that he got someone to say he had a detached retina, certainly a convenient affliction and hard to diagnose, and wound up classified as physically unfit. I wonder what happened to him after that."

"For all his delaying," said Koji, "he must have graduated from Hokkaido by this time. He's a smooth operator. You know, he swore he'd never let himself be killed."

Ibuki took out a pocket notebook and checked the time of the next train to Yokosuka.

They finished their beer, went to Shimbashi by subway, and waited for the train. A dry wind blew across the platform in the elevated train station. A middle-aged field-grade officer wearing a short overcoat walked back and forth, his shoes sounding on the concrete. Several people, probably a family from the Kamakura area, waited in the chilling cold for their train.

"You know," Ibuki said suddenly, "human life really comes cheap."

The Yokosuka train pulled into the station. The second-class cars were empty.

"Koji, just how do you think this war is going to turn out?"

"I really don't know. We've come this far so all we can do now is do our jobs as well we can and hope that Japan will find the best way out."

"Is your work in communications intelligence?"

"Right on the mark," said Koji, "but I don't think we ought to talk about it here on the train."

"Well," explained Ibuki, "there were Special Services people in the Third Fleet too. I've heard it said that in modern warfare, a country can't afford to start fighting without having the terms of the peace treaty already in mind. How do they intend to deal with this? What's the thinking in the government?"

"I don't know," Koji answered. "I may work under the General Staff, but what I do is pretty specialized. I don't know anything about that sort of thing. Prince Takamatsu is a captain in charge of a department, but every day he goes to the Officers' Mess, hands in pockets and without his cap, for archery practice. Maybe even the Prince is disturbed about all this."

"There's no point in thinking about it, really," said Ibuki, "but when you're with the fleet, you've got a surprising amount of spare time. Even at Kavieng we saw nothing that bore any resemblance to actual war. Just once, I amputated a chief petty officer's arm. The chair legs under the wardroom mess tables get worn down a little more each morning, but not much else happens. With that extra time on my hands I think about all sorts of irrelevant things."

The train passed Yokohama and went through a tunnel. Koji wasn't exactly sure where they were. Ibuki was having second thoughts about visiting Lieutenant Katsuta's next-of-kin. It was forbidden for a private individual to bring a family news of kin killed in action before an official announcement, but besides that, Ibuki apparently couldn't deal with the prospect of breaking the news to the Katsuta family face-to-face. Still, the idea of giving up and going back to Yokosuka also seemed to bother him. In the end, when the train arrived in Kamakura the two of them got off. They went through the dark streets looking for the Katsuta house, a scribbled address in Ibuki's hand.

The houses around them, all of the same sort of design, were deathly still. When they turned onto a narrow street, they could hear the sound of the surf coming from the direction of the ocean. The Katsuta home, found after a brief search, was in the clinic where the father practiced. It was surrounded by a wooden fence, high and weathered. The front gate was closed and a bell was attached to the gatepost.

A dog began barking behind the house, apparently sensing intruders, whereupon all the dogs in the neighborhood started barking. They could hear a piano from the back of the house; perhaps it was Katsuta's younger sister. The player would come to a particular part and misplay, then begin once more from the beginning. She repeated the passage over and over again. The two men listened to this mediocre piano playing for a few moments, the dogs still barking.

"Hey," said Ibuki suddenly, "enough of this. Let's go back."

"Yeah, to tell you the truth," said Koji, "the accompaniment is more than I can handle."

"Right."

They hurried away from the house as though fleeing the scene of a crime and headed back toward the station.

That night Koji drank at the Officers' Club in Yokosuka and stayed over with Ibuki. Ibuki avoided mentioning Hiroshima and Chieko.

* * *

Clear days followed one after the other and in the morning sky over Tokyo one could often see the vapor trails of army aircraft. The papers announced the "heroic defeats" at Makin and Tarawa. Koji learned that a fellow officer, an ensign, had been killed in action on Makin Island. This was the first death in battle of an officer that Koji had trained with. It had now been four months since Koji and his fellow officers were commissioned, and they were quite familiar with their work. The end of 1943 drew near.

Tanii was moved to B Section and ordered to study Great Britain's Naval Code, a random distribution cipher. It was a thankless task, involving a daily search for the repetition of one number out of one or two thousand in endless columns of numbers written on large sheets of blue graph paper. The work thoroughly depressed him and he complained about it often. Kurimura, a friend of Koji and Tanii, was in reserve officer school in Sendai. Koji got a letter from him saying he was training every day on a drill field from which he could see the snow-capped Mount Zao and that he would become a cadet in the not-too-distant future.

Lieutenant Iwamoto, head of C Section and Koji's immediate superior, was on temporary duty in Sasebo to strengthen the new Z Section that Special Services had set up there because of the gradual buildup of American air strength in China. During his absence Commander Ezaki, head of the Soviet section, was also in charge of C Section, the China group.

As Lieutenant Iwamoto had requested, Koji kept an eye on the messages between Chungking and the military attaché in Washington on the question of supplying American intelligence to Chungking, and one day he found such a message, one sent by Chungking. It was in the Domic cipher, an improved form of the Blue Secret system, and a somewhat elaborate cipher which had no repetitions. It was made by first enciphering in Blue Secret, then, using a key which contained numbers from 1 to 25 in random order, writing the text in vertical lines, but transmitting it horizontally, line by line. However, since Blue Secret, the basic cipher, had already been broken, they were able to decrypt it without too much effort, and to exchange keys with the army unit that was doing the same work, the General Staff's Section 18.

The decrypted message read as follows.

The Military Command's Signal Intelligence Group is scheduled to commence utilization of a new cipher system, revising the military-attaché ciphers as of January 1, 1944, and has already completed the dispatch of codebooks and appended revised tables, in addition to notifying all areas of the change. Given that said new cipher system is to achieve the level of the Anglo-American systems, we want you now to negotiate as best you can with the U.S. Department of the Navy and request that they provide intelligence.

When Koji read this he knew his work as of the new year would not be easy. He had no idea, in terms of technique, what was meant by "appended revised tables." His feelings were mixed, both a sense of foreboding that Chungking was confident its cryptography would reach the level of the Americans and the British, and hopeful expectation: it would be fantastic if they could break the new system. He took the message to Commander Ezaki, the acting section chief.

Commander Ezaki showed little interest.

"Leave it there," he said, his eyes scarcely leaving the book he was reading. There was a tendency in the navy to not take Nationalist China seriously, and the Commander seemed to share this attitude. And he generally did not show too much interest in the work of the Special Services Group itself. This was something of a letdown for Koji.

Commander Ezaki had been in charge of Special Services' S Section for only a month, but he had already made known his view that Special Services was merely, in his words, "a place to hole up for the winter." There were zealous young officers in S Section who took offense at this. He possessed a massive, ruddy and well-nourished face into which broad, deep lines were etched, a rugged, good-looking sort of face which only rarely broke into a grin. He was thoroughly unenthusiastic about his work and, incongruously, he was inordinately sensitive to cold and cared for nothing save his electric stove.

Whenever an American plane loaded with aid for the Soviet Union would go across the Bering Straits from Nome to the Soviet Union, there would be an exchange of pilots, Soviet for American, at the first airfield, and then the supplies, plane included, would be ferried westward, relayed from point to point. This was the Mazruk Line, so called for the American colonel who had established it. Should it develop that the planes were heading not toward the European front, but south toward Vladivostok on the Soviet-Manchurian border, that would mean that the time when the Soviets would open hostilities with Japan was drawing near. Messages from Mazruk Line aircraft and ground stations were an important source of intelligence for the Soviet section, yet Commander Ezaki simply glanced at this material, and as for the rest, the messages and intelligence of the Soviet section and the China section he now had responsibility for inevitably lay untouched on his desk. Having had a petty officer in General Affairs make him a table to go over the electric stove, he would spread a navy blanket on top of it and the stove, and ensconce his legs deep within. Then he would fill his well-burnished Dunhill pipe from his large store of English tobacco and silently lose himself in a book, projecting the aroma of fine tobacco to those around him. Close inspection would reveal he was reading Ranke's *The Great Powers* or somebody's treatise on currency, which he would skim through before grandly drifting off to sleep. It was said he put a bright red cover around his favorite book, the detective novel *Hanshichi's Convict Register*, so that it would look like a classified document.

When he wore his overcoat, Commander Ezaki would leave work without his short sword. This was, of course, contrary to naval protocol. The first time he did this an ensign from S Section, thinking he had forgotten it, went running after the Commander with the sword, only to be sent back with it. The Commander didn't want it, he said, because it was a damned nuisance. Koji, nonetheless, looked upon this man with relative amity.

* * *

Whenever he arrived at the office or was coming off the watch, Koji did not wait for the petty officer responsible for sorting and distributing the intercepts to the appropriate officers and civilians to come around. He would hurriedly go through the file of intercepted transmissions from the night before, pulling out and scanning cryptograms relevant to what he was working on in the hope that he might find something significant. He enjoyed unearthing unusual intelligence, of course, but he also relished the sense of doing his part, however trivial, in a war which was little by little drawing nearer to Japan.

One morning he took back to his desk a half dozen or so Blue Secret and Domic intercepts he had found. None of the typists had come yet, so he began decrypting and making rough translations of each, using his own portable typewriter.

The first one, from Chungking to Moscow, was a rather long Blue Secret. Koji wrote in the characters with some anticipation, but he soon saw that it was December's payroll. He put a check mark on it and tossed it aside. The second message, a Domic, was to Washington and gave the scheduled arrival time in New York of a Secretary Ch'en. It was a frigid, frosty morning. As Koji blew on his hands to warm them, typing or writing in pencil, the women typists and his fellow officers eventually all put in their appearance, greeting him as they arrived. Commander Ezaki also came in, and Koji watched as he turned on the electric stove the instant he got to his desk in S Section on the other side of the room divider. The third intercept was a query from New Delhi about pay. It would seem that payroll disbursement by the Chungking government was inevitably late.

It was when he decrypted the fourth one that Koji felt a tingle of tension. It was a brief dispatch in Blue Secret from the Chinese naval attaché stationed in Bombay to headquarters in Chungking, and the Chinese characters were in the following order: *chien carrier and in -age deputy-chief air hui destroy bay English HMS one bom chun craft huang -er anchor.*

Using a key, this partially decrypted message could be broken up into several parts, then re-assembled. All one had to do was manipulate the characters. Koji divided the text into four lines.

1	*chien*	carrier	and	in	-age
2	deputy-chief	air	*hui*	destroy	bay
3	English	HMS	one	bom	
4	*chun*	craft	*huang*	-er	anchor

He then changed the line order to 2-4-1-3 and got

2	deputy-chief	air	*hui*	destroy	bay
4	*chun*	craft	*huang*	-er	anchor
1	*chien*	carrier	and	in	-age
3	English	HMS	one	bom	

Read from top to bottom, starting on the left-hand side, the plaintext read *Deputy Chief Chun Chien: British aircraft carrier HMS Huihuang and one destroyer in Bombay anchorage.*

Koji wrote it out—in Japanese this time—on a message form.

Sender: Chungking Naval Attaché Stationed in Bombay
Recipient: Deputy Chief, Headquarters, Chungking
Message: British aircraft carrier *Glorious* and one destroyer at anchor in Bombay harbor.

He took it immediately to his section chief. It was rare for China-related messages to produce this sort of intelligence, the kind that might well be directly related to tactical operations. Koji put the report in the chief's basket and saluted. Commander Ezaki, as usual, continued to scrutinize the morning paper, pipe in mouth, and gave no immediate indication he might take a look at it.

Koji spoke up. "Section Chief, we have intercepted a message from Bombay. It would appear that a British naval squadron is there."

The Commander set aside his newspaper, glanced at Koji and looked down at the report.

"The *Glorious* is there?" he asked.

"Yes, sir."

"Are you sure? What does the message itself say?"

"It says the British aircraft carrier *Glorious, Hui-huang* in Chinese."

"The *Hui-huang*?" The Commander had Koji write the characters—which literally meant illumined brilliance—on his desk note pad.

"This is *Glorious* in Chinese?" he asked.

"Well . . . uh . . ." Now Koji was not so sure. He looked at the characters *hui-huang*. "Glorious" had come to him as soon as he had seen the words "English carrier," and that was how he had translated it, but now it didn't seem quite right.

"Well," the Commander demanded, "what about it?"

Koji said nothing.

"The *Glorious* is supposed to have sunk a good while back. Have we got a ghost carrier turning up in Bombay? We've got real problems when an officer of the Special Services Group comes up with disgraceful intelligence like this." He thrust the paper at Koji. "Go back and check it again!"

Koji was offended and angry, but he kept his resentment to himself. *And what will you do if the* Glorious *hasn't been sunk? I'm not sure of the word, but you can't blame me if the China-boy attaché made a mistake! You sit there and give me hell and yet you loaf the day away!* Koji returned to his desk and vented his anger at the petty officer who worked with him.

"Bring me the naval yearbook!" he barked.

He began going through all the British aircraft carriers listed in the 1941 edition of *Jane's Ships*. The photo and specifications of the *Illustrious* caught his eye. He checked the meaning of its name in his English-Japanese dictionary: superior, brilliant, outstanding.

Damn! This comes much closer in meaning to the characters hui huang *than* Glorious. He immediately rewrote the whole report and, irritation in his face, once more turned it in to Commander Ezaki.

"I have checked it again, sir. I seem to have confused it with the *Illustrious*."

"Okay." The Commander picked up his phone and asked to be put through to Department Three of the Naval General Staff. Department Three responded that it had had other intelligence about the squadron for some time and was now able to confirm it with this new information. It praised them for a job well done. In a very short while the Tokyo Communications Corps' primary net sent its own enciphered message into the ether.

One British carrier and one destroyer now at anchor Bombay. This can be taken as sign of possible operations by Britain's Eastern Fleet. Vigilance required in Bengal and Sumatra areas.

Thus it was that Commander Ezaki came to learn Koji's name. Several days later, on the night of December 30, Koji had the watch and found himself together with Commander Ezaki. After dinner Koji had gone for a leisurely bath in the Tokyo Communications Corps' *furo* in the Ministry compound. Warmed to the bone, he returned to S Section to find Ensign Fujita, who was assigned to the section and was on duty, and the Commander sitting face-to-face under the blanket at the electric stove, warming themselves and talking.

"Special Services Group," Commander Ezaki was saying, "doesn't treat its people right. Here we are standing watch at year's end and there's nothing to eat."

He rose slowly to his feet and took a flat flask from the pocket of his overcoat, hanging on a hanger.

"How about it? We're a day early, but what do you say the three of us welcome in the new year. There's not much, but at least it's Johnny Walker. Fujita, have a man in General Affairs bring glasses and something to nibble on."

A little later Petty Officer Izawa from General Affairs shuffled in listlessly with a single whiskey glass on the tray, his sandals slapping the floor sharply as he walked.

"Hey, you gotta bring us three!" Commander spoke as though to a servant.

"Three, sir? . . . And sir, there's nothing to eat."

"If there's nothing to eat, brew some tea."

"We've used all the hot water."

"If there's no more, then heat up some! Do I have to tell you each and every damned thing to do?!" The Commander glared at the man. "And telephone Hamada's in Shimbashi and tell them to send over three good-size meals, something good, on the double. Tell 'em it's for Ezaki with the Naval General Staff."

Petty Officer Izawa left, his face expressing his displeasure. Ensign Fujita was furious. The petty officers in General Affairs, true to form, had been telling dirty jokes and eating food they had filched somewhere.

"He told me there was no hot water even though it was sitting right there."

It was another instance of a young officer fresh out of college being taken advantage of by the veteran petty officers.

After a 30-minute wait another petty officer brought in cold tempura and soup and the like, nothing you could really call good food, but common enough fare for the times, together with a chipped teapot and cups. Koji and Fujita, at the Commander's urging, drank whiskey and snacked on the food. On the second floor telephones rang continuously as A and B Sections, which were on duty, busily charted the position of enemy warships detected by direction-finding. Downstairs, however, where C and S Sections were off duty nights, it was deserted. From time to time they would hear the laughter of the petty officers coming from the General Affairs room.

"Where're you from, Obata?" asked Commander Ezaki.

"Hiroshima, sir."

"You're not going home during the New Year's break?"

"Well, sir," said Koji, tilting his head doubtfully, "if I were to leave here the night of the thirty-first I would not arrive in Hiroshima until the afternoon of the first, so I cannot request a pass."

Since January 2 was a regular working day, Koji could have requested a pass over New Year's had his home been close enough so that he could finish work on New Year's Eve, immediately leave Tokyo and return for duty the morning of the second. Thus one could go no further west than Kobe; Hiroshima was out of the question. Personal trips violated the articles in the Naval Communications Codes concerned with "leaving one's duty station without permission."

The previous year Koji had come down with malaria at the training base in Taiwan, and while still recuperating had left the ward without authorization. He had been found out and reprimanded, and was now leery of such a misstep. Around noon he had watched with some envy men from Fukushima and Nagoya and such relatively nearby places busily making ready to return home, and had promised a man who was going back to Osaka that he would stand duty for him on New Year's Day.

"Are your parents alive?"

"Yes, sir. They are old, but in good health in Hiroshima."

Commander Ezaki puffed wordlessly on his pipe for a moment.

"How would it be, Ensign Obata," he asked with sudden casualness, "if you caught cold tomorrow afternoon?"

Fujita drained his whiskey glass and grinned and Koji laughed in spite of himself.

"I could catch a cold, but I have agreed to pull duty for someone else New Year's Day."

Commander Ezaki frowned. "Can't be helped if you've got a fever."

"Yes, sir, uh . . ." Koji was hesitant now, his nerve faltering. Fujita gave Koji's elbow an encouraging poke under the blanket, and he at last responded.

"Then, Section Chief, I shall telephone and see if I can somehow get a special express ticket for tomorrow. If I find one," he said, emerging from the blanket, "I shall catch cold."

"Hey! Make sure the men don't hear more than they need to!" A wreath of smoke from his pipe billowed thickly about the Commander's face.

Koji first called the ticket office at the Tokyo Station, but was curtly told the expresses for the next day, New Year's Eve, were already sold out. He remembered that Tanii's father had once had some sort of position with the Rail Ministry, so he next phoned the Tanii residence in the West Okubo district of the city. The connection was poor and Koji had to shout, but he tried valiantly to get his message across just to Tanii, and not the petty officers on duty right next door in the General Affairs room. Sweat dappled his brow as he tried both speaking in German and using Morse code.

"Can you hear me? I'll say it in German one more time. *Nach* and dash-dash-dot-dot-dash, dot-dash-dot-dash..."

"How's that? What?" shouted Tanii, "I can't hear you! What's *nach*?"

With no small difficulty Koji got his message across and was greeted with chuckling from the other end of the line.

"That's great! Hirokawa, Kuki, Wada, and Tsutsumi are here, and the five of us are sending off the old year with a marathon mahjong game! We were just talking about you, buddy. If I can't come up with a ticket, Hirokawa or someone should be able to find one. One ticket . . . can you hear me? . . . on the *Fuji* express tomorrow . . . Okay? You'd have no problem if you had proof you're on official military business, but that's not in the cards, right? In any case, we'll get it to you somehow tomorrow morning."

Koji, dabbing at the sweat on his forehead, returned to his place at the electric stove.

"What a botched job that was!" said Commander Ezaki, assiduously coaxing the last drops of whiskey into his glass. "You're a flop as an intelligence officer. It goes without saying, does it not, that the men in General Affairs are better at Morse Code than you? You blew that one. In any case, whether it's simple lying or something more serious, you've got to be audacious, able to pull it off with flair, without the hint of a blush."

The three of them talked into the wee hours of the night, warmed by the heat of the electric stove. Koji was cheerful now, suddenly able to go on a totally unexpected home leave, and Commander Ezaki was also in a good mood.

Commander Ezaki, like Commander Morii, the head of A Section, had served many years overseas and had stories to tell, which he related with obvious pride. There was the time, for example, he was traveling through Siberia by train and the GPU, the Soviet secret police, was after secret documents he was carrying. Another time he was journeying through the high plains of Central Asia and was surrounded one moonlit night by wolves. Once he was stopped by customs on his way back from Harbin with two half-gallon saké bottles he had filled with vodka. He told the customs officer it was water from the Sungari and Amur rivers that he had collected to take back for a water-quality analysis as part of his inspection report to the Navy Ministry, and he said he would open it and let the man taste it, if he liked. The inspector passed him through with a sardonic grin.

The Commander also told them that when you are tailing someone there's much less chance of losing your man if you stay across the street at a diagonal, and when it's necessary to listen in on a conversation in an adjoining hotel room and there's a door between the two rooms, you can paste a sheet of thin brown envelope paper over the keyhole, creating a natural microphone.

Koji found all this interesting, but he could not forget what Ibuki had said some days earlier. He wanted to ask someone like the Commander how he thought the war was going to turn out.

"To change the subject somewhat," said Koji, "I don't suppose ending this war with a series of decisive, clear-cut victories will be a simple matter, will it."

He was attempting to draw the Commander out, but the latter chose not to respond to the overture. A little later, however, he did have some comment.

"Navy Minister Shimada is really no more than an aide-de-camp to Premier Tojo. The navy has more impressive people than that."

His remarks ended on a platitudinous note.

"Men, we must resolve to do our very best!" He knocked the ash out of his pipe. "Well, let's call it a night."

* * *

The special express to Nagasaki on New Year's Eve was filled to capacity. Koji could see several naval officers in the compartments, but no Special Services people. His comrades who were going back home would be taking the regular express that night after they got off duty, so it turned out that Koji had done very well for himself.

Tanii had not been able to provide him with a special express ticket, but Hirokawa had somehow managed to find one and brought it over.

"I couldn't get a sleeping berth," he said, handing it to Koji the next morning. It was concealed in a paper wrapper. Immediately after lunch Koji reported to Commander Ezaki and told him that he seemed to have a fever and requested permission to leave early. The Commander looked up from his book only for a moment.

"Right."

Koji hurried back to the barracks, took only one suitcase, already packed, and ran off to catch the three o'clock train.

He sent his family a telegram from Yokohama. The train sped down the Tokai line, tracks that Koji had gone back and forth on many times each year when he had been a student in college. He knew each station name by heart. Hayakawa. Nebukawa. Manazuru. Then Yugawara and Atami. The winter sun began its early descent, and as they emerged from a tunnel, Koji saw the beauty of the sea visible far below and the surf surging over a black strand.

The sun set as they were passing through Shizuoka. Koji went to the dining car and ate dinner, then stayed awake reading paperback fiction until late at night when the train passed through the Kyoto-Osaka area. Shukugawa and Ashiya, where he and Chieko had strolled, went past in the darkness beyond the window. As the train crossed the road to the detached palace in Suma, Koji at last fell asleep leaning back against the seat, his overcoat wrapped around his hips and legs against the cold.

The *Fuji* pulled into Hiroshima at 5:40 in the morning, New Year's Day. It was not yet light. Koji, suitcase in hand, leisurely walked from the station to his home. The lights were on in the living room, the entryway and the kitchen. His mother was up already, heating up rice-cake soup, the traditional New Year's breakfast.

"Welcome home!" Koji's mother came out to greet him, blinking her failing eyes, operated on several years before for cataracts. "I'm surprised they let you return home! You're even thinner than you were in the spring when we visited you in Kure after you got back from Taiwan."

"Where's Haru?" The maid was nowhere to be seen.

"She left us at the end of November," answered Koji's mother in her broad Kansai dialect. "We looked around and saw that no one was employing maids anymore. Besides, she said she wanted to go back home. And with your father and me doing things together, there's no problem."

Koji's father had been asleep in a six-mat room toward the back of the house, but Koji soon heard him moving about, and then he came out.

"What a pleasant surprise this is!"

"My section chief is a bit unconventional," explained Koji. "I'm supposed to have a cold. I don't have to return to Tokyo until the morning of the fourth. There's no hurry this time."

"That's fine!" said his father. "Well, the first thing to do is go inside and pay your respects to our ancestors."

Koji entered the room with the Buddhist altar. He was not at all religious, but every year his parents had had him pay his respects to the memorial tablets on New Year's Day morning, so he rang the bell and, observing the ritual in form, at least, brought his hands together. At that moment he felt that he was truly home for the New Year.

His mother came in with the offerings. "Is there incense?"

"I don't need any."

His mother sat down next to Koji in front of the altar.

"Your father's been quite out of it since fall. Now and again he comes out with some strange comments. The other day he asked if you were still in Taiwan. 'What are you talking about?' I said, 'He's in Tokyo.' He laughed and said it'd just slipped his mind. You don't suppose there's any danger he'll suddenly pass away, do you?"

Koji grunted his concern, but he did not think there was any cause for alarm.

"All right," said his mother, "let's go and celebrate the New Year."

The New Year meal had gotten leaner over the last few years, but they were still able to enjoy spiced saké and regular saké and rice cakes. Hardwood charcoal glowed red in the brazier and the tea kettle boiled noisily.

"Happy New Year! It's wonderful that the family—just the family—can be together like this."

The three of them raised their drinking cups.

"Happy New Year!"

After they had begun eating, Koji said, "Father, do you remember Mr. Kawai's daughter, Kawai from Antung?"

"Oh, you mean Kawai with Tamura Trading?"

"Yes. You remember the girl, the one everybody was calling O-Chu, the tall, stylish one. Last year—no, it's a new year now, so it would have been summer the year before last—she came to see us off at Antung station. You'll be surprised to hear she's now working where I'm stationed. I found out she was there the other day when she called out to me."

"Eh? At the Naval General Staff? I'd heard that her father had been transferred to the head office."

"Oh? I didn't know that. The General Staff is made up of any number of departments, of course, but it turns out that just by chance we're in the same one. Of course, a lot of the girls are there to avoid the civil draft, you know."

"Is that right?" his mother said, obviously interested. She had apparently been giving very considerable thought to a suitable bride for Koji ever since he had had—in her eyes—the good fortune to be assigned to Tokyo.

"And what sort of work do you do where you two are?" asked Koji's father.

"Well, I can't tell you that."

"You're helping the General Staff officers, something like that?"

"You could say that."

"What field is it, roughly speaking? You went to communications school, so it's related to that?"

"I really can't go into the details."

"Why not?"

His father's interest was piqued but Koji told him nothing.

The morning saké was having its effect and Koji's cheeks were flushed. He took off his uniform, changed into a kimono with a *kurume* splash pattern his mother had made, and sat across from his father to drink more saké.

"You know, you're a fortunate lad," his father began. "You have the honor of being assigned to the Naval General Staff, you're out of harm's way there, and you can come home like this for New Year's. You must give proper thought to your obligations to your ancestors, His Majesty, your parents and brothers, and your teacher. Today or tomorrow go pay your respects to Mr. Yashiro, and while you're about it, let him see you in your uniform."

"I'm not so sure Mr. Yashiro would be pleased to see me as an ensign in the navy."

Koji had told his fellow ensigns, Tanii, Hirokawa, and Wada, that they should be thankful for getting duty in Tokyo which, at the very least, meant their death sentences had been stayed: "And if our chow were on a par with fleet air unit food we would be in absolute paradise." Yet he felt himself resisting when his father told him of his good luck.

"It bothers me that you think only about how your own child is faring or how lucky he is or what his obligations are. You know, even I might be sent off somewhere as early as next month. No matter how you look at it, Japan is now facing real difficulties. We can't just think of what's best for ourselves, Father. I'm beginning to hear of my own classmates being killed in action. And I'll tell you, a lot more will die this year. I myself might well find myself in the thick of it. In any case, I can't think in terms of obligation and the like. Even Ibuki—"

"Now, now, that's enough," Koji's mother interjected. "Don't talk to your poor father like that. Stop it, now."

Her tone softened. "Young Ibuki is on a warship. He's been transferred to Iwakuni."

"You know *that*?"

"Yes. Chieko came over the other day and told us her brother had returned from southern waters and had said he'd seen you in Tokyo."

Surprised, Koji wondered why Chieko had visited his parents.

"She asked if she could have the address of your lodgings and was quite intent on getting it, which put us in an awkward position. Not to cause you any problems, I told her that while it was true that you were in Tokyo, sluggard that you are, you hadn't sent us any letters, so we didn't know where you were living."

It seemed to Koji that his mother's evasion had been transparent. Surely Chieko had known that he was in Tokyo, but had been intimidated at the thought of sending him a letter at the Navy Ministry, and had come to his house. Their feminine attitudes, both his mother's and Chieko's, struck him as somehow repugnant.

"Of course, she's a nice young lady," his mother continued in her broad dialect. "She's petite and girlish and looks young, though in fact she'll be 26 next year. She brought over an apple pie, I think it was, a fine pastry that you don't see much nowadays, that she said she'd baked herself."

"Your mother, you know, thinks highly of anyone who brings us something good to eat these days," said Koji's father, laughing.

"I was talking with Ibuki the other day," said Koji, changing the subject, "and we were wondering what in the world Ishikawa was doing."

"Isn't he back at the family clinic helping his father?" his mother said. "He told everyone he wouldn't go into the military and that apparently is how it stands. Even though he's healthy-looking enough."

"Is that right? Then tomorrow I'll see if he's in."

The next morning, the second day of the new year, Koji donned his uniform and left the house to visit Mr. Yashiro and his friend Ishikawa. The city was rundown somehow: houses all over displayed the flag, but they looked shabby and seemed to him perfectly attuned to this frigid morning early in the new year. He crossed a bridge and saw clear, cold water flowing beneath him.

The two Yashiro children were fascinated by his naval attire and noisily amused themselves, playing with his short sword and trying on his cap. His former teacher expressed his disgust with the recent formation of a so-called Patriotic Corps and how fanatical people at the high school had become. Mr. Yashiro told him of the many others who had graduated and followed him into the service.

Koji had lunch at his teacher's house and in the afternoon went to Ishikawa's. Ishikawa came out in an Oshima kimono, the sleeves of his shirt sticking out from under the sleeves of the kimono, looking every inch the local doctor on his New Year's break. He waxed eloquent on his clever evasion of the draft, on how they must be resourceful enough to contrive to somehow survive the war, that since, by and large, the war itself was hugely idiotic, it was preposterous to get caught up in it, that he was no longer interested in doing research, so if he ever wanted an advanced degree, the fastest way to get one would be to make a lot of money and buy it. It was vintage Ishikawa.

He brought out a padded kimono.

"Why don't you change into this. That uniform will spoil the taste of your saké."

"Not at all, you traitor," laughed Koji.

69

Koji left Hiroshima the next day, the third, on the daylight express. His mother went to the station with him.

"If you should find someone suitable, would you consider marrying while you're stationed in Tokyo? The war is getting worse and your father and I aren't getting any younger."

Koji did not reply.

Whenever he had gone out during his three days in Hiroshima, he had wondered if he might run into Chieko on a street corner. He could not, however, bring himself to go visit her house. He had rejected her offer, yet an unrelieved ambiguity somehow persisted in his mind, unsettling him.

When he arrived in Tokyo on the fourth he temporarily checked his baggage and went directly to Special Services.

He attempted to buttonhole Commander Ezaki in the hallway to tell him his "cold" was better, but the latter, without a backward glance, merely gave a slight nod.

His assistant, Petty Officer Sano, brought him the mass of messages that had accumulated while he was gone. Sano commiserated on Koji's coming down with a cold during the New Year's holiday and asked, among other things, if he had had the opportunity to eat the traditional rice cakes.

It was clearly unavoidable, so Koji told his assistant—and only him—the story behind his "cold."

"What? Really? You certainly pulled one off, sir," the petty officer said, laughing loudly and affecting an odd, archly dramatic tone of voice.

When Koji flipped through the file of messages he found the completely new attaché cipher mentioned in the year-end messages amongst those in the already-accessible Blue Secret and Domic ciphers.

The first such message was sent January 1 from New Delhi to Chungking. Koji found it beginning to turn up sporadically in messages dispatched from Moscow, Washington, Chungking and Tehran from around the seventh on. Like Blue Secret, it was a letter cipher using the Western alphabet, and there would be the words "Level

Secret" or "Oblique Secret" in cleartext at the beginning of each message, but with the seven or eight intercepts he had to work with Koji had no way of telling if they referred to two codes or if they were, in fact, a single code, "Level-Oblique Secret." He had no idea how many letters one letter group was made up of, or what the basic codebook was. Except for what appeared to be random repetition, Koji detected absolutely no potentially significant repetition in the messages and the usage frequency of the letters was pretty much the same for all 26. Koji hadn't a clue where he should begin.

*　　*　　*

From Koji's diary:

A day in January, 1944
　　Received letter and package from Antung. Brother was delighted Commander let me catch cold for New Year's. He is saying he will send him something tasty. Fired off a letter asking him not to. As always, he is playing lord of the manor. The package contains whiskey-chocolates and sugar, which is a treat. I'll take the chocolate to Tanii and Wada tomorrow for them to eat. These days everyone's down in the dumps somehow. They're talking about going to Yokosuka again and raising hell. Sung-hui Ch'oe is dancing at Imperial Theater, so Hirokawa and Kuki are suggesting we go.
　　Both movies and fiction are worthless. You finish a novel called *Navy*, and one titled *Army* comes out. The Moulin Rouge has changed its name to Sakubunkan. I doubt you can drop a name much beloved for over twelve years that easily. Tiresome business. To have all our energies in the military channeled into war is fine, since that's what we're about, but why must they paint with such a broad brush? First of all, the use of "hostile languages" is certainly not being abolished in the navy. As always, a wash basin is still called *osutappu*—from the English washtub—and the *furo* is *basu*, from English bath.
　　On the less serious side, several days ago in the Research Jottings

column of the paper a doctor quotes a certain professor at the University of Berlin lecturing his class.

Gentlemen, he who would be a doctor of renown must approach his work possessing a highly-developed sense of struggle and meticulous, scrupulous powers of observation. In ancient times a physician would taste his patient's urine and thereby determine whether or not there was sugar in it.

The professor then dipped a finger in some urine and licked his finger. The students, doleful expressions on their faces, did likewise. The professor addressed them when they had finished.

My joy at seeing your highly developed sense of struggle knows no bounds. As for your meticulous, scrupulous powers of observation, they have failed. Not one of you noticed that I dipped my index finger in the urine and then licked my middle finger. You can never become great doctors, observing as you do.

When the *Mainichi* newspaper ran an editorial calling for large increase in production of naval aircraft, Premier Tojo is said to have suddenly jumped up and said, "Destroy the *Mainichi*!" Don't know to what extent this true, but have the feeling it's probably not credible story, even making allowances for Tojo.

Another day in January

Tanii came an hour and a half late to the class reunion at Yokosuka with the surprising news that Kurimura passed through Tokyo today. Said Kurimura had called from a pay phone to tell him he had come from Sendai to Ueno Station in Tokyo and wanted to see him for two hours before his southbound train left Tokyo Station. He sounded fine and when Tanii asked where he was going he responded "south, far south." Tanii flew over to the station, but in spite of fact that a great many cadets were there, he could find Kurimura nowhere. Knew neither unit nor train Kurimura was taking. I wish Kurimura best of luck.

A day in February

Defenders of Ruotta at Kwajalein apparently made their final attack last night. Since Prince Otowa, son of Imperial Prince Asaka, is at Kwajalein, there was talk of dispatching a rescue flying boat, but nothing seems to have come of it. What must everyone feel in such a situation, when a rescue craft accommodating no more than 10 or 15 men arrives?

Appears Innami also was killed in action. News of death in battle of classmates comes one after the other these days. Guys here in Tokyo must feel pressure, because there is continual arranging of marriages going on. Hirokawa is making arrangements with Chizuko Kayama, a young pianist who studied in Paris. He told me he's "crazy about her," but wanted to know what I thought. Seen on stage, she appears cute, naive girl. I've also felt it might be okay for me to marry. Strikes me as curiously sordid to say one loses if he dies in war without ever knowing the pleasures of married life, yet when I think of Chieko, it seems clearly preferable for me to marry someone at this point.

Another day in February

Received a telegram informing me Father is seriously ill.

In the evening a bunch of us, Wada, Hirokawa, Tanii, Tsutsumi and Kuki, went to Imperial Theater to see Sung-hui Ch'oe dance. Very interesting, and a beautiful sight to see him dance traditional Korean folk pieces in his national costume. When he had finished dancing, the stage went dark, and when the spotlight came on again Ch'oe was kneeling at center, still dressed in his Korean clothes. He cast a steady, intense gaze at the balcony where fellow Koreans sat watching and smiled engagingly. Koreans responded with tremendous, fervid cheer and for a moment theater was engulfed in the unspoken force of human will. Was astounded at national consciousness, if that's what it was, of Koreans. When I mentioned this to Kuki after we had left the theater, he said at rugby matches and the like between Korean and Japanese teams, the response is even more overwhelming. When Korean rooting section gets worked up, they shout "Kill them! Kill them!"

When I came back a telegram was waiting: "Father slight cerebral hemorrhage. Unable to get up this morning." Been expecting this, so wasn't that surprised; if next informed he has passed away, I'm sure I'll have to go, so I'll get a new dress uniform and mourning band. It's now a little before one. No word has come.

Another day in February

Details received from Mother. That morning they were hulling millet grown in garden, heads bent. Father said he was going to rest a bit. As he raised his head he experienced dizziness and lost control of his hands. Even so, she says he went into the toilet by himself. He fell down in hallway returning, and crawled back to the room. Doctor came immediately and gave him a shot, but he had absolutely no sensation on the left side of his body, so he's being kept in bed. He's alert and not in poor spirits. Doctor said he'll survive if this is not followed by a bad one, but I think his remaining partially paralyzed like this with the war gradually worsening will be a thorny problem. My mind's set on returning home, but haven't broached matter, and this pains me, yet doubt I can return home simply because Father is seriously ill. Understand my brother has wired that his wife is returning to Japan.

Another day in February

There has been a rash of thefts. The other day Kuki had an alligator belt taken on way to or at the office, Wada had a raincoat taken, and someone else lost his shoes. As one would expect where protecting military secrets is taken very seriously, this caused a considerable stir for a bit. Today Kuki was away from his desk and returned just in time to catch Kihara, lieutenant junior grade in the class just before ours, start off, quick as a wink, with his gloves, so he took them back. Indeed appears thief taking things over the last few days is Kihara. Word is there was a cover-up in his class. Light-fingered or not, we've got a weird one on our hands.

At the junior officer's formation today we were lectured on the impropriety of young officers chatting familiarly with typists. May be due to Wada's loudly rhapsodizing over the beauty of his very own Blue—she always wears a blue sweater—on whom he lays exclusive claim.

I really seem to be preoccupied with this sort of talk these days. My work has run smack into a stone wall. Can't go into detail in this diary, of course, but in such a situation I'm immobilized, really confronted with a wall that blocks progress. Sight of work every day is torture.

A day in March

Snowed, good two or three inches piling up, then snowed again. On return from attendance at the naval college graduation ceremony, His Majesty The Emperor stopped by at the Naval section of Imperial General Headquarters. We welcomed him in the snow at the side of the Ministry front entrance in full formal dress. He took lunch at the Ministry and the mess hall provided us a repast as spare and simple as a department store child's plate.

"Getting a peek at our little Emp sure as hell isn't going to make my day," said annoyed Kuki, brushing snow off his shoulders. Kuki, son of an aristocratic family descended from a feudal lord, has no compunctions about talking like that, which struck me somehow as oddly amusing, singular. Yet later when I stole a glance at the Emperor descending the front stairs as a military band played the national anthem, I was nonetheless deeply moved. His Majesty's face looked almost translucently pale and his expression extremely troubled, though it may have been way the light hit him. Struck me that His Majesty is most certainly more affected by war than we are. Later said this to Kuki.

"That's only as it should be," he responded. "Every day hordes of people go to their deaths calling out his name, and the Emp can't stand the thought of it."

As for the ancient exhortation, be loyal to your lord and love your country, Kuki said, though he and Wada may do the latter, in no case would they subscribe to the former.

Today the Prince, Captain Takamatsu, who normally does navy calisthenics with the women typists and returns our salutes with obvious cheer, did not respond to our most formal salute. He may not have seen us, or that may be the way he's supposed to act.

Another day in March

Read in paper that as of April 1 use of special expresses, sleeping and dining cars and first class will end throughout Japan. This causes no great difficulties, yet one somehow catches the scent of defeat in the air now. There's no food in the city, people's clothes are ragged and it seems once a month we are told of another "glorious defeat." Today Hirokawa, face incredulous, told me there was large banner on front of Imperial Rule Assistance Association building proclaiming "Divine Winds Will Soon Save Us."

When I get home from drinking at the Officers' Club, the landlord's wife needles me cynically. As for work, am completely in the dark and do not know where to turn.

In Hiroshima, Father's condition is unchanged, but unfortunately he has a ravenous appetite these days and from time to time will ask for something extravagant.

Another day in March

Heard that Commander Hori, second in command when we were in Taiwan, is now Executive Officer of warship *Takao*, and that it was berthed in Yokosuka, so yesterday a large group of us went down to Yokosuka en masse to visit with him. He said he thought he was a dead man when they landed at Menado, so has no attachment to life now and feels not the slightest distress in ignoring hunger for food, sex, fame, or sleep. We had some saké and did some folk dancing. After seeing intelligence types here in Tokyo affecting a curious sort of intellectual pose when they talk, an honest-to-God warrior like Commander Hori is a breath of fresh air. Stayed in Yokosuka one night, returning early the next morning. The snow from the night before which lay heavily on telephone wires was melting in the sun and falling in large droplets, which glistened as they fell. Spring coming, I thought to myself. Love the feeling of crisp, clear mornings in the wake of large snowflakes that fall at the end of the winter season. Slushy roads, bundled-up children, pure-white, harvested rice paddies and groves of bamboo bending under snow, saw all these to my delight glistening from the train window as I returned to Tokyo. And today is Sunday. Hear that the office is to be moved to the Meguro district first part of April.

Four

There were many trees on the grounds of the Navy College near the Meguro station in Tokyo, and with the arrival of spring the lawn atop a knoll used as a croquet court turned green, and the trees that had lost their leaves set forth their tender buds. When the wild cherry and Yoshino cherry trees scattered throughout the garden were at last bedecked with blossoms, the azaleas also burst into bloom and all was transformed for a time into a beauteous array.

An often sunny warehouse-like building standing on a corner of the knoll and adjacent to the tennis courts was a temporary mess for the young officers. Special Services Group, which had been in the Kasumigaseki district of Tokyo, had moved onto the grounds of the Navy College early in April 1944.

In the mess hall, rows of long, narrow tables extended to the back of the room. On the white tablecloths sat a string of white plates emblazoned with the anchor emblem, two for each setting, which held the midday meal of ham and bread, and a name card stood at each place. One man disputed loudly with another as he broke off a piece from his bread, another smoked, and yet another yelled for tea. There were few windows, so the room reverberated with the sound of voices. In the midst of this hubbub Wada and Tanii were quickly finishing their meal. Wada was the one with the thin pale face and in the seat across from him was the portly Tanii. Koji, Kuki, and Tsutsumi sat on either side of them.

Wada lit up a cigarette, leaving half his roll uneaten.

"Say! I'll take that!" said Koji, his hand shooting out at Wada's discarded bread. Tsutsumi's face betrayed his chagrin. For someone with a decent appetite, one piece of bread was nowhere near enough. Koji had already broken the roll-half in two.

"Want some?" he asked, thrusting a piece under Tsutsumi's and Tanii's noses.

They snickered derisively.

"No thanks."

"I've had plenty."

The hand Koji had extended now hung awkwardly in the air. He was suddenly self-conscious.

"What's the matter, Wada?" he said. "You're always leaving something."

"Oh, my stomach's been out of sorts lately." Wada answered, nervously knitting his brow. Kuki, who had been reading something, suddenly looked up at them.

"Hey! Listen, I, uh, the fact is, I finally got my orders today."

"What?"

"I'm heading out," laughed Kuki, wrinkling his nose. "Going to Third Fleet Headquarters. I'm trading places with Ensign Suzuki, from the first class."

This was news to everyone. There was a sudden flurry of questions.

"Really?" they cried.

"When?"

At which point a lieutenant junior grade from the first class, Nakada, who worked in A Section, came in behind Koji, his small frame bent over, and looked each man in the face.

"Anyone want to go out and play croquet?"

The first class of reserve officers, the class ahead of Koji and his mates, had all been promoted to lieutenant junior grade several days earlier, and at the same time, Commander Morii had been made captain and Lieutenant Iwamoto, back from Sasebo, had been promoted to lieutenant commander.

"Kuki says he's leaving."

"I know that," said Nakada. "They didn't want to send him, but it was up to Captain Morii, either Hirokawa or Kuki. Hirokawa's about to get married, so Kuki was odd man out."

Like Nakada, Hirokawa and Kuki worked in A Section.

"Third Fleet. That's tough."

"You'll die, you bastard," said Wada, a matter-of-fact expression on his face. He had been closest to Kuki since the time when the group had been in Taiwan.

"No way! No way, dammit!" said Kuki, shaking his head and affecting a clownish tone. "I refuse to die in battle!"

"Hey! You don't wanna play?" Nakada persisted.

"Croquet?"

They put out their cigarettes and stood up.

After they had set up the iron wickets in the grass beside the mess hall, they brought out the mallets and wooden balls from the box and—resorting to the scissors, paper, rock game—chose up sides.

"The Mobile Fleets were doing splendidly up to Midway," said Kuki, "so I even thought Japan might just win."

"What do you mean 'might,'" Koji said with a laugh.

Nakada and Wada formed one team, Tsutsumi and Kuki the other. Tanii and Koji had to wait for the next game. It struck Koji as ironic that Kuki, the most pessimistic about the war of all his comrades, should be about to be transferred to Task Force (Third Fleet) Headquarters at a time when rumors were flying that a decisive naval battle was near.

Gavel-shaped mallets struck the balls with light wooden reports, sending them rolling over the young grass. Wada expertly hit Tsutsumi's ball over the boundary line with his own. Kuki must have lost his concentration, for he succeeded in getting his ball through the first wicket only after several tries.

"Hey," Tanii quietly asked Koji, "Isn't that Blue?"

"Where? Oh, yeah. On the end, at the right."

The typists who had finished eating, Blue Kizu and O-Chu Kawai and a couple of other young women, passed along the far side of the croquet court, chopstick cases in hand.

"Not so loud. You know, I really wonder if she's pretty enough to fuss that much over."

"I suppose," Koji responded. "I myself don't find her that attractive. But I suspect Wada does. To hear Kuki tell it, Wada is inventing useless jobs just for Blue to do."

Miss Kizu, wearing a bright blue half-coat, her smartly coiffeured hair dancing on her shoulders, went off together with the Kawai girl toward their office building, her calves flashing white as she strode along.

"Kuki gets carried away and exaggerates," said Tanii. "I don't think Wada has anything special going. In fact, I wonder if he isn't a little off his feed these days. Look. He looks awfully pale. He's always working."

Wada had developed a new lead in the breaking of the American strip cipher and, surmising what sort of message the enemy might send in a given situation, was working backward from hypothetical plaintext. He was single-mindedly working on re-creating the system's cipher disks. Miss Kizu had been assigned to him as his typist.

The four men worked their way around the course to the sound of wood smacking wood.

"You know, Kuki—" Koji said to the others, "our friend Kuki is a bit upset. And we'll miss him too."

A little later the Nakada-Wada team returned victorious.

"You wanna play next?" Nakada asked, holding out his mallet.

"Let's not," said Tanii. "It's about time for the Exalted Ones to make their appearance."

The section chiefs and staff officers had no compunction about taking the court away from the junior officers when they emerged from the other mess hall.

"It's blazing hot," said Wada, taking out a white handkerchief and mopping his brow. "Let's go back to my room. We have to plan a going-away party for Kuki."

Koji and Tanii broke off from the others and began strolling through the grounds.

Four or five typists had formed a circle and were hitting a volleyball back and forth with an officer who had removed his jacket and was playing in his blue trousers and dress shirt. The circle expanded, contracted, then broke up. The young women stood chatting together around a girl in a yellow sweater, their backs against a sun-drenched wall. Three ensigns were playing catch with a baseball. The two men descended the low knoll and walked on.

"What d'you think of that bunch?" asked Tanii, thrusting his jaw toward them. "Don't look! Don't look! There's a real knockout there."

Several childlike girls, a little younger than Blue and O-Chu, were boisterously bouncing about near two petty officers playing ping-pong.

"You mean the one holding the petty officer's jacket?"

"Yeah, that one, that one," said Tanii, now directing his gaze toward the top of the office building. "She's better than Blue."

Among the half-dozen or so girls who were so noisily enjoying themselves, unable to stand still even for a moment, one typist obviously did not share their pleasure. Koji saw a suggestion of melancholy in her face. She leaned her slender, spare frame against a honey-locust tree, the petty officer's jacket draped over her arm.

"Uh-huh, I've noticed her before. She's attractive," said Koji. "It's that obvious boredom of hers. Know her name?"

"Dunno."

The two of them passed by the group, walking toward the rear of the archery range. A grove of trees stood on the grounds of the adjacent Asaka Imperial Mansion. They were struck by the colors of the young leaves, layer upon beautiful layer, of every imaginable shade. When they doubled back once again to the croquet court it was already almost one o'clock and the lunch break was ending. People were putting away the game equipment and others were putting on their coats. By ones and twos, figures began to leave the grassy knoll and the sun-drenched wall.

"By the way," asked Koji as he left Tanii, "what would be a good day for Kuki's going-away party?"

*　　*　　*

82

The more the intercepts accumulated, the clearer it became that the Chungking government's new military-attaché cipher would be extremely troublesome. The name of the cipher was Level-Oblique Secret after all, not two ciphers named "Level" and "Oblique," as Koji had thought. Early in March a message was sent in Blue Secret from Chungking to New Delhi saying that because the revised code tables appended to Level-Oblique Secret had an error in them, corrected tables were being forwarded by air mail. This was broken and confirmed, but the basic cipher book and the transposition keys were apparently entirely new, so the prospects for decryption did not look good. Even Section 18 at the Army's General Staff Headquarters was working frantically on it, but the word was that they had hit a dead end.

Koji and his assistant, Petty Officer Sano, were experimenting with this cipher every day. Sano was a workaholic who loved his job, and he had previously broken several simple systems. He had noticed that in one Level-Oblique Secret message the letters O and V turned up in a curious fashion. The 26 letters of the alphabet were used with more or less the same frequency in Level-Oblique Secret, but this one particular message contained an unusually large number of O's and V's and in the interval between two O's and two V's, he saw—though did not understand—a curious configuration: an apparent rule that required the intervals to be multiples of 3 or 4. The two men were able to get only a hint of the basic nature of the cipher, but made not the least progress beyond that.

Each of the Level-Oblique Secret letter groups seemed to consist of three letters. The total number of combinations of such trigrams, in a codebook employing all 26 letters of the alphabet, would be 26 to the third power, or 17,576. This seemed a reasonable number for the codebook that had succeeded Blue Secret, in practical terms. If each letter group consisted of four letters, however, the total number of possible groups would be 26 to the fourth power, or 456,976 combinations, far too many to be practical for the codebooks of any country. And it was probably correct to assume that messages enciphered in three-letter groups were composed, as Domic was, in horizontal rows, and then, after a given key was applied, transmitted as vertical columns following the order prescribed by the key.

There was absolutely no way of knowing, however, whether there were 15, 20, or 30 keys, on top of which, there seemed to be provisions for individual attachés to resort to differing stratagems depending on their locations, so that the Japanese side could detect subtle differences in the frequency-of-usage curve for individual letters. The secret to unravelling this riddle was probably the revised code tables Chungking had referred to, but the nature of these was not known.

Level-Oblique Secret began gradually to replace Blue Secret and Domic, the attaché ciphers they had broken, and with the phasing out of these ciphers there was a precipitous drop in the production of intelligence. The heads of A and B Sections, not to mention Lieutenant Commander Iwamoto, Koji's own section chief, queried him endlessly about it, leaving him depressed and frustrated each time.

The fact that there might well be a passage of critical importance to Japan's fate hidden within the columns of letters Koji saw before him made him uneasy. The decryption of military-attaché cipher systems had been relentlessly pursued ever since the Special Services Group's Chinese section had been established, but now, thanks to this Level-Oblique Secret, the whole operation could come to an abrupt end. The effort to stop this rested squarely on his shoulders, which in itself strengthened, willy-nilly, his sense of responsibility.

The Chinese military attaché stationed in Bern was the only one not to use the new cipher system. He employed the cipher known as ABKF, 70 per cent of which C Section could read. Bern had used it even when Blue Secret was being used everywhere else. Switzerland was neutral, and so friendly and hostile diplomats and military attachés rubbed shoulders in the city, and thus its use was apparently a measure taken for fear Level-Oblique Secret might be stolen. Precisely for that reason, however, prospects for expanding at a stroke the decryptable text of Level-Oblique Secret would be good if even only a part of the Level-Oblique Secret were to be broken, provided they were able to snare a message transmitted to Switzerland in ABKF that was identical in content to one sent from Chungking to America or Russia. But even then, little would be gained if they couldn't break the basic formulation of Level-Oblique Secret.

Koji sat down and calculated the possibilities for achieving effective recovery, using all the theoretically possible combinations. He got the preposterous answer that in order to test completely all instances it would take 100 typists working 8 hours a day at least a dozen years. It would be nonsensical to make a work request of anywhere near this magnitude when things were so bad these days that Special Services was even having trouble getting typing paper.

One day Koji invited Tanii to the Officers' Club and on the way over he told him about Level-Oblique Secret.

"I'll tell you, nothing's worse than grappling with a cipher you can't crack. I can really appreciate the sense of desperation and depression you guys felt when you were working on Naval Code traffic and the strip cipher."

Since Koji had taken his friend to task for what he had seen as his endless complaining, Tanii now turned and gave his friend a knowing look.

"The Americans, of course, would put 10,000 typists on it and solve it in a month. That's how the Americans are."

"They'd probably invent a machine of some kind to do it, rather than use typists. I think Japan's handicraft mentality is really the problem," Koji said. "If the enemy scores a hit in one out of a hundred rounds, they'll bring out a thousand cannons."

Koji and the others had talked before about how sheer quantity transformed itself into quality. The slogan "Better one gun scoring a hundred hits in as many tries than a hundred guns scoring one" was considered to epitomize the spirit of the Imperial Navy, but everywhere today the unfolding reality was that even if Japan had guns which scored a hundred hits out of a hundred, the Americans would overwhelm them with a thousand—or ten thousand—one-hit-in-a-hundred guns. This was true even in communications security. Japanese forces, no matter the circumstances, never transmitted in the clear. In emergency situations American naval forces, however, did so with equanimity.

"Enough! Enough! Let's quit this damn shop talk when we're going off to drink."

Koji had begun to be drawn to saké in a way that he hadn't been before. Gradually, however, saké was becoming an unobtainable luxury.

By this time his friend Kuki had had his farewell party and was already on his way to his new post with the fleet. He hadn't been able to tell Koji and the others what ship he'd be on, or where his duty station was, until he got to Kure, so when he left, Koji drew a map showing where his house was and told Kuki that if he were to be in Kure for a while he should go over to Hiroshima and stay at Koji's house. His father had had a stroke, he told him, but if that didn't bother Kuki, the old man would still be able to offer him a drink.

And Commander Ezaki, head of S Section, had been transferred from Special Services to the aircraft carrier *Zuiho*, where he was now executive officer, leaving, in fact, before Kuki. It looked as though the time was approaching for the decisive battle in the western Pacific between the Japanese and American fleets, though Koji and the others did not know precisely how the situation stood now.

"Hey, I've found out her name!" Koji told Tanii, sitting across from him in the Officers' Club mess.

"What're you talking about?"

"That typist I told you the other day I found attractive. You know Tamura, the baby of the Kindergarten Set? She told me."

"Really."

"Her name is Noriko Yano. You write *Nori* with the character for 'decorum.' The feel of the name's not half bad, is it?"

Tanii said nothing.

"No interest in her today?"

"It's not that," Tanii answered, draining his saké cup yet again. He looked about, seemingly unsettled. "The fact is I've got something to celebrate today."

"What? Not again!" Tanii had always been proud of his success with the fair sex, so Koji was alluding to that.

"No, that's not it at all," Tanii interrupted quickly. "I can't talk about it yet."

"Then don't bring it up in the first place. I'm certainly not going to press you about anything secret."

Saying no more, Koji reached over to the plate of whale meat that had been brought in. The fare at the Officers' Club was growing plainer by the day. Young officers with Special Services were scattered about the room eating. When they spotted a colleague they would smile weakly and raise their knives slightly in a meaningless sort of gesture.

"I wonder if I could tell just you," Tanii began uneasily.

Koji did not respond.

Tanii suddenly closed his eyes. He drained his saké cup again.

"Ding! Ding! Dong! Starboard rudder!" he said, pretending he was commanding a motor launch, his shoulders hunched.

"Ah-ha! You, too," said Koji, setting his fork down and fixing Tanii with his gaze. "You're shipping out, right?"

"Yeah."

"Where to?"

"Can't say yet."

"Don't worry. Tell me. Don't make such a big thing of it. Where?"

"Headquarters, Combined Fleet. It's tentative at this point. I talked with Commander Ozawa at noon."

Combined Fleet Headquarters was not considered to be in as hazardous a deployment as the Third Fleet.

"Really? How 'bout that! Sounds great."

"Fare thee well, Naval Code traffic!"

Dazzling sunlight, the deep-hued sea, its shining billows, the intense interplay of tension and release—Koji and Tanii had originally elected to go into communications for the same reason: the desire to have a go at sea duty. Koji left his friend that night feeling a tinge of excitement.

Three days later, however, the matter of Tanii's "tentative" assignment abruptly took a new and different turn. Summoned by Commander Ozawa, head of B Section, he was asked if he were the eldest son in his family. Tanii replied that he and his younger sister were the only children.

"There are no circumstances at home that might cause concern?"

"No sir."

"The other day I said you might be posted at Combined Fleet Headquarters, but given our needs now—it will be difficult for you, of course—we'd like you to leave for Northeast Area Fleet Headquarters as of May 1."

Tanii felt the blood drain from his face. Even from their daily briefings it was obvious that the course of events in the north these days was cause for serious concern. It was generally believed that an enemy invasion of the Kurile Islands was essentially a matter of time. And though it was referred to as a fleet, where Tanii would be going was actually a land-based communications unit on Shumushu Island at the northern tip of the Kurile chain.

Koji was convinced his friend would not return to Japan alive.

*   *   *

His fellow ensigns he had trained with gave Tanii the traditional going-away party before he left.

They reserved a room at the Officers' Club in the Shiba district, closed the door, and immediately reverted to the free and easy student mentality, proceeding to have a good and boisterous time of it. Only Tanii, the guest of honor, was obviously forcing the gaiety, looking ill at ease. He would abruptly fall into a gloomy silence, then just as abruptly and absurdly burst into paroxysms of uncontrollable laughter. One of the more adept men got on the good side of the waitress and soon the saké was flowing in incredibly vast quantities. Everyone was feeling the effects of the alcohol. Tsutsumi and Wada and Hirokawa were all chattering at once, so practically no one could be heard. Their talking—every man for himself—was more like shouting. Amidst all this, Tanii's transfer was forgotten, and they drank to the good health of Kuki, who had already left, the recovery of Wada's sick father, and just about anything they could think of.

Tsutsumi stood up.

"Next, then, we drink to Ao."

He was talking about Miss Kizu, the typist, whom he normally referred to as *Blue*, using the English word, instead of the Japanese *Ao*. By obscure custom, foreign words were strictly taboo at farewell parties for those leaving Japan proper and every time someone accidentally used such a word, he was fined 10 *sen*. The money thus accumulated was given to the leavetaker as a farewell gift. It was an ironic twist to the wartime abolition of English in Japan as a whole.

"Who's Ao?!" asked the dreadfully nearsighted ensign named Ono. "I'll be damned if I'll drink to someone I don't even know!"

"Damn!" Tsutsumi, interrupted in the middle of his toast, looked down at Ono. "Whatta pain you are! Listen, you've got to have noticed that pretty typist whose nickname is the English word for blue. Learn something about women, too!"

Ono had worked with Wada on the strip cipher, and was something of a *wunderkind*, but aside from his exceptional ability in English and a talent for holding his liquor, he was decidedly the unworldly type. Ever since Taiwan he had been making a mess of his day-to-day work. He came to the office in a dirty, grimy uniform and his breath inevitably smelled of Jintan, the popular antacid he took so much of. Once when someone suggested they all go to Yokosuka and hire some geisha, he actually began to tremble. He had been terrified, absolutely panic-stricken.

"There's one like that?" Ono responded, undefeated by Tsutsumi's jab.

"You can't possibly be unaware of her! She always wears a blue *sweater*," Tsutsumi said, using the English word. "Oh-oh!" He threw a 10-*sen* coin on the table. Ono let a smug smile crease his maldeveloped, comic face.

"She wears a vest made of blue yarn and every day the color of her *skirt* changes like a piece of *China Marble* taffy. Oh-oh. I give up. Enough, already."

Ono and Wada laughed together, as did Hirokawa and Koji. Tanii, however, was obviously tired and growing impatient.

A little later Koji took Hirokawa, who had made all the arrangements, off to one side and suggested the party break up. Following Hirokawa's lead, they all stood up, raised their saké cups, each offering Tanii the stock farewells, after which they rambunctiously exited out onto Iikura Boulevard and went their separate ways.

Koji and Tanii, wanting to lose the others, took off at a trot toward the Toranomon area and left the rest behind. Tanii, looking straight ahead, now walked briskly along.

"Hey," he began imperiously, "I know it's late, but come with me down to Yokosuka."

Koji smiled to himself in the darkness. The usually diffident Tanii spoke in a peremptory way, an unusually contentious manner.

"Well, today I'll go with you anywhere you want. Where do we get the train?"

"Hamamatsucho," Tanii replied without turning to look at Koji.

The evening's "fines" came to train fare for two, exactly. They took the Yamanote line train from Hamamatsucho to Shinagawa, and by the time they had transferred to the Yokosuka line there, Tanii was obviously exhausted and had the air of someone sorely put upon. He flopped down on the seat and closed his eyes.

"Buck up, you calculating bastard! When you thought you were going to the Combined Fleet you were happy enough."

"You're damned right!" Tanii opened his eyes and fixed Koji with a defiant stare. "How come Commander Ozawa went out of his way to pick me to go up north?"

"I don't think he really 'went out of his way' to pick you."

"Shit! One order, and I have to go off somewhere and die." Slouching, Tanii threw out his legs and lay there limply like a long-dead fish.

"Listen, you're in the military, so you have to accept that. Nobody can know what the hell fate has in store for him. Kuki went off without complaint, didn't he? Hang tough! You think you won't have to go if you try sulking?"

"You'd be delighted to go, would you?"

"I wouldn't be delighted, but if I had no choice, I think I'd keep a stiff upper lip and try to look as nonchalant about it as possible."

"Wow, you know what?" Tanii said peevishly. "You don't know a damned thing about me!" He smiled sardonically and closed his eyes once again.

The train was almost deserted by the time it arrived in Yokosuka. It was a balmy night toward the end of April and a salt-laden breeze blew in from the ocean. The streets of the navy town were dark, and the hordes of seamen and petty officers who came walking along the sidewalk would peer at the two men in the darkness and, when they realized that they were officers, would suddenly salute as though given a jolt of electricity. Koji and Tanii could see high above them a string of red warning lights.

The two men entered a Japanese-style restaurant reserved for naval officers that they had often been to. O-Shin, a waitress they knew, greeted them.

"Congratulations!" she said when she heard of Tanii's transfer. "But why the long face?"

Tanii forced a smile in spite of himself.

It was late, so there were practically no other customers. After they'd been there an hour or so, however, a pretty geisha named Kikuchiyo, a big draw in the restaurants in Yokosuka that catered to the navy, made her slightly tipsy appearance. Nonetheless, Tanii's ill-humor remained undisguised. He had been drinking saké like water, and was now close to oblivion.

"I tell you, I'm really fed up with the military."

"Goodness, that's unusual, isn't it," Kikuchiyo said. "But some people feel that way, don't they."

Tanii ignored her and turned to Koji.

"You like the military, don't you," said Tanii, putting the needle to his friend. "It's fine for you. Am I right? You like it, don't you? But I shouldn't have gone into the navy. What is the damned navy? A mass of stupidity and fraud!"

"What? Then you mean you should've let the army take you? I

think, when all's said and done, the navy's better than the army."

"Just as I thought. You like the military after all," guffawed Tanii. "You should've joined the marines when you finished middle school and forgotten about literature!"

Tanii laughed hysterically.

He suddenly grabbed Kikuchiyo by the neck and pulled her toward him.

"Stop it! What d'you think you're doing!?" She pushed him away. "You're a coward, you know that? There's not a single officer in the Naval Air Force like you! My boyfriend died at Makin. I'm gonna keep on working right here until we win."

"What'd you say?! You mouth off to me and I'll smack you one!"

It was then that O-Shin returned.

"What's going on here? Please don't argue. Kiku," she said, sending the geisha off, "you have a phone call."

After Kikuchiyo left, O-Shin told the men that the geisha would take out a map of the world every day and scratch at Makin Island in the Gilberts with her fingernails.

That was all they saw of Kikuchiyo. She didn't come back. Tanii then turned his querulousness on Koji, who at last exploded.

"Knock it off, you damned fool!" he shouted, giving Tanii's shoulder a solid shove. "You know we're all going to miss you when you're gone."

Tanii was all but knocked over backward, and put his hand out on the *tatami* to keep from falling. He abruptly fell silent and pushed himself upright. He stared into his saké cup, looking as though he were on the verge of tears. The two men left the next morning, each dogged by a lingering discomfiture.

Soon afterward, Tanii left Ueno Station on the morning train for Aomori. The only flights to the Kuriles were from the airbase at Chitose in Hokkaido, so he would first have to travel to Chitose by train. When Koji went to see him off, Tanii, at last looking halfway cheerful, was there with his parents and sister. Tanii pulled him aside as he came out onto the station platform.

"Haven't told the family where I'm headed. I've led them to

believe it's somewhere in Hokkaido. Go along with me on this. When we took a short sword—an heirloom—out of the family storehouse, the old scabbard came apart. My mother's really worried about what that might mean."

He handed Koji his fingernail clippings wrapped, as tradition demanded, in Japanese paper. "For my funeral in case I don't come back.

"There's something else," he continued. "I've told my folks that after I leave you'll be coming to the house to pick up some things I've written of a classified nature. I want you to remove something from the inside coat pocket of my suit and take care of it. I put something out of the ordinary there and forgot about it."

"What is it?" Koji asked, then suddenly understood. "You're telling me to do your dirty work, huh?" he said, with an unconcealed grimace.

The departure bell began ringing. A large number of navy and army personnel being posted to the north were aboard the train already.

"Well," said Tanii to his father, "I'm on my way."

He got aboard and stood in the vestibule. They had not let his mother and sister onto the departure platform, and the two women stood dejectedly on the next platform looking across the tracks. Interurban trains were pulling in every few minutes, blocking their view and making Tanii's mother all the more anxious.

"With any luck, the Yanks will invade the Kuriles while I'm still waiting around for my flight out of Chitose."

"Fainthearted bastard to the end."

"Yep." Tanii smiled. "I even miss the Kindergarten Set. I've really blown it."

The train jolted forward, then began moving slowly down the track. Koji, fist on hip, took off his cap and waved it. Tanii started waving his cap too. Koji saw the receding face stiffen. At the end of the platform the wheels of the locomotive raced spasmodically, noisily, and billows of white steam rose into the air. The train gathered speed and Tanii's figure at last rounded the end of the platform and disappeared.

Koji went down the stairs with Tanii's father and once again exchanged pleasantries with the mother and sister. Tanii's mother, her face flushed, a handkerchief gripped tightly in her hand, thanked Koji again and again for all he had done for her son.

*　　*　　*

Koji's work in decrypting Level-Oblique Secret was getting nowhere. The fresh spring greenery on the grounds of the government building Koji worked in had changed now to the darker shades of summer. He wanted nothing to do with paperwork. When he pulled the night watch he was no longer able to work through the night with the intensity he had shown before, and more often than not he would pass the time vacantly staring off into space. A number of A and B Section men would be on duty, encamped around the telephones and the large locator board used for plotting enemy activity.

One day when Lieutenant Commander Fukuda, who was with A Section, was standing watch, and Nakada and Tsutsumi were scheduled to sleep in the duty room, Koji joined the group in conversation. They were talking about how the army was attempting, as always, to seize the initiative from the navy over the allocation of materials for the building of aircraft.

"Is it actually true that the army types have made a transport submarine?" Nakada asked the lieutenant commander, slapping at the locator chart with the pointer used in briefings. To a man the younger officers had been infected by their superiors' dislike of the army. They disdained it and believed Japan would not now be a hostage to destiny had not the army acted so highhandedly. As a matter of course they contemptuously referred to the army as the army types, Mr. Land, the landlubbers, and so on.

"Well," began Fukuda, originally a submariner, with an amiable smile and a wink, "it might be true, mightn't it. It would seem Mr. Land has now realized—finally—that transporting by sea is no simple matter. And even if you do make yourself a submarine, you can't easily submerge and surface and the like with a crew you've just thrown together."

Tsutsumi, ensconced at the telephone, shouted out plotting information as he received it from the communications unit at Owada.

"1830. BIMEC strip cipher, bearing 87 degrees from Penang. Next, 1840. Same BIMEC cipher . . ."

Reports on enemy vessels and aircraft from various direction-finding stations arrived in condensed form from Owada. A and B Section personnel on duty would process these and record them on the board in preparation for the briefing the following morning.

"Does it look as though there will be a major engagement in the near future?" Koji asked.

"In about a month, I'd guess. If Japan loses that one the odds will be against us, I'm afraid. After that it'll be a whittling process, the Philippines, Taiwan. And then," Fukuda added with another smile, "we'll all cut our bellies open together.

"I know it's rude," Fukuda continued, but on a different tack, "to say something that doesn't give due weight to everyone's individuality, but I think everybody knows more than they need to of our own tactical operations. The English, in contrast, are much more consistent on this point."

He then went on to tell them that when English spies coming from India by plane arrived in Burma's interior they changed into regular Burmese dress, wrapped an antenna around their waists, and with a portable radio disguised as a carrying case, began their work. They might be captured and interrogated, but they turned out to be surprisingly ignorant of what their own side was doing. They had very precise knowledge of how Japan's military was organized and what the names of its ships were, but nonetheless knew nothing about their own ships at anchor in Calcutta, save perhaps for the number of vessels. Anticipating the danger of capture, the British intelligence services apparently trained their people according to the principle that you can't divulge what you don't know.

Lieutenant Commander Fukuda also said that research seemed to be well along on a bomb so powerful it that could lay waste a city the size of New York using no more than a matchbox of uranium, though it was not clear if it was Japan that was well ahead or the Americans.

"1925. Callsign NERK, bearing 48 degrees from Kaohsiung. 1927. FEMYH strip cipher, bearing 145 degrees from Truk."

"Everyone's enjoying himself playing volleyball and the like with the typists again," said the lieutenant commander, almost as an afterthought, "but the senior staff officer takes a dim view of it, I assure you."

Koji knew this comment was not directed at him, but he was momentarily flustered. He had said goodbye to his friends Kuki and Tanii in quick succession and his work was getting nowhere, so his mind had inevitably turned in another direction. Only a little more than a week after Tanii had departed from Ueno Station he had begun to feel a kind of emotional turmoil he had not felt since Chieko. Lately he would stroll along the corridors of Special Services even when he had no business to attend to, or pretend at quitting time that he had forgotten something and run repeatedly up and down the stairs. He was looking for the typist Noriko Yano, the young woman he and Tanii had earlier agreed was attractive. Noriko was a typist in B Section, so Koji had absolutely no work-related link with her, which meant that he had no occasion to talk with her, and was forced to invent pretexts of one sort or another.

"Well then," he might say, having asked her to undertake some trivial task, "please tell Ensign Tsutsumi for me."

"I shall," Noriko would answer shyly, softly, with a tilt of her head and a smile. In Special Services, where most of the women came from well-to-do families and had developed a taste for ostentation, Noriko's clothes were almost conspicuous for their plainness. For example, her *mompe*, the baggy work pantaloons all women wore, were made of wash-worn cotton of a simple dark blue splash pattern. Paradoxically, Koji was impressed by this. And he liked the expression in her ever-melancholy eyes, which always seemed on the verge of tears. Wrapped up in his thoughts of her, he was startled by Lieutenant Commander Fukuda's comment. The latter, however, said no more about the matter that night, and those who had no work to do retired one by one to their cots in the duty room.

By June his lack of progress at work and his intensifying physical urges were disturbing Koji more and more. During lunch breaks he would go up to the roof and furtively watch Noriko amongst the so-called Kindergarten Set, the young girls amusing themselves next to the volleyball court far below, gazing at her slim waist and her thin legs.

It's time for me to get married.

He began to think seriously about marriage. When he thought about himself and Chieko again, there was that always-ambiguous—and thus oppressive—feeling. It occurred to him that if he married Noriko he would, for better or worse, not have to worry about his relationship with Chieko anymore.

"I want to talk to you guys about something," Koji said one day, inviting Wada and Tsutsumi to dinner. "Eat with me tonight."

His mind was just about made up, but he wanted to talk with them about the practical side of it, and in any case he wanted to share his secret with someone. The three men went to a club for army and navy officers near the Navy Ministry building for beer.

"Fact is, I'm thinking about getting married to one of the typists."

"What? What're you talking about?" Tsutsumi was more than surprised, he was stunned.

"The one I'm interested in is Yano."

Koji explained how his feelings for her had grown over time.

"I know there'll be all sorts of problems to deal with, but it would be awkward for me to be open about it. You guys can carry the ball for me, play the intermediary, if you would."

"Yano?" exclaimed Tsutsumi. "You want us to—I'll be damned!"

"You know," cautioned Wada, "if you're not extremely careful you could have a scandal on your hands."

"I really like her eyes," said Koji, embarrassed by his own words.

"Maybe I shouldn't say this," Tsutsumi began, "but just what's so good about her eyes? Listen, I ask her to prepare final copies for me all the time. Have you really taken a good look at her? Her eyes are disgusting and greedy! For someone so young she seems awfully interested in the opposite sex. She's shifty-eyed, I tell you. I can't say I'm behind you on this. Give it some more thought. If you're really sure you want to go ahead with it, I'll help you, but you'd be better off taking a good cold shower in the meantime."

"I'm going ahead with it no matter what you say," said Koji, reflexively dropping his intimate tone.

"Hold on!" Wada interjected. "Isn't she the same Yano that Tanii said was attractive?"

"The same. Tanii and I said so at almost the same time."

"Now I see. You're imagining things. Which is to say," Wada continued, "Tanii, your good friend since college, goes off to the Kuriles, you get lonely, and what Tanii had said sticks in your mind. Think about it. I'll bet that's what happened."

"That might be true. But who cares? I know what I feel, and I'm not imagining anything, not at all. I've got everything under control."

"Everything under control?" asked Wada. "But if you're so determined to go ahead with it, you better watch your step. Have you looked into her family background at all?"

"No. I don't know anything. Where's she from?"

"You're a real hothead, you know? No two ways about it."

Koji, at Wada's urging, agreed to have an agency specializing in pre-marital investigations check into things, but for the rest, he left it all in the hands of his two friends, convincing them to do it in spite of themselves, and in the face of their passive opposition.

The next day Koji put on a civilian suit and called at an agency in the Ginza district that he had learned of from Wada, who said he had gone there once before in connection with a family marriage investigation. In the hallway, files of family registers, yellow with age and covered with dust, were piled precariously along the wall up to the ceiling. He met the manager, a funereal sort, in a partitioned room, and was told that since the person to be investigated worked on a military installation, military security would present all kinds of complications, but that he should be able to come up with something in ten days or so. Koji concealed his identity with an assumed name. Meanwhile, Tsutsumi and Wada, stealing snatches of time from their work, slowly began to dig into Noriko Yano's background.

The Level-Oblique Secret decryption work lay untouched on Koji's desk. Only his assistant, Petty Officer Sano, wordlessly put pencil to the columns of letters every day. As for Noriko, Koji was certain that, investigate though they might, they would turn up nothing out of the ordinary. They would doubtless discover that she had graduated with middling grades from some girl's high school, that her father was a retired government official or something of the sort, that she had several brothers and sisters, and that the family was not very well off, but tranquil and ordinary. Koji might be marrying a poor woman, but this did not mean that he must fall into poverty, and he felt it would be good for him to take as his wife an ordinary woman from an ordinary family. Soon those eyes and that waist, those slender arms would be his, and he would be content and treasure them, and live as he was destined to, and that would be enough. As he considered this he felt a kind of happiness, together with a hint of wistfulness, as though the course of his life had now been irrevocably determined.

*   *   *

One morning several days later Wada dropped by C Section for Koji, calling to him casually.

"Obata. Come up to the roof for a bit, would you?"

Koji nodded with equal casualness, responding as he might to a work request from someone in another office, grabbing up a bundle of papers as he left his office. Tsutsumi was waiting for them on the roof.

"I've found out where Yano went to school," Tsutsumi began.

"You have? Thanks."

"You're going to be disappointed. She graduated from the Kawamura Girls' School of Home Economics. Her friend Tamura told me."

"Hmm." Even Koji could not claim this was good news. Kawamura Home Economics was not the sort of school the so-called better families of Tokyo sent their daughters to, but Koji was quick to reply, as though to dispel his own doubts.

"Well, that sort of thing doesn't bother me in the least. Tamura knows a lot about Noriko?"

"She knows about her school, but for someone who goes around with her she doesn't know much else. And of course I couldn't ask too many probing questions without arousing suspicion."

"And another thing," Wada interjected. "The word is that Yano will be quitting work before long."

"How come? Why is that?" An uneasy expression crossed Koji's face. When a typist quit, it usually meant she was about to get married.

"I was on duty last night and was helping plot DF vectors in A Section. Things were slack and Mitsui and Sakai started critiquing the typists. I saw this as my chance, and, playing along, asked about her. It sure sounds like she'll be quitting soon. Yano or Tamura or someone in that kiddy clique is distantly related to Mitsui. It seems that both Tamura and Yano from time to time visit the Mitsui home on the sly."

Koji did not like the sound of this.

"I'll be damned. That's no good, is it. If the senior staff officer finds out he'll be ticked off."

"Don't be so self-centered," Tsutsumi laughed, a hint of reproach in his voice. "If anything's going to tick off the senior staff officer it's what you're up to."

"But you really don't suppose Noriko would quit to marry Mitsui."

"Don't be a fool!" exclaimed the thoroughly exasperated Tsutsumi. "Who besides you is going to make a fuss over Yano?"

"Well, at this point that's all there is," said Wada. "But to change the subject, a large number of American submarines were detected last night off Borneo. Looks like the Third Fleet is in the area. I wonder how Kuki's doing."

The next day during lunch break Koji, mulling over what his two friends had told him, was walking by himself toward the deserted archery range when he noticed the typist Blue and a co-worker sitting off the walkway in the lush clover. Apparently set upon by tiny insects, Blue was moving her hand back and forth in front of her face to fend them off as she talked, her legs thrown out in front of her. Koji caught snatches of what she was saying.

"They say it's been decided. . . . Lieutenant Mitsui."

He started. Straining to hear as he passed by, he could again catch only bits and pieces.

". . . Mitsubishi Heavy Industries . . . any day now."

He kept walking, going to the far side of the archery range. There was a long row of trees, branches growing from their supple-seeming trunks and their large, paulownia-like leaves lush in their abundance. Koji broke off several of the leaves and casually started back toward where Blue was. The two young women stopped talking and watched him approach.

"Typist Kizu," Koji asked, flourishing the leaves as he came to a halt before them, "would you happen to know what kind of tree this is?"

"Do you know?" Blue asked, turning to the other typist, then asking Koji: "Isn't it from one of the those trees behind the range? If it is, I'll bet it's called a catalpa. In the fall it bears cowpea-like fruit."

"Well, you really know your trees." He felt ridiculous in spite of himself, and he could hardly work in an abrupt change of subject: *What were you talking about just now?*

"Ensign Obata," asked Blue, turning the conversational tables on him, a slightly coquettish lilt in her voice, "I understand you went to Fujimidai."

Koji reddened slightly.

"Yes. Why do you ask?"

"I went there too." She told him this with a beguiling smile, making a show of thumping her chest with obvious pride. Fujimidai was the name of the primary school he had gone to in Hiroshima.

"But I only went as far as the second grade because my father was transferred. I don't suppose you remember me."

"Is that right? I didn't know that."

The fact was, this was the least of his concerns at the moment. He left the two women, hurried back to the office building, and went looking for Wada and Tsutsumi. He had felt uneasy all morning, and now he was thoroughly convinced that Mitsui was to marry Noriko and obviously that was what Blue and her companion had been talking about. Wada was not around, having gone to the main Ministry building on business before noon. Tsutsumi would not take him seriously.

"Why should you jump to that conclusion? You've heard the saying, 'the doubting heart sees demons in the darkness.' That's what you're doing! Listen, they were talking about Mitsui's finding work on the outside, in the real world. Just relax and wait until you know what the agency has come up with."

Koji waited well into the evening for Wada to return, but he didn't appear; perhaps he had gone straight home from the Ministry. Koji, tired of waiting, left the office, then, an idea coming to him, headed toward the Kawamura Girls' School of Home Economics, not far from Shirogane Boulevard.

Through the glass door at the main entrance Koji could see many shoe lockers lining the now-hushed hall. The students and faculty had all apparently gone for the day and none of the glass doors yielded. It was then he noticed that the dark sheet-glass doors were like mirrors, reflecting his awkward uniformed figure, bent over, peering in. Koji hurriedly left. He went around to the back and found that there was a cottage attached to the building. This door opened when he pushed on it and the caretaker, an old woman, came to the door. She told him there was no one at the school then, but if he went to the residence hall two blocks down the road he would doubtless find the instructor who was hall manager. He set off to find the hall.

The name of the dormitory was engraved on a low stone gate, and a long and narrow pathway of flagstone led from it to the building, where Koji could hear from a dimly lit room the unpleasantly metallic tinkling of a piano. The faces of several of the residents peered out at him from a second-story window, only to draw back in surprise as he looked up at them. He asked around for someone to talk to. A fortyish woman instructor in dark blue traditional clothes came out and asked him, rather nervously, what he wanted. Koji now regretted coming in his uniform. Ushered into the visitor's room, he came right to the point and asked the instructor, his tone nonchalant, about Noriko.

"Miss Yano? A student named Yano? We have had several, but I don't recall anyone called Noriko Yano. I have been employed here for eight years, and I remember all who graduated during that period, for the most part. But please wait a moment. I'll take a look at the register."

She leafed through the book, but found nothing.

"Perhaps she has changed her last name?"

"No, I doubt that's the case."

Unable to understand what was amiss, the bewildered Koji left the residence hall and returned to his lodgings.

As soon as Koji got to work the next morning Wada came for him, and the two went up to the roof again.

"Tsutsumi told me early this morning what happened yesterday," Wada began, his expression uncommonly serious.

"He did? I really can't shake the uneasy feeling I have," Koji said, somewhat embarrassed.

"This business about Yano and Mitsui—you can certainly find things to wonder about if you look for them. But I want to take this opportunity to say what I said before."

Koji did not respond.

"I want you to know it's not that I think you're particularly insincere. But her as the wife of an officer? And in the future if you're going to write . . . when I try to picture Yano as your wife in those circumstances, it just doesn't come into focus, not at all. I don't know how the agency investigation will go, but I just can't think of her as a fine young woman. You praise her to the skies, but I'm telling you her eyes are the eyes of a flirt. You yourself may not be conscious of what's happened, but as I told you before, I think

Tanii's words affected your feelings a lot. What about it? Are you willing to give it more thought?"

"I don't want to, I tell you!" Koji faced his friend feeling defiant, though against what he was not quite sure. "My becoming a writer, your becoming an anthropologist, Kuki returning to the Foreign Service, just how realistic is it to envision ourselves doing these things? Somehow I think it's stretching it a bit to suppose the time will come when I'll once again be going on carefree trips or thumbing through a manuscript or a novel I've written. Understand, I'm not saying I should go off half-cocked. But I have to be true to my gut feelings. I don't want to muddy the waters. Listen, it's something that may never happen again for me. I may die, so I don't have time any more to be calculating or coy. I don't give a damn whether the staff officers and the guys in the first class tell me I'm creating a scandal or think I'm a fool. On the contrary, it gives me courage. Falling in love and marrying right away is a lot more respectable than worrying about protocol and society."

"And haven't I been telling you I don't think you're being dishonest? She's the problem, not you."

"You're wrong. I'm going to make it happen, come hell or high water. And the sooner we marry the better."

"Then what would you do if there really was something going on between Lieutenant Mitsui and Yano? You'd still push ahead with it?"

"Of course I would. It's worth it to me. I wouldn't hesitate for a second to fight it out with Mitsui for her."

"If you're going to do that—if you act like that, won't it only mean that all three of you will come to grief?"

"I don't care."

"No matter what?"

"No matter what."

Wada stepped back from Koji. He abruptly turned on his heel and, looking at his feet, walked across the concrete to the edge of the roof, his shoes sounding. Koji, not moving, watched him silently. Wada leaned against the iron railing for some time, apparently lost in thought. He then came back to where Koji was, his gaze still downcast. His pale, aristocratic face looked curiously morose, and his eyebrows twitched.

"The fact is," Wada began with obvious reluctance, "I never thought I'd tell anyone, but I'm in the same sort of situation you are."

"You?!" Koji was stunned.

"But it's over now."

Just then the door to the roof opened and a typist poked her head out, then another face appeared.

"Whoops," one of the young women said when she saw it was Koji and his friend, then: "She's not here." They slammed the door shut and fled down the staircase, their shoes clattering on the stairs.

"It's Blue," Wada said.

"Ah, is it? So it's Kizu after all."

Wada explained what had happened. In the fall of the previous year, two months after Koji and his classmates were commissioned ensigns, several new typists had been hired, including Kawai and Akie Kizu. Kizu, the prettiest of the group, immediately became a favorite subject of conversation among the young officers. She was assigned to Wada to work with him exclusively on a new method he was devising to break the American strip cipher. The two of them secluded themselves in a room where day after day, from morning until night, they worked together with the same message files, the same statistical tables, the same hypothetical plaintexts. Wada gradually fell under the spell of the enchanting Miss Kizu, unable, in the end, to deny his feelings for her. He told his parents how he felt, then had the agency now investigating Noriko for Koji do a background check. The result was not unfavorable. Blue had graduated from a Christian girls' school, though she was not herself a believer. Her father had been a retired rear admiral, but had been recalled to active duty and was presently at Surabaja on Java. Her elder brother, a graduate of the Naval Academy, was a fighter pilot, a lieutenant with an air unit at Yokosuka. She also had an elder and a younger sister.

Wada's father was in a hospital and bedridden with a difficult liver ailment, and as he considered the little time he might have left to him, he was absolutely delighted that his only son might be getting married soon. Wada's mother had also been in favor of the match. Wada had intended to bring things along in the utmost secrecy so that it would not develop into a scandal, and if all went well he would have Blue quit her job at Special Services at the appropriate moment. Then, after she had dimmed in everyone's memory, he would unobtrusively finalize the talks. In mid-March, however, his mother, who had been assiduously searching out rumors of one sort or another on her own, came home with information from a fairly reliable source that his prospective bride was already engaged. Wada was disheartened and his ailing father greatly disappointed. They concluded that pushing ahead would only bring the matter gratuitously into the open and make a bad situation worse, so Wada, unwilling to make both himself and his parents miserable, decided to put an end to the matter. Unfortunately, because of their work at Special Services they were together every day. It was very difficult for Wada because he had continually to talk with Blue and could sense her near him, yet had to pretend that she meant nothing to him.

"So it was Blue. I'll bet that's why you didn't eat your bread."

"Not really. My stomach's been bothering me," Wada responded, a dour expression on his face.

"What sort of guy is he, this fiancé?"

"That I don't know. I told you I've put a stop to my pursuit. I suppose you could say that in my case I've given up. It's not like your situation."

Koji was not convinced. He found his friend's attitude a bit hard to take.

"In my case, I may be charging the machine-gun nest, but I think you're being a little too quick to concede defeat, a bit fainthearted."

"I shouldn't have told you so much," said Wada. "Don't tell anybody, not even Tsutsumi or Hirokawa."

The door to the roof opened again. Tsutsumi stepped out onto the roof, a knowing smile on his face.

"I thought you'd be out here," he said as he approached. "Hey, we've got to be careful! The three of us are always getting together and talking. Tamura suspects something. This morning when I met her in the hallway out of the blue she says 'Ensign Tsutsumi, Noriko is off today.' You could have knocked me over with a feather, but I thought to myself, *you little so-and-so, you're not the child you seem,* and said 'Really? You don't say. But why are you telling me that?' At which point the damned girl, not knowing what to say, blushed beet-red and scurried off."

"Okay, okay. Let's go back down. We've been away from our desks a good while."

A burst of clacking typewriters greeted them as they opened the door and started down the stairs. Koji met Hirokawa in the hall on his way back to C Section. He looked extremely tense for some reason.

"Come here a minute, Obata," he said, pulling Koji toward the A. Section office.

"You guys," he said as he went along, "have been skulking around lately, not getting any work done. What're you talking about?"

Koji was guarded.

"What difference does it make? I'm discussing something with Wada. I'll be talking with you as well before long. You don't have any work to talk to me about, right? I'm going back to my office."

He shook off Hirokawa's hand.

"Whatever. Anyway, come to A Section. I've got something to show you," Hirokawa said, pulling Koji along with him.

"Look at this," he said, pointing at what was on his desk: copies of two Japanese operational messages. Koji glanced at them casually, then started, and stood transfixed.

Initiate Battle Operation A.

The fate of the Empire rests with this one battle. All hands will renew their resolve to die for their country and discharge their duties with every fiber of their being.

Five

Koji's friend Kuki, with the Mobile Fleet as it steamed northward through the Sulu Sea toward the battle zone in the western Pacific, was looking at the same message. His ship was the *Taiho*, flagship of both the First Mobile Fleet and the First Air Division. It was a new aircraft carrier which, unlike carriers converted from seaplane tenders or auxiliary carriers converted from merchantmen, had been designed from the keel up as an aircraft carrier. It had just been commissioned in March. Kuki had gone from Special Services in Tokyo to Kure, and had flown then to Singapore, where he reported to the *Taiho*. Its armor was thick and because there was little wasted space and few scuttles, the ship was hot and living quarters very cramped. Still, the wardroom and other common areas all had air-conditioning and fluorescent lighting, and the ship was fitted with the very latest that Japanese technology had to offer in radar, gyrocompasses, optical rangefinders, radios, anti-aircraft guns, and the like. The First Air Division at this time was made up of three regular aircraft carriers: besides the *Taiho*, there was the *Zuikaku* and the *Shokaku*.

At the same time, 30 knots ahead, Yukio Ibuki stood on the flight deck of the aircraft carrier *Hiyo* in the Second Air Division and listened in the ranks at general formation as his captain read the statement initiating Battle Operation A. The Second Air Division consisted of three aircraft carriers, the *Junyo*, the flagship, the *Hiyo,* and the *Ryuho*. The *Ryuho* had been the submarine tender *Taigei* before it had been converted, and the auxiliary carriers *Junyo* and

Hiyo had been, respectively, the *Kashihara-maru* and *Izumo-maru*, both with the Japan Mail Line.

The Third Air Division, the carriers *Chiyoda* (flagship), *Chitose*, and *Zuiho*—the first two converted seaplane tenders—was another thirty knots ahead. These three air divisions, in total a nine-carrier flotilla, were escorted in a ring defense by a large task force consisting of battleships, cruisers, and destroyers, and other ships, including the *Yamato*, the *Musashi*, the *Nagato,* and the *Kongo*. Thus the fleet flagship *Taiho* that Kuki was aboard was steaming at the end of a formation of ships strung out over a considerable distance. Commander Ezaki, who had been head of Special Services S Section, was aboard the *Zuiho* as executive officer. Just as Admiral Togo's victorious ships had done in the battle of the Japan Sea during the Russo-Japanese War, each vessel flew from its masthead the Z signal flag of combat. As for the aircraft on the nine carriers, there were Tenzan torpedo attack planes, Comet light bombers, and the Zero fighter, improved Model 52. Except for the Comets, though, the planes were now obsolete. Even the Zero, so feared at the time of the fierce fighting over Guadalcanal—and flown by superb pilots—was no longer a match for American aircraft because of its poor defensive capabilities and a reversal in the quality of pilots on the two sides. It was now dismissed as a "paper plane" or a "Zero lighter." The plane's glory days were epitomized by an often-told story of a message being sent in the clear to an advance command post that B-17s should avoid a particular area because Zeroes were there. And even in the case of the new Comet, the pilots had not achieved proficiency, so they were not able to fully exploit its capabilities.

While the *Taiho* was on maneuvers at its anchorage in the Singapore area, Comets stalled time and again thanks to the insufficient training of the pilots, and 50 lives were lost. The vast majority of the Naval Air Force's fine pilots flying at the onset of the war were now gone. The young, green pilots had been given an accelerated three-month training, and had been drilled in only one method of attack. Concern about this cast an ineffaceable unease over the warships steaming toward the decisive battle in the Marianas.

Kuki, aboard the *Taiho*, which had left its Lingga anchorage in April 1944 and put to sea for training, had seen countless young, ruddy-cheeked petty officers, fresh out of training, go to their deaths almost daily as the ship steamed back and forth across the equator for almost a month, until mid-May. The principal cause of the mishaps was underdeveloped flying skills. During landing practice the bridge presented a terrible psychological barrier for a pilot, who would, in his attempt to stay away from it, stall the bomber and plunge it into the sea. Once a plane was in the water it would sink as soon as the canopy was opened, taking its crew with it. Seeing all this with his own eyes, Kuki had become increasingly pessimistic, and wrote letters to Wada, Hirokawa, and Koji that were shot through with cynical comments on the utterly unfavorable progress of the war. He would stamp these personal communications with an official seal and enclose them with classified papers bound for Japan by air.

In mid-May all units, anticipating the battle, left their training areas and began to rendezvous off Tawi-Tawi Island, northeast of Borneo and southwest of Mindanao. Both Kuki's *Taiho* and Ibuki's *Hiyo* were part of this. There were five battleships, nine aircraft carriers, 13 cruisers, some 30 destroyers, many oilers and supply ships, practically all the ships left in the Japanese Imperial Navy. The waters off Tawi-Tawi were a bright and beautiful light blue, and Kuki, together with two fellow idlers from the junior officers' quarters, the paymaster and the medical officer, was constantly neglecting his duties to go to the bow of the ship to cool off and discuss the possibility of defeat and what that would mean. The bow was in the shade of the flight deck and provided a nice breeze, and when the carrier was sailing on maneuvers they could see silver flying fish flashing up out of the water before them and sailing over the waves like seagulls. The idlers enjoyed their inactivity, to which they gave the name "shade-bathing."

Immediately after the fleet had rendezvoused, however, enemy submarines began to swarm in Tawi-Tawi waters like schools of porpoises. Destroyers that went out to challenge them were themselves sunk, so exercises beyond where the carriers were anchored became impossible. Thus the carrier planes could not practice take-offs and landings. The half-trained flight crews futilely waited on standby, their level of proficiency dropping even more.

The U.S. Navy's Task Force 58 struck Saipan on June 11. The Japanese fleet off-loaded all inflammables from its ships, all hands drank to victory, and at 8 o'clock on the morning of the 13th set off from Tawi-Tawi, the whole of the Imperial Navy's surviving forces. That afternoon one of the three carrier-based bombers that had been out on anti-submarine patrol crashed on landing because of pilot error, coming in on top of the plane landing in front of it and bursting into flames. There were no injuries on the carrier itself, but since the bomber had been carrying bombs, they could not attempt to extinguish the fire because of the danger of explosion. All hands went below to wait for the fire to burn itself out, but this meant that five men and three officers perished in the flames. That evening the fleet temporarily dropped anchor in the channel northeast of Iloilo in the Philippines to take off the dead and take on provisions. Looking at the large, blue-black form of a nearby island, Kuki could not help but feel it was an omen of ill fortune.

As they were leaving the San Bernardino Channel the following day they could see a fire set by the natives on a headland on Samar Island. It appeared to be a signal to the American submarines, and, as if in response, a lookout on the *Taiho* reported sighting a periscope. Moments later Kuki's signal intelligence group in the First Mobile Fleet intercepted a transmission by what appeared to be the same sub of an O message, used for especially urgent tactical communication, in the BIMEC strip cipher employed by submarines. It was an extremely loud signal; the sub was apparently transmitting very close to the fleet, audaciously so. They could not break the cipher, but it seemed obvious the sub was reporting its discovery of the Japanese fleet. Kuki immediately notified the communications staff officers, but they were slow to take action and the Japanese side lost contact with the submarine. This was one of the immediate causes for the failure of Operation A.

An at-sea refueling was conducted on June 16. On the 18th the fleet arrived in the battle area, and in the afternoon information on at least part of the American task force became available, but since the sun was about to set, the attack was called off. Scout planes went out before dawn the next morning, the 19th, in several waves. These early sorties should have passed over the enemy task force, which was in the immediate area, but no sighting reports came back from them, and by the time the enemy's deployment became generally known, the sun had already risen. The initial attack, which should have begun at daybreak, thus suffered a delay of several hours. The American task force, centered on Saipan, was divided into several flotillas, each of which was virtually equivalent in firepower to the entire Japanese fleet. At seven o'clock the carriers turned their bows into the wind. By 8:30 the first wave of attacking planes had taken off from the *Taiho*. Preparations for sending off the second wave began immediately. But at that moment the the last carrier-bomber in the first wave off the *Taiho* suddenly veered strangely, then abruptly dived into the sea, where it quickly sank beneath the waves. At almost the same instant a *Taiho* lookout spotted torpedo wakes 30 degrees off the starboard bow. The *Taiho* responded with a hard-over rudder, evading three torpedoes. One, however, struck the starboard bow. The bomber pilot had spotted the torpedo wakes as he took off and had tried to protect the carrier by crashing into the torpedoes, but had missed them.

Kuki was at his station, and felt a jolt, like a car riding up over a large rock. The *Taiho* did not catch fire, but the gas tanks at the bow ruptured, part of the flight deck was ripped up, planes in the second wave that were on deck were blown about, and the forward elevator jammed as it was descending to the hangar deck. Gasoline fumes spread through the ship and some of the men who inhaled too much became disoriented. The order was issued to open the side-scuttles and for those with hobnails on their soles to go up and down ladders carefully, since the fumes would be ignited if a hobnail created a spark against an iron ladder rung. The *Taiho*, without reducing its authorized top battle speed of 33 knots or its immediate standby status, was able to make headway unimpeded, but with the flight deck elevator dropped below deck level, leaving a gaping void above it, the next group of planes could not be sent off. A work crew in gas masks had gathered lumber together and hastened to repair the damage.

The First Air Division, however, was now caught in the net of the American submarines. Almost immediately afterward the *Shokaku*, close by the *Taiho*, was hit by a torpedo. A huge hole was opened amidships and she immediately started to burn and very quickly lost speed. At first, her crew was able to keep her afloat. She pulled out of the line and attempted to return to base at Yokosuka under destroyer escort, but in the end the 29,000-ton carrier sank beneath the waves.

Meanwhile, the *Taiho* had received no reports at all from the planes that had gone off to attack the American ships. Those back on the carrier waited uneasily. The planes were scheduled to skim over the water as low as possible, and when they had closed to 50 knots of the enemy they were to climb steeply, then, having achieved a high altitude, were to swoop down in a surprise attack. By making a low-level attack they would exploit the curvature of the earth and evade detection by the enemy's radar. They were to gain altitude before attacking because it was assumed that enemy fighters would be flying cover over their carriers. This was the only tactic the pilots who had gone through accelerated training had been taught. They would not have known what maneuver to adopt had they be called upon to respond to a different situation. They carried out the maneuver they had been taught faithfully and accurately. The enemy, however, had prepared a surprise for them. It was not clear whether the Americans' analysis of the situation was simply superior or they had broken an enciphered message. In any case, a large formation of enemy fighters was waiting above them as they began their climb— their speed lower because the climb was steep—50 knots short of the enemy carriers.

The Japanese losses were huge. Of the first and second wave of approximately 400 aircraft that had taken off from the nine carriers—excluding those planes that landed at airfields on Tinian, Guam, and Rota—no more than a hundred were able to return.

As the surviving planes began to return to the *Taiho* in small groups in the afternoon, Kuki was at his duty station, having had a late lunch in the officers' lounge next to the radio room. Suddenly a tremendous, rending explosion resounded through the ship. Kuki lost consciousness.

When he came to he was in utter darkness. He did not know how long he had been knocked out. Neither his vision nor his hearing had entirely returned to normal; he was still only semi-conscious. He had the sensation that he was lolling half asleep in bed, as he had during his tranquil student days. Then his consciousness, the feeling of having just awakened, seemed about to desert him once again. He could hear people groaning.

"Damn! We've been hit," he said, and in that instant tried to jump up. It was then he felt a spasm of pain from his legs to his back. Something held his legs; he couldn't move them. He heard the sound of something rolling about or burning, a powerful, rumbling sound, in the hangar at his back. A bright shaft of light shone through a crack in the steel bulkhead.

He gradually realized what had happened to him. The deafening explosion had knocked his heavy desk on top of him, something had hit him hard on the head, and he had fallen beside the desk, his legs pinned by it. When he realized this, he was able to calm himself somewhat. Flames were now leaping through the crack in the bulkhead behind him and he could smell his hair singeing.

Well, so this is how I'm to die.

He felt no sadness, nothing. Images of his family and people who had been close to him seemed to float before his eyes. He had no idea what was happening elsewhere on this huge carrier. It seemed to him that it was sailing along under its own power. Two men, seamen apparently, rushed out of the darkness, intending to flee toward the passageway through another bulkhead break through which light was visible, next to a bomb hoist.

"Hey! Wait!" Kuki shouted before he realized it. The two men ran off without so much as a glance in his direction.

"Is that you, Ensign Kuki?" a voice asked in the darkness from a corner of the room. It was Chief Petty Officer Tajima. "Petty Officers Kato and Yamada have had it."

"How are you? Can you get out of there?"

"I'm afraid I can't," the CPO answered. "It's my legs."

"My legs are caught too. And my hair is starting to burn, unfortunately." His own words struck him as extraordinarily casual. He did, however, shift himself around, pivoting on his legs, so that the flames could not get at his hair. It was an awkward position, so his abdomen was uncomfortably distended and, without really thinking about it, he put his hand on his belt. When he loosened it, his pants started to slip off. Surprised, he kicked his legs, and they slipped free of his pants. His pants cuff had been caught and he hadn't been able to pull it free, that was all. The desire to live surged within him like a raging river.

"Take off your pants!" he shouted at CPO Tajima. "Then you can escape."

He ran into the lounge. He had eaten lunch here only fifteen minutes before the explosion and now all the men he and others had relieved were dead. The bone of a broken leg, jutting up like a crutch, had pieces of dark red flesh adhering to it. Enameled plates and food, covered with blood, were scattered all about. As he was about to step through the hatch he noticed a man's head, split open like a pomegranate, wedged between the door and the jamb. He stepped on the head with his bare foot, then hopped to the passageway at the side of the ship. As soon as he got to the passageway he saw an ensign-midshipman and two seamen who were obviously confused. Black smoke rose from the carrier, which was almost dead in the water.

"What the devil's happened?"

"Secondary explosions from the gasoline," the midshipman answered. "Shouldn't we lower the aft cutter?"

In that instant Kuki recalled hearing that when the mixture of gasoline fumes and air reaches a certain ratio, its explosive force is more destructive than any bomb. He was still unable, however, to comprehend the condition of the ship as a whole.

"The order to abandon ship hasn't been given yet, has it," Kuki said sharply to the other three. "Let's go up on deck."

"But Ensign Kuki, you're badly injured."

For the first time Kuki realized something had happened to him. He had a deep gash diagonally across his right leg. He had left behind his shoes and pants, so only his *fundoshi* loincloth covered him. He put his hand to his right ear; it was hanging from his head like a piece of meat. One of the seamen improvised a bandage out of a hand towel and tied it securely around his head. The four men headed for the flight deck. A body was lodged between the rungs of the ladder, its arms dangling, looking as though it would fall over the side of the ship at any moment. Those who were not injured ran about aimlessly.

The huge flight deck had buckled down its middle, which had heaved up, roof-like. Crimson flames wrapped in oily smoke leapt up everywhere, and the bridge was already engulfed in smoke. When Kuki saw this from the ladder he doubled back and made his way to the quarterdeck, the only part of the ship that still remained intact. A helter-skelter sort of abandon ship had already started and men were throwing anything that would float into the water. The young, uninjured men jumped boldly from the ship. Kuki looked over the side of the ship in despair: he was so high up over the water; ever since training, high diving into the water had been just about the hardest thing for him to do. His leg and ear began to throb unbearably. The midshipman and the seamen had gone their separate ways. A destroyer, apparently unable to approach because of the explosions, circled the *Taiho*, flashing its signal light endlessly. Kuki made it down to the next lower deck. There he found that the head of maintenance, a commander, had taken command of the ship. He had had the men take off their shoes and was beginning to put the men into the water.

He called out to Kuki as soon as he saw him.

"Hey, Ensign! You're hurt pretty bad, aren't you. Go first."

The seamen silently made way for Kuki. He saluted the commander, took hold of the heavy line hanging over the side of the ship and slid down it. As soon as he dropped into the water a huge swell washed over him. He had cut his hands on the prickly rope and now they stung painfully. As Kuki came back up to the surface he saw a sofa that he had often sat on floating nearby, and grabbed onto it. There was another man holding onto the other end, his face black with fuel oil. The man was bobbing up and down like a rubber ball, which Kuki found encouraging, but his wounds were now beginning to pain him horribly in the sea water, and because of the deep gash on his right leg it was difficult for him to kick; he could scarcely move the sofa along at all paddling only with his hands. He looked back when he was sure they had covered a good distance, but the huge vessel was still immediately behind him, looming over him as it listed. A severed hand floated toward Kuki and seemed about to trail after the sofa, then drifted away, horribly pale in the water as it was gently carried off by the current, palm down. It seemed to Kuki that the sinking of the *Taiho* was now only a matter of time. He had been desperately pushing the sofa as far away from the ship as he could get it and all the while it was gradually absorbing more water, so that finally each time he pushed against it, it would drop precipitously.

A destroyer came within about 200 meters of Kuki and he could see they were lowering a cutter. The current seemed to be taking the sofa in the opposite direction, so Kuki, after some hesitation, screwed up his courage and left it, swimming unaided toward the destroyer. He was tense and he was losing control of his legs. The *Taiho* grew more distant, but he was unable to get any nearer to the destroyer before him. He could see that it had lowered away the cutter, gone astern, then turned to its starboard and was now starting to get underway. The men in the cutter began rowing, taking the boat to his left and at a right angle to the direction Kuki was swimming. The sofa was gone now; he could see it nowhere. Kuki's spirits plummeted. The fuel oil was thick and black, and swells remorselessly hurled it and sea water into his mouth and nose. There was now almost no one to be seen on the deck of the *Taiho*. The carrier, still listing to port, red hull exposed, was about to sink, its stern in the air. An officer stood on the sloping deck waving his cap in farewell. The battle flag, which should have been lowered, still flew at the mast. On the destroyer, now fully underway, Kuki could see countless crewmen lining the railing on the *Taiho* side of the ship like statuettes, their arms raised in salute.

The actual sinking was over quickly. The 44,000-ton vessel thrust its stern up into space and slipped beneath the waves in the twinkling of an eye. Tears coursed down Kuki's cheeks, and these the oily sea washed away.

Kuki once again began to drift into unconsciousness, overcome by a not-unpleasant drowsiness. One hour after the *Taiho* went to the bottom, as the colors of evening deepened in the waters west of the Marianas, devoid now of ships, Kuki's body also disappeared quietly beneath the huge swells. He was 26.

*   *   *

Lieutenant Yukio Ibuki, after meeting Koji in Tokyo, had gone on to his post with an air unit at Iwakuni as medical officer attached to Headquarters. He had been stationed there throughout the reorganization and retraining of the First Air Division, so he had had several opportunities to return home to Hiroshima. His younger sister Chieko had been in bed with pyelitis since January. She had told friends it was pyelitis and nothing more, but she was having difficulty breathing, too. A doctor, an old friend of her father's who often played *go* with him, had been examining her occasionally. Mrs. Ibuki told her son that his sister Chieko was turning aside all attempts to find her a suitable mate. Chieko showed nothing but delight—not a bit of envy—now that her younger sister Ikuko's marriage to a naval air cadet was being arranged. It was as though, with a continually narrowing, single-minded focus, she lived only for Koji's return to Hiroshima. Her brother had no idea how the war would go, on top of which, it seemed to Ibuki that Koji's feelings for Chieko had cooled considerably. He was uneasy about her attitude, but did not say anything to her about it.

In the spring Chieko recovered from her illness. Meanwhile, the Third Fleet's main force would sail to Singapore, where fuel was plentiful, wrap up its training, and prepare for the coming decisive battle, and Ibuki was to accompany it. The commander of the Third Fleet held a banquet in Kagoshima and Ibuki attended this, flying in on a DC-3 together with the entire officer corps at Iwakuni, but afterward he was re-assigned and sent to Singapore on the carrier *Zuikaku*, and when he returned to Kure he was transferred to the *Junyo*, then put on the *Ryuho*, feeling somewhat like a aircraft-carrier bird of passage. At the beginning of May he joined the crew of the *Hiyo*, at which point he at last felt settled in. The *Hiyo*, originally named the *Izumo*, was a comfortable ship with good food and quarters, which would have been Japan's largest luxury liner had it been built as originally designed. Instead, midway through construction it had been converted into a large aircraft carrier.

When the Second Air Division, made up of the *Junyo*, the *Hiyo*, and the *Ryuho*, sailed forth from Tawi-Tawi on June 13, it took the same heading as the Third Air Division ahead of it and the First Air Division, which followed, sailing from the Negros Channel through the San Bernardino Channel, directly toward where the battle would be fought in the Marianas. In the *Hiyo*'s wardroom the flight leader was delivering himself of the opinion that the enemy's strike at Saipan was merely a feint, that the Americans were actually intending to invade Truk, since it would not be easy to conduct large-scale operations on Saipan because it would mean an over-extended supply line. But the flight leader's prediction was to prove wrong.

By 10:30 on the morning of the 19th all planes of the first and second waves had been sent aloft. The aft warrant officers' wardroom on the starboard side had been turned into the starboard sick bay; this was Ibuki's battle station. Judging from experience, if the departure of the attacking planes went without a hitch you could figure that the odds were in favor of the Japanese side, so he waited for word that they had been victorious.

When he went on deck around 1:00 p.m., he saw in the distance, near the horizon, a ship afire. He could not tell whether it was friend or foe, but before long two different rumors were making the rounds: one, that it was the *Shokaku*, which had been hit and was under tow; the other, that it was the *Taiho*. Before the ship's identity could be determined, however, it was shaken again and again by secondary explosions which rumbled in the distance like faraway thunder, after which it sank.

Clearly visible from the *Hiyo* were the aircraft carriers *Junyo* and *Ryuho*, the battleship *Nagato*, the heavy cruiser *Mogami*, and four or five destroyers, all of which were sound and sailing as night fell. The reason only a small number of their planes had returned, they were told, was that most had put down at Tinian or Rota, or some other island. While Ibuki had no wounded to tend to, it was apparent that his carrier's planes had gained essentially nothing in battle. The divisions had sent off the planes that day rather a good distance from their targets to assure the safety of the carriers, then had withdrawn yet further, closing at night to prepare for launching planes the following morning. Ibuki had heard that when the battle between the two fleets was over, the battleships *Yamato* and *Musashi* could be expected to shell the enemy's beachhead at Saipan with their big guns. Since he was a medical officer, however, he wasn't too clear on the details.

On the next morning, the 20th, the *Hiyo* rendezvoused with a supply squadron and took on supplies. If no word of victory had come that day either, neither had an enemy attack, and it appeared that the sea battle, the prospect of which had stretched nerves taut, might well end indecisively. The tension Ibuki had been feeling eased and he returned briefly from the sick bay to his quarters. He returned his glasses and wallet and the other personal belongings that he had been keeping with him to his foot locker, and because it was so hot, changed into lighter attire, just a non-dress khaki uniform over his loincloth and a gas mask. His orderly put away the tables for the wounded who never came and began feeding the patients dinner. It was then that the P.A. system crackled into life.

"Large enemy formation approaching! Large enemy formation approaching! All hands man your battle stations. On the double!"

Not now!

Ibuki sent one of his corpsmen to the quarterdeck to see what was happening. The man returned much excited: the carriers of the Third Air Division, at a distance of some 3,000 meters, were putting up a fierce barrage of fire against enemy planes as they zigzagged to evade their torpedoes. Ibuki tensed up at the corpsman's words. Almost immediately there was the sound of explosions directly overhead, and several minutes later a strong, dullish shock reverberated heavily through the sick bay, sending the jars of medicine on his desk crashing to the deck in a shattering of glass. The sick bay began to list steeply to port.

Moments later several men with minor injuries came into the sick bay. The enemy had begun its attack on the *Hiyo*, which had been hit by a bomb and a torpedo and was now apparently afire. Ibuki set about treating those who were injured. He could feel his cheek twitching from the tension. His only relief came from throwing himself into the work of treating the wounded. A petty officer who had been asphyxiated was carried in by a comrade. Ibuki immediately injected him with a heart stimulant. He bandaged up burn patients with sterilized gauze. The jolt to the ship had broken his medicine jars, and he was quickly running out.

Ibuki heard a rumbling sound overhead. When smoke from the fire began filling the room, he put on his gas mask and went on mechanically tending to his patients one after the other. In a little while, however, they were scarcely able to breathe, so he led the 30 or so patients out onto the quarterdeck and had them lie down. Most were burn victims, their faces swathed in bandages, but he seemed not to have any really severe cases. Perhaps, he thought, all the seriously injured had died before they got to him. Fierce crimson flames were burning their way down the passageway toward the quarterdeck. A young ensign, an engineer, leapt out of the flames in a swirl of smoke, sword clutched tightly in his hand, and fell to the deck. Ibuki watched him for a moment, making no move to treat his wounds. The ensign suddenly opened his eyes, got to his feet wordlessly and, grasping his sword, attempted to run back into the flames. Three firemen quickly grabbed hold of him and he went limp in their arms.

It was then that the *Hiyo* took two more torpedoes, these in the stern. The fires were spreading. A sailor, the whole of his face burned, sprinted along the deck, jumping over the bodies that lay there as he ran.

"The flight leader has been killed!" he shouted.

A lieutenant junior grade with Special Services had left the bridge with a message, but now as the bridge began to burn he was unable to return to it, and ground his teeth in frustration. He told them that the switching room had been knocked out by one of the torpedoes, and that because the fire-fighting equipment was not operating, efforts to combat the fires were going nowhere.

Ibuki now realized they would have to abandon ship. He and the Special Services officer took whatever lumber they could find around them and threw it into the sea, then led the injured men into the water. The waves instantly came between Ibuki and his patients. As he swam, hanging on to a piece of lumber, he could see crewmen at the fore end of the ship jumping one after the other into the sea. One side of the vessel was already down in the water and she was starting to go under. The enemy planes had left and the sky was now tranquil.

Ibuki was uninjured, so his swimming was unimpaired, but as time wore on his legs grew colder and he could feel them growing numb. The sea was heavy with fuel oil. Every swallow of its water was torment. He caught between the waves now and again the sound of voices: "*Banzai* for the warship *Hiyo!*" When he turned back, the carrier, sheathed in flames, was almost perpendicular in the water, and just starting to slip beneath the waves. It was getting dark. Someone somewhere began singing the *Dreadnought March* and the sound of men singing spread gradually amongst the seamen and officers scattered over the sea. They wept as they sang, their faces smeared with oil.

Ibuki floated face up to avoid any shock waves, but he heard little, only sharp, sibilant reports, perhaps machine gun rounds going off, and this only briefly. When he again rolled over on his stomach and began swimming, the *Hiyo* had already disappeared, leaving above it only many large whirlpools turning in the sea.

The sun set. Two Japanese aircraft, their speed reduced almost to stalling, skimmed over the surface of the ocean; the soft, low throb of their engines was like soothing music. Four destroyers cruised the area playing searchlights on the water. Night had fallen, which made them loom larger in the darkness, looking more like *Mogami*-class cruisers, and this was reassuring. The many steam- and gas-powered launches and cutters that the destroyers had put into the water set about their rescue work, but Ibuki could not stop thinking that it would be all over if the American submarines returned.

Almost immediately a steam launch appeared before Ibuki, its engine purring smoothly as it approached. There began a lively exchange of shouts between the men on the boat and those scattered here and there in the water. They had apparently spotted Ibuki, for a long line flew its length out to him. However, a number of wounded men with no lumber to hang onto were swimming in the same area, and Ibuki yelled out to the boat, indicating where the others were. He would wait for the next rescue boat. As the steam launch went out of sight one of the destroyers drew near at reduced speed. He was thrown a line again, and this he took. His legs, however, were numb and his hands swollen, and climbing up the side was almost beyond him. When he reached the deck he collapsed, utterly exhausted. A foul-tasting mixture of sea water and fuel oil gushed from his mouth. He could hear excited voices over him: "He's a pilot! He's a pilot!" This was probably because his hair was longer than most navy men's. He lay face down on the deck and listened, as though he were hearing them talk about someone else. A man slapped his body again and again with a piece of rope to keep him from slipping off into unconsciousness. Someone then took him by the arms and brought him into the wardroom. He lay down on a sofa and was given a soft drink. Once again he vomited, ridding his stomach of the last of the salt water and oil. It was agony. It was impossible to eat the crackers offered him. Thirty minutes later, however, his sea-chilled body rubbed dry and wearing thoroughly dry cotton clothes that had been lent him, he was fully conscious, and, comfortably warm, was overwhelmed, absurdly so, with a feeling of happiness.

The destroyer that had rescued Ibuki was the *Hamakaze*. Before it had picked up Ibuki and the men from the *Hiyo*, it had rescued some 300 survivors of another sunken warship, so the ship was jammed to the gunwales with men. It just so happened, however, that the gunnery officer had been head of the junior officers' quarters when Ibuki had been on the *Zuikaku*.

"Well," he said with a grimace when he caught sight of Ibuki, "they really got you, didn't they. Better come to my quarters."

In the gunnery officer's quarters Ibuki put four or five chairs together, lay down on them, and talked with the other man of many things, including Lieutenant Katsuta, the medical officer of the *Chuyo*, who had gone down with his ship. The gunnery officer told Ibuki that probably two-thirds of the *Hiyo's* crew had been rescued. As they talked, Ibuki felt as if the cabin was growing hotter and hotter. He knew he was all right now. The gunnery officer's quarters were directly over the engine room, and the cold water the orderly had given him was now lukewarm.

The ships that had survived Operation A began withdrawing to the safety of Okinawa at a cruising speed of about 16 knots, sharing their fuel as they went. Japanese gains in the battle were limited: one plane had dived into the battleship *Indiana*, the battleship *South Dakota* had taken one direct hit from Japanese guns, and 130 enemy aircraft had been shot down. In exchange, the Japanese side had had three of its aircraft carriers sunk, a total of 91,500 tons, and approximately 400 carrier-based planes lost. The American navy would later call this battle the Marianas Turkey Shoot.

Dawn the next morning, June 21. They were told they would be within range of enemy planes until around noon. Should American attack planes appear again, how effectively could the fleet—a mere remnant now—respond? Resting in a deck chair he had put out on the fore deck, Ibuki sat and abstractedly pondered the cheapness of life.

When the *Hamakaze* entered Nakagusuku Bay in Okinawa two mornings later, most of the other ships, including the six surviving carriers, were already there. Soon afterward the big warships *Nagato*, *Mogami*, *Zuikaku*, *Junyo*, *Chitose*, *Ryuho*, and *Chiyoda* weighed anchor for Kure. The *Hamakaze* was moored alongside the cruiser *Toné* and Ibuki and the other *Hiyo* survivors moved to the *Toné*, which weighed anchor and left Nakagusuku Bay around noon that same day.

Vessels carrying survivors from ships that had been sunk were not permitted entrance to Kure lest word of the loss get out. The *Toné* and the others were forced to drop anchor for a week at the Hashirajima anchorage in the Seto Inland Sea. In the waters of Hashirajima, not far from Hiroshima, the rains of the wet season were gently falling. The Inland Sea was absurdly serene, its crinkled surface extending to the furthest reaches of its rugged islands, wet with rain.

Ibuki's wallet and glasses had been lost with his foot locker, victims of his momentary carelessness, so he borrowed some money from the *Toné* paymaster when they made port in Kure and went ashore. Later he was transferred to the *Zuikaku*, then toward the end of July ordered to the Sasebo Naval Station for assignment there.

Six

When the order was given to put Operation A into effect and the Americans began their invasion of Saipan, the men of the General Staff's Special Services Group in the Meguro district of Tokyo began working late into the evening on a daily basis. This included Captain Morii and Lieutenant Commander Fukuda, almost everyone in A Section, Wada and Ono from B Section, and even Koji and Fujita of C and S Sections, whose work had no direct connection with what was happening in the Marianas. They all wanted to contribute in some way, however trivial, to the Japanese effort in this fateful battle, and they were eager to hear word of an outcome that promised some measure of hope. As was to be expected, only Tsutsumi among them went home every day promptly at the regular quitting time.

"You can't expect me to become a rubbernecker at this point," he said.

Nakada and several other officers were assigned to the code room of the Tokyo Communications Corps in Kasumigaseki on a rotating basis. The Corps handled Japanese cryptograms. A direct phone line had been set up between there and Meguro, so that they could quickly compare situation reports and operational messages on the one hand, and information garnered from their communications intelligence on the other.

Yet not one salutary battle report from the fleet arrived to relieve the tense atmosphere of Special Services Group. And the men at their desks in A Section, concentrating on enemy callsigns, the amount of traffic, and the ships and aircraft detected, uncovered no particularly unusual phenomena in the signal traffic.

Once an American submarine was detected sending an O message along the projected course of the Mobile Fleet, and a *kin* message—an operational special emergency message similar to the U.S. Navy's O dispatch—urging caution was sent to the task force, but because the fleet was observing radio silence, Special Services could get no response, so they did not know what effect their message had had, if any. Kuki, of course, had intercepted this same transmission on the *Taiho*, but the sub had been allowed to escape.

On what was supposed to be the second day of the battle, they located what appeared to be the enemy task force in a semi-circle of three flotillas west of the Marianas group. In the end, these two instances would be the only work Special Services Group would have a hand in.

From time to time a message would come in from a Japanese scout plane: *No sign of the enemy.* There were no battle reports, yet they now began getting unsettling reports like one message that came in from Rota.

We have one surviving operational Milky Way plane. In daylight we put all efforts into concealment; at night we are scheduled to attack enemy fleet with above aircraft.

Their impatience and tension began by degrees to turn into a feeling of boredom. Gradually people started to indulge themselves in idle chatter.

"I suppose," someone ventured, referring to the craft of cryptanalysis, "that in America the Black Chamber is busy now too."

"Absolutely," said Captain Morii, taking his jacket, draped with the sash of a staff officer, off its hook. Captain Morii had been in communications intelligence since it had been established in the navy and had a reputation as a man who, if you gave him a nail, could crack just about any safe. The captain told them that when he had been assigned to the Japanese embassy in Washington as a military attaché he noticed that the boy who came to deliver the telegrams every day had extra copies. When Captain Morii stopped him and asked about them, the youth at first would tell him nothing, but finally admitted that one was for the Department of War and another was for the State Department.

"'And the last one,'" said the Captain in English, repeating the boy's words, "'is for you.'"

That was how he learned the Americans were studying Japan's enciphered messages. And when the dirigible *Akron* crashed, he, as military attaché, was expected to make a condolence call at the U.S. Navy Department, but the official message of condolence he was waiting for was slow in coming, so rather than take over a message belatedly, he called on the Assistant Secretary of the Navy, pretending that he had received such a message of condolence. The Assistant Secretary courteously expressed his gratitude, then his face broke into a broad grin.

"But I expect you haven't yet received the telegram from Tokyo."

"What the devil will happen if we've lost Saipan?" Koji asked after Captain Morii had left.

"Lieutenant Commander Fukuda told us what would happen," Nakada responded. "Next will be the Philippines, then Taiwan, then Okinawa. A whittling process."

Mitsui was nearby. When Mitsui was around Koji had trouble keeping his mind off Noriko Yano.

"'*If* we've lost Saipan'?" Wada said *sotto voce*. "You can bet your life we have! I feel sorry for Suzuki." Suzuki was a classmate, an ensign, who had been sent to Saipan.

"I wonder about Kuki, too."

"If Saipan falls," said Hirokawa, applying a compass to a nautical chart, "they'll start bombing Tokyo."

"How many miles is it?" Wada asked as he stood to peer at the chart. "I'd say it's just a matter of time. I wonder how many months it'll take the enemy to build B-29 bases."

"And they won't let us off with the kind of small-scale bombing Kyushu had the other day."

And so the conversation went as they ate an unappetizing late-night snack of *sushi* made with boiled barley and rice. There was a call from the Tokyo Communications Corps; they had received a message that had been delayed. It was from the attack force.

Have discovered enemy task force we lost contact with last night. It is 150 knots off Saipan, bearing 260 degrees, distance 280 to 300 knots.

This caused something of a stir, but no other messages followed it.

Wada was pale and haggard-looking. He was putting up a tranquil front, but he was utterly depressed, and not because of the loss of Saipan. Only Koji was aware of this. Ever since Wada had told him about his secret feelings for the typist Blue, Koji had kept needling him about it, and now Wada was definitely uncomfortable.

The men on duty were tired and began to retire to their bunks in the duty room. Koji quietly asked Wada up onto the roof. The temperature abruptly dropped as they passed through the blackout curtains; there was a wind and the night sky was clear, not what one expects during the rainy season.

"You're pretty restless, aren't you. I'll do what I can to help, not just because I've asked you to check up on Noriko. How about giving it one more try with Blue?"

"You're still on that track?"

"I'm a pain, right?"

"You're not a pain," said Wada, "but I'm just not as devil-may-care as you."

"I tell you, I don't get it at all. You say she's engaged, but that's just what someone else says, or someone's misinterpretation of the situation. And even if it were true, anything could've happened since then. Either one could've broken it off, or the engagement might've fallen apart by itself."

Because of the blackout the city was dark, so they could see countless stars, sprinkled across the sky like sand. The outline of the big Ebisu brewery building loomed in silhouette beyond the rows of houses.

"I'm sure you mean well," Wada said, "but no amount of talk from you is going to change things."

"I wonder. I just don't think a man can turn his back on such strong feelings with no regrets."

"Forget me. What about you? No report from the agency yet?"

"Not yet."

"Hey look," said Wada, "there goes a shooting star! You know how big a shooting star is?"

"Hey, dammit, don't change the subject."

But Wada had heard enough from Koji.

"Listen, I'm tired. What do you say we turn in? I guess Saipan is done for. I sure hope Kuki lives to tell about it."

* * *

A notice arrived from the investigation agency several days later. That evening Koji changed into a business suit and went to pick up the report at the office in the Yurakucho district. He paid the fee and received a thick sheaf of papers in a sturdy envelope. He went outside, opened the envelope and read the report as he walked toward Hibiya. It was an impressive document, carbon copies neatly typed on fancy lined paper, and began with the Yano lineage starting with Noriko's grandparents.

Koji had already decided that Noriko was an ordinary young woman from an ordinary family. In his heart of hearts a certain feeling had developed without his knowing it: he saw her ordinariness as the absolute minimum, and should he find out that things were better—even a little bit better—he would be even more delighted. The reality, as recorded by the typed symbols on the page before him, however, was worse.

The Yanos had been a low-ranking samurai family that had lost its status at the time of the Meiji Restoration. The father was currently working as a guard at the Ministry of Finance. The family was poor and, were one to rank it, would fall at the lower reaches of the middle class. So far, so good, but when he came to the section on her mother, most of it was negative: she didn't pay enough attention to her children, she was considered a busybody within the neighborhood association, she had more than her share of rationed goods, and so on, all doubtless information picked up in her neighborhood.

As Koji read on he could visualize the woman: fiftyish, a flat, uncultured face, gold teeth in her mouth. He was less than enchanted now. But the worst was yet to come. When he came to the section on Noriko herself, the report noted that the information that she had graduated from the Kawamura Girls' School of Home Economics was either an error or a complete fabrication.

While the subject may not be considered mentally deficient, she has never, even as a child, evinced an affinity for academics, her performance inevitably being at the lowest level of her class. She enrolled in the Nakamura Commercial School for Girls, but had absolutely no interest in her studies and voluntarily withdrew after a year and a half. She subsequently remained at home helping with household chores. She is, by nature, fickle in all things. In March of her 18th year she enrolled in the Tanaka Typewriter Institute to learn the use of the Japanese typewriter.

Noriko Yano had older brothers and younger sisters, but nothing good was recorded about them either. In particular, a student at a technical school, a friend of an older brother, had some sort of relationship with Noriko, the closeness of which was unknown. The report noted that "this matter would require a separate investigation."

Koji almost collided with a bicycle and looked up, startled.

"'While the subject may not be considered mentally deficient'!" Koji muttered to himself, the report clutched in his hands. He jumped on a Shinjuku-bound streetcar that had just stopped in front of him. The car began to move. He turned toward the window, and, shielding the document with his body, dropped his gaze to the passage.

It struck him as a dreadful phrase. Nonetheless, it was because of this dreadful phrase that he now felt he could breathe more freely, and he read the entire report again, skimming this time. When he had finished he could feel his attachment to Noriko begin to fade within him; it was as though a fog was slowly lifting. His mind was clear: *It's no good.* He felt no pain whatsoever. He was full of cheer that evening, joking with the landlady, and slept like a log that night.

The next morning when he went to Special Services he called

Tsutsumi and Wada and told them what had happened and expressed his gratitude.

"Thanks. It's over."

"You're kidding!" Wada exclaimed. "That was a close one! But it worked out all right, didn't it."

"You're sure you have no regrets?" Tsutsumi asked.

"Strangely enough, I don't. I caught sight of Noriko this morning, and when I took a good look at her I could see her eyes are shifty, just as you said."

Wada and Tsutsumi burst into laughter.

"You're quick to fall in love," observed Tsutsumi, "and quick to cast it aside. Now I feel a little sorry for Miss Yano."

"Say whatever you want. Anyway, it's really a load off my mind."

"I'll bet. You were haunted by Tanii's comment about her, just as Wada said."

"I guess I did lean in that direction. I wonder why."

"You're awfully accommodating today, aren't you."

"What about her and Mitsui?"

"The funny thing is, there seems to be nothing at all between them."

The three men laughed uproariously.

"You know, they were able to breach security. They found out that Noriko took the rolls Special Services served for lunch home for her family. Those agencies are really something. And even when it came to her work here they wrote that she was relatively reliable."

"Well then, wouldn't you say she's a fine young woman, pure of heart?" Tsutsumi teased.

*   *   *

For the first time in a good while Koji began to pay some attention to the file of cryptograms in Level-Oblique Secret.

His assistant, Petty Officer Sano, had divided the messages according to point of origin, New Delhi, Washington, Sydney, and so on, and he showed that the messages that used a lot of O's and

V's—something they had paid particular attention to earlier—were always out of New Delhi. Sano was constantly reminding Koji of this fact and advancing various hypotheses about it. Koji, however, was able to draw no inspired ideas from the file of messages he half-heartedly went through. He hadn't a clue what this special, suspicious relationship between O and V meant, or how he ought to go about formulating effective retrieval from it.

Soon afterwards he again abandoned his work. He could see that Petty Officer Sano was not very satisfied with his lack of enthusiasm for cipher-breaking. Koji was away from his desk almost daily, trying to persuade Wada to rekindle his feelings for Akie Kizu. Koji himself might have failed in matters of the heart, but he was determined to drag Wada out of his abject withdrawal.

For Wada this was apparently unwelcome solicitude, but day after day Koji's friend thought of nothing else, a funereal expression on his face. After a week of this Wada finally asked Koji if he would look into the situation with Blue just one more time.

"And make damned sure you don't talk directly with Blue herself! All I need to know is about the guy's she's engaged to. If I can find out just how far along things are, then I can finally say adieu to talking nonsense with you and being depressed."

If this was how Wada felt, Koji decided it would be best to go directly to the heart of the problem, and the sooner the better. He was determined to disrupt any other marriage talks if he could, though he hadn't told Wada that. The only problem was where to meet with Blue. For the senior staff officer, a milk-sop officer named Tada who had been a captain forever, fraternization served as a peg to hang his fault-finding on: younger officers will *not* talk with the women typists except in the course of their duties; they will *not* play volleyball or ping-pong with them.

After some thought, Koji decided to use O-Chu Kawai. O-Chu was a friend of Blue's, her parents had asked him to visit them sometime, and their home was not far from the office. He was sorry to take advantage of O-Chu, but what had to be done had to be done. Having made his decision, Koji immediately waited for a time when no one was about, then slipped into the small office Blue was working in. Luckily, the other woman there was O-Chu. They were apparently taking a break and were deep in conversation. Each was almost embracing the new Remington typewriter in front of her, leaning toward the other woman over her machine. Koji called out.

"Typist Kizu."

Blue said nothing.

"I'm sorry to break in on you so abruptly, but there's something I'd like to talk with you about after you get off work today."

"Goodness, what could that be?" She sat back in her chair, the smile leaving her lips.

"I just want to talk briefly. It's nothing to worry about. And, uh, it wouldn't be a good idea to meet in public. Typist Kawai, I wonder if we couldn't use your house."

"Yes, that's all right," O-Chu replied, "but what for?"

"This is a bit odd, wouldn't you say?" Blue said, somewhat disconcerted.

The room was reserved for typists working on the strip cipher, and it would have been unfortunate for Koji if he had been seen chatting away in a room he had no business being in. Adopting a peremptory tone, he got them to agree on a time, then left the room. Another typist came in as he was going out.

Koji had dinner at the Special Services dining hall, then went to the Kawai house in Shiroganedai. O-Chu invited him in and led him to a Western-style room at the back of the house, where Blue was sitting on a sofa. O-Chu sat down next to her and they exchanged comments on the weather.

"Well, let me know when you're finished talking," said O-Chu as she left. "I'll bring some tea."

Once again Koji could not help but feel a bit sorry for her.

"How may I be of assistance?" Blue asked, speaking with uncommon formality.

"I hope you'll forgive me, but I should like to ask you about a marriage proposal."

"A what?"

134

Koji, heedless of her surprise, rushed on.

"I understand you are engaged to be married."

"Why should I be obliged to respond to you on such a subject, Ensign Obata?"

"I'll tell you why later. What sort of person is he, your fiancé?"

"What do you mean? I'm not engaged, most assuredly not."

"Please tell me the truth. This is a serious matter."

"This is too much. There's nothing to lie about. I am *not* engaged."

"Is that really true?" Koji's face flushed.

"If you have any doubts, you can call my home in the Omori district and ask my mother. But why are you asking me this?"

"Really? But you were supposed to have become engaged sometime around March this year."

For an instant a barely perceptible smile flickered at Blue's lips.

"That . . . oh . . . I suspect you're referring to my elder sister. She married an engineer in the navy, a lieutenant, at the beginning of May."

There could no longer be any doubt. In his mind's eye Koji saw Wada's pale face with its expression verging these last few months on nervous exhaustion. *What'd I tell you!*

"Let me explain. I'm sorry to have pried. It's not much of an explanation. If that's the actual situation, may I ask how you feel about Ensign Wada?"

Thus did Koji launch into his exposition, informing her of his friend's proper family background, Wada's training as an anthropologist, his parents, and just about everything he could think of, as he described the emotional see-saw Wada had been on since the previous fall. He was unable to tell her just how it came about that he, Koji, was interjecting himself into these marriage talks, but he talked of his friend's suffering.

"No doubt this sounds completely off the wall, but I assure you it isn't," Koji said, making his last comments. "Wada's a good man. In his stead, I ask you to by all means accept his proposal."

Blue heard Koji out, eyes lowered and posture unchanging, but when he pressed her to respond she told him it was most awkward having the proposal suddenly thrust upon her. She said she respected Ensign Wada for the work he was doing, but that she would leave the question of marriage to her mother. And besides, she wanted to think things over herself. She spoke with relative assurance and ease. At this point the mood lightened. Blue raised her head and he could see her usual charming smile.

"But Ensign Wada can be so amusing. Even though he's so methodical, he loses track of documents sometimes. He'll get this worried look on his face and shuffle papers around searching the shelves for a good 20 or 30 minutes!"

"Oh, that. He's a bit of a blockhead. But maybe that's his charm. Shall we call Miss Kawai now?"

O-Chu came in with a tray of tea and cakes for the three of them.

"Would you like some? Did you have a good talk?" She peered into Blue's face as she spoke.

"It was about Miss Kizu's getting married," said Koji, responding for her. "I'll give you the details later."

"I see. I told her it was sure to be a marriage proposal."

Blue apparently felt uncomfortable staying there with Koji any longer. She took several sips of tea, then left.

"Anyway," said Koji as he saw her to the entranceway, "please say yes. I don't want to be responsible for what happens if you don't."

He returned to the living room and, for the first time since his summer visit to Antung, paid his respects to O-Chu's mother. Her father, a friend of Koji's elder brother, was not there. Koji made an effort at conversation with O-Chu's mother about Antung, Mukden, and Dairen, and about his brother and his wife, who were then in Antung, but he could see a hint of resistance in her face.

Koji hastily quit the Kawai house and called Wada from the nearest public telephone. He told him to wait for him, that he had good news, then headed for Wada's house in the Shitaya district on the next streetcar.

Wada, sitting bolt-upright in his chair, listened to Koji's account, silent and pale from beginning to end.

"Well, what did I tell you? All you have to do now is press ahead. What more do you need than to confidently take the initiative? It'll be okay, believe me."

Wada took a deep breath, his shoulders rising.

"Okay."

He went downstairs and did not return for a while.

Wada's room was a jumble of small foreign oil paintings, dishes, and Western furniture that his father had apparently collected, and Wada's technical books and shell, bone, and hair specimens.

Wada came back up to the second floor with his diminutive, elderly mother in tow. She was obviously delighted. Secretly, Koji was quite proud of himself.

That night the Wadas had him stay over. His friend brought out a bottle of fine old wine from the storeroom.

"With you confronting her, I'll bet even Blue couldn't resist," he said, pulling the moldy cork from the bottle.

*　　*　　*

By the time the main force of the Second and Third Fleets, defeated in Operation A, dropped anchor at the western end of the Inland Sea, it was already clear which way the tide of battle on Saipan was running, and on June 22 Special Services verified through intercepts that American aircraft had taken over its Aslito airfield. Very soon after the battle the young officers heard that three of the Third Fleet's aircraft carriers, the *Taiho*, the *Shokaku,* and the *Hiyo,* had been lost and that Kuki, who had been on the *Taiho*, had perished in the fighting. Koji and several men who had been especially close to Kuki gathered one night at the Shiba Officers' Club and mourned him at the table off in a corner where until that spring Kuki had regularly installed himself to drink.

At about the same time Koji received his first letter from Tanii, who was in the northern Kuriles. Notwithstanding the fact that Tanii had left looking like a condemned man, unanticipated tranquility reigned in the northeast.

There have been no significant changes in the overall situation since my posting here, so daily life is pleasant. Spring is briefly here and a flower called the Ganko Orchid is blooming everywhere. It's a tiny purple flower the size of a grain of rice, and the leaves are also tiny, though very thick. It has glossy nodes on its stem shaped like beetle shells. It bears fruit you can make a wine with. Between the rocks at the seashore there are sea urchins everywhere you look, and plenty of seaweed of all sorts. It will soon be time for the salmon to lay their eggs and I look forward to watching them swim upstream. It's a peaceful landscape here that one cannot conceive of as part of a life and death struggle. On those rare days when the sky is clear, we can see the snow-covered mountains of Kamchatka across the water.

I miss Tokyo. How are the typists, I wonder? I look forward to mail from everyone, but have yet to receive even one letter. Say hello to Wada and Tsutsumi and Hirokawa for me. And please don't forget my family. I can't write anything to them that would suggest I'm in the Kuriles.

Koji circulated the letter among his friends.

Tsutsumi, Hirokawa, Wada, Koji, and the others in their class, save for several whose progress had been delayed by illness, were promoted to lieutenant junior grade, effective July 1.

A week later, in the midst of the commotion over the news that radio contact with Saipan had at last been completely cut off, Lieutenant Commander Iwamoto, head of C Section, returned to the office, furiously dabbing at the sweat on his face and neck. He called Koji over to him and took some papers from his thick briefcase.

"Army General Staff Headquarters says it's broken Level-Oblique Secret."

Koji was stunned.

"Apparently they've got a handle on only a very small part of it, and they were not about to give us anything, but I asked them, practically begged them, so from here on there'll be joint decrypting and we're also going to put more people on Level-Oblique Secret and exchange what we've solved every day. You're to go over to General Staff Headquarters right away."

Koji could only utter a startled "yes, sir." He was incredulous: how had they had broken Level-Oblique Secret? He packed his briefcase with material the navy had on the system, paper, and pencils, quickly left Special Services, and headed for General Staff Headquarters' Section 18 in the Ichigaya district.

In contrast to what one found in the navy, in the army's cryptanalytical section there hung in the air the seedy, gloomy atmosphere peculiar to that branch of the service. Koji met with a bovine captain named Hori. He was the one who had partially decrypted the code-cipher, actually a code within a cipher system.

According to the soft-spoken Captain Hori, the Army General Staff had also concluded that theoretically it would require several years of cryptanalysis to break the code, and at one point work had come to a virtual standstill. Around the end of May, however, Captain Hori's wife, who had been living in Dairen, suddenly fell sick and died, so the captain took a leave and went to Dairen to put his wife's affairs in order. He returned to Tokyo ten days later, able now to look at the cipher-code from a fresh perspective. He noticed that messages out of New Delhi often appeared in special ways, and he realized that this could be the system's Achilles heel. He was on the right track.

It's those O's and V's after all.

For the first time Koji felt that his behavior toward Petty Officer Sano had been indefensible, almost ignoring the decryption problem in his preoccupation with Noriko and Blue. It seemed bizarre to him that throughout Japan only he himself, Captain Hori, and Petty Officer Sano, along with no more than two or three other people, were actually studying this cipher-code, and even in a world-wide context they were but a few in a handful. Because the work was cloaked in secrecy, any success or failure happened behind the scenes. But he found himself thinking—rather self-importantly—that if his work were of a public nature, like scientific research on a particular problem, his negligence would have destroyed his reputation throughout the world.

Koji sat across the table from Captain Hori taking in his explanation of the data piece by piece, and then returned to Special Services.

As he had expected, Level-Oblique Secret was a three-letter group code in which BUS, for example, meant enemy, GOL meant English, and IIC was ship. The code used the so-called single-book system, and, just as with Blue Secret, the sender and the receiver had identical books. The ordering of the Chinese characters followed a kind of dictionary used with civil telegrams called the Chinese Commercial Telegraphic Code, widely available in China. The New Delhi codebook, for example, was simply this dictionary, arranged into 26 pages. Each page, column, and line was given a letter—beginning with Z and continuing alphabetically to Y—in which, for example, following the usual dictionary order, the character for "enemy." was on the B page, line U, column S. Chungking's military attachés would leaf through the codebook, transforming the Chinese text to be sent into several hundred letters in the English alphabet; this was the first level of encipherment. Unchanged, however, it would permit quick recovery, as in the case of Blue Secret. That is, were the word "enemy" used five times in a text, the trigram BUS would also appear five times in the encipherment. To avoid this, they did a second level of encipherment, or superencipherment.

The text of the first-level encipherment was written out horizontally on special lined forms which had 25 squares per line. The first few squares were left blank, just as though you were starting a paragraph in a Western language. Each of the military attachés, regardless of location, had his own special key, which was a random arrangement of the numbers from one to twenty-five. Each of the 25 columns of letters written out on the form would be assigned numbers in order of the attaché's key. Then the columns were reshuffled in numerical order from 1 to 25, thereby setting up the second level of encipherment, which would mean there would no longer be any repetition whatsoever.

Given the nature of the Chinese language, however, there were many instances where English or another foreign language had to be used for Western place names, personal names, and other special terminology. For this reason the requisite letters were to be found in alphabetical order on page O, line V of New Delhi's codebook. Thus the letter A was OVA; B, OVB; C, OVC; and so on. And because a plaintext message might have somewhat lengthy English phrases like *Port Blair* or *tactical air force* embedded in it, the enciphered message would make conspicuous use of O's and V's. While the structure could be broken down with a key, because of the cyclical nature of the use of the 25 squares, O and V would appear in certain specific patterns.

Also, indicators were inserted at the beginning of a cryptogram so that the recipient would not make a mistake in keying. In the case of, for example, ABSEF HHFXX, the first indicator showed how many squares down on the special message form the columns of ciphertext extended. In this case five, the distance alphabetically from the first letter, A, to the fourth letter, E. The second indicator told the recipient how many squares to leave blank at the beginning of the first line, eleven here, the number of letters from X at the end to H (XYZABC....H). The S and F at the middle of each letter group had no meaning, and the doubling of the X and the linking of A and B were to avoid errors in the indicators themselves.

Koji and Petty Officer Sano were overwhelmed with work. Since the Army General Staff as yet had only broken the New Delhi key, they had to break the keys of the attachés in Moscow, Washington, Sydney, Melbourne, Tehran, London, Chungking, and elsewhere, and their substitution table, the so-called Appended Revised Tables published at the end of the last year, as well as compiling a code-book and increasing the number of known characters. They also had to read the flood of Level-Oblique Secret messages that poured in every day for which they had the key and generate intelligence, and reprocess the several hundred messages that had accumulated since

January. All of this could most certainly not be accomplished only during regular duty hours. Several men were assigned to help Koji, including a Lieutenant Shibasaki from the class ahead of his who had returned from posting with X Group in Shanghai. Of course, Koji, who had been dealing with the problem for some time, inevitably became the central player in the effort. On the several nights a week when he pulled watch he would usually voluntarily work on the project through the night out of a sense of responsibility and simple concern. Because this was the cryptosystem the Chungking General Staff had earlier claimed with pride had achieved parity with the codes and ciphers of the U.S. and Great Britain, it seemed to Koji that the Chinese would encipher and transmit matters of quite high sensitivity with it, and he thought about the sort of intelligence it might produce: the time when enemy forces might begin landing operations on the Chinese mainland, for example, or conciliatory moves toward peace that might be made by one or more of the Allied countries.

Within a week both the Army General Staff and Special Services had figured out a good number of keys and decryption procedures. It was obvious that Chungking had put considerable thought into the system. The same character was represented by different letter groups, depending on location; while "enemy" was BUS in New Delhi, in Washington it was KDB, and in Chungking it changed to FYW. Koji had even thought at first that each attaché was provided with his own codebook, but when they broke it, they found the changes were based on a single uncomplicated substitution table. That is, if New Delhi had as its basic table ZABCDE . . . WXY, then Washington's would be IJKLMN . . . FGH, and Chungking's DEFGHI . . . ABC, the latter two shifting a number of letters down the alphabet from the one before it, so that a Z in New Delhi was an I in Washington and a D in Chungking.

They also determined that the Chinese naval, air force and army attachés in Washington, Moscow and elsewhere used different key numbers.

Koji and his co-workers developed a basic codebook for all the

142

other locations using the New Delhi traffic they had broken, and went on to decipher all the keys and the substitution table. The work proceeded quickly. The fact that the last letter of New Delhi's OV combination was always the same as the letter of the original proved to be a serious blunder on Chungking's part.

* * *

One afternoon an office boy came to tell Koji he had a telephone call. The call had come to the guard room at the entrance downstairs. Koji went down to the ground floor and picked up the receiver.

"Hello," the caller began. "This is Akie Kizu's mother."

She told him she would like to talk with him briefly and asked if he wouldn't mind coming by one day at his convenience. Koji was amenable and agreed to visit her that evening and asked the way to her house from Omori station.

The city was well into summer. Days of endless sun had covered the leaves with dust, and the street lights, back-lit by the failing light of sunset, looked for all the world like lamps shining under water. Koji had managed no more than two or three hours of fitful sleep near dawn on some wooden chairs in Special Services, so he was tense from fatigue and the heat. He had readily agreed to her request, but he could not dispel the anxiety that Blue's mother would come down hard on him for his presuming to mediate.

He walked toward the Sanno area from Omori station. Houses of similar construction stood along both sides of the narrow lane. Few people were about, and the area had the tranquility one expects of a residential neighborhood. Cedar doors, bamboo fences, well-tended pine trees, these things suddenly evoked within him a nostalgia for the peaceful world he had left behind, and to which his return was problematic. Koji located the house and, standing in the entrance-way, announced himself.

"This is Lieutenant Obata," he called out, his voice a little tense. "You telephoned me earlier today."

Blue's mother hurried out. She was still relatively young.

143

"My goodness! Sorry you had to come so far out of your way! Well, please come in. Excuse the mess."

She showed him into a room to the side of the entranceway and immediately brought him a damp face towel and something cold to drink.

"Don't stand on ceremony so! Take off your jacket," she said, her tone straightforward.

Koji at last relaxed.

"Akie took today off, as you probably know," her mother began. "She said she was going to visit her sister's when she left, and she's not back yet. You know, the other day she told me she was going to O-Chu's house, and came home late. She said she didn't feel well, didn't eat, just sat there playing the piano. After enough of my questions, she told me about the proposal, which was a shock, I'll tell you."

The fact that Blue's mother was from Hiroshima and that Blue and Koji had gone to the same primary school loosened his tongue somewhat. Though it embarrassed him to do so, he assiduously praised Wada and told her what a fine person he was, as a go-between is expected to.

Blue's mother said she thought the proposal reasonable enough, but wondered whether there might not be trouble in the future due to the difference in their family backgrounds. Everyone in her family was in the navy. Lieutenant Wada was certainly a navy man, but he would, in due time, go back to his academic specialty. As for anthropologists, she hadn't any idea what sort of things they did, and this made her uneasy.

"How would it be, do you suppose? Would Akie make a good wife for a scholar, I wonder?" she asked, but her tone suggested she had halfway accepted the match.

Mosquitoes whined about their legs. Blue's mother lit a mosquito coil and fanned the smoke around their legs as she talked. She told him she would have liked to have been able to discuss the proposal with her husband, who was in Surabaja, but the situation being what it was, it would be difficult to get in touch with him, so those in the family who were in Japan proper could decide the matter.

A little later Blue returned from Kamakura. The three of them were together now, but there was nothing more they had to talk about, so Koji, among other things, told them about Wada's research, parroting what Wada had told him about how the periodization of the Stone Age was determined, and left the Kizu residence an hour later.

Thereafter the Wada-Kizu talks seemed to progress smoothly and there was nothing further for Koji to do, so he disengaged himself from the process. One of Wada's aunts visited the house in Omori and formally made a proposal of marriage on behalf of Wada's family, and this was accepted. Since the head of Special Services, Rear Admiral Kato, and Captain Tada, its senior staff officer, were friends of Blue's father, also a rear admiral, Rear Admiral Kato was delighted at the match and actively took over the role of go-between. It was decided that Blue would soon quit her job at Special Services, before word of the match leaked out.

"How's it been going?" Koji asked Blue when he happened to meet her in the hallway.

"Things seem to be moving along quite nicely," she answered self-consciously, though with obvious friendliness.

Koji's work on Level-Oblique Secret became all the more frenetic as they solved the various keys. As he had anticipated at the outset, only the attaché stationed in Bern, Switzerland, continued to use the ABKF system. Thus every time Chungking transmitted its regular report on the war situation in China, identical messages in Level-Oblique Secret and ABKF were sent, increasing at each instance the number of known characters in the codebook. Koji was intrigued that in the war reports on the continent Chungking inevitably referred to Manchukuo as "the pseudo-state."

They also recovered valuable intelligence from old message files, notwithstanding their lack of timeliness. The Chinese attaché stationed in Australia, the liaison with Allied forces headquarters in the southwest Pacific, appeared to be extremely capable, and was always dispatching fresh intelligence to Chungking. More than once he received a message from the head of the Chungking General Staff praising him for his work. Once the system was broken, they found that the intelligence that came into the hands of the enemy attaché was excellent and nicely suited their needs. It was from dispatches from Chungking that Koji learned the name of a new Japanese aircraft, and that a Japanese submarine had been detected with American radar and sunk, and that the subs were now covered with rubber in an attempt to thwart radar.

Before long the next class of student reservists had completed their training and been commissioned; 40 or 50 of the new ensigns were assigned to Special Services. Five were attached to C Section under Koji, who was ordered to teach them a basic knowledge of Chungking's codes and ciphers. The new ensigns, however, had a good deal of trouble understanding their work, frequently leaving Koji irritated and exasperated.

Hoping to get his charges to recite the names of the various attachés throughout the world, he asked them to tell him who used Blue Secret. He got back answers like "the user is Lieutenant Shibasaki." He gave them a cryptanalytical exercise in simple substitution hardly more difficult to read than a detective novel. Even though he told them it was an English passage on the war, one man spent three hours on it and still couldn't solve it.

"You sure as hell can't do your job in Special Services if you're a half-wit!" he shouted at the ensigns, just as Commander Ezaki had berated him.

Phonetic transliteration or sense translations of foreign personal and place names appearing regularly in the news facilitated the decryption of Chinese characters that would have been otherwise hard to solve, names like MacArthur, Mountbatten, Midway, *Pravda*, Hitler. The new men could not even read these, and yet it was his job to somehow make one of these men competent to take his place in the work on Level-Oblique Secret.

Along the route he took to his office every day, soldiers in the Engineering Corps had been dispatched to begin the work of pulling down old houses that stood wall to wall, to make fire-breaks. The loss of Saipan seemed already to be exercising its unmistakable influence. Koji passed his days with his mind somehow flushed and feverish. He made time to sit down and write a long letter to Tanii in the Kuriles. There was much to write about: Noriko Yano, Blue and Wada, Level-Oblique Secret, Hirokawa, who had recently decided to marry the pianist Chizuko Kayama.

The day Akie Kizu was to quit her job at last arrived. Word that the fabled Blue was quitting caused a sensation in the ranks of the officers, but Koji feigned ignorance throughout. Wada appeared even more unruffled, the very soul of serenity. It was the custom whenever a civilian employee quit for her to make the rounds of the section chiefs and the officers she had dealings with to show them her resignation and say her goodbyes. Blue, in kimono, arrived at the office later than usual that morning. She gathered up her personal belongings and began the circuit of the sections, B first, then A and D.

Some time later when he saw the door of C Section open and Akie enter, Koji jumped up, an incipient blush on his face, and left the room.

Out in the hall Noriko Yano and her friend Tamura hung back, arms linked, like gawking children trailing after a bride. Koji stole a glance at Noriko's problematic eyes as he went by. *Rather pretty at that.* But he thought no more about her.

*   *   *

After Akie Kizu had left the building, seen off by typists lining the corridor, Koji returned to his desk and began working again on Level-Oblique Secret. That afternoon Lieutenant Commander Iwamoto, the section chief, summoned him. The section chief had just come from the office of the head of Special Services, and Koji thought with an unpleasant chill of anticipation that he would now be lectured about the Blue business.

It was, however, something quite different. He was being transferred to Fleet Headquarters, China theater.

Koji, Wada, and Tsutsumi went off to the traditional Japanese restaurant in Yokosuka they frequented for a kind of bachelor's party, but it would also be a send-off for Koji. Ever since the business about Noriko, Tsutsumi had noticed Wada and Koji constantly talking off in a corner about something and had not hidden his resentment, so now his two friends revealed all the details about Koji's matchmaking.

"You don't say! Congratulations! Obata was his usual rash self." Tsutsumi laughed, but it was a strained laugh. "You know, Obata, I'm impressed that you were able to pull it off and not even I had a clue."

As he drank, Koji thought about the flurry of changes in his life over these last few years: from life as a student to the military, from Taiwan to Yokosuka, Tokyo, and now Shanghai; he had come this far unaware of where the tangled threads of his life would lead. Had he at some point taken another turn, he would no doubt now be doing something entirely different in an entirely different setting. His taking Chinese in college on the whim of the moment had proved to be a fork in the road that determined his present position, and if Tanii had not been ordered to the Kuriles, which had led him to Noriko and then Blue, Wada's situation would most certainly be different. He knew this kind of thing happened in normal times, of course, but in war, where individual will plays no role, such dramatic changes in destiny seemed so arbitrary. Koji felt almost hopeless, and wondered where today's threads would lead him.

"Well then, tonight," Tsutsumi was saying, "this get-together for Obata is also Wada's celebration, but as a matter of fact, I'm also being transferred. They told me today."

"Where?!"

"I'll be going into plywood torpedo boats," Tsutsumi responded, raising his cup and striking a mock-heroic pose.

"The hell you say!"

He laughed.

"I'm gonna be an instructor at the communications school. Making the likes of me an instructor means that the navy's beaten, not the force it used to be. But the food's good here in Yokosuka, so I'm not complaining, I'll tell you."

"One by one everybody's leaving," said Wada. "Looks like I'm the only one staying behind."

"Well," Koji said, "if you're staying behind—Saipan's fallen, so who knows what will happen next—you ought to have the wedding early, even if it means braving the heat. I've put my affairs in order, so I can go off to Shanghai with a clear conscience."

Kikuchiyo and another geisha who catered to naval officers came and sat with them.

"Whatever became of that faint-hearted, cowardly ensign who came with you a while back?" she asked Koji. She seemed unable to settle down, however, and kept leaving the room and coming back. A little later Kikuchiyo returned accompanied by the waitress O-Shin, and then a short man, his head shaved and wearing a sport shirt, suddenly appeared. It was Lieutenant Kizu, Blue's elder brother. He had asked the women to call him if Wada came to the restaurant.

"I wanted to meet you, but I haven't had a chance to get to Tokyo," the brother said, fanning himself vigorously.

The three other men were at first a bit reserved and inhibited, but Blue's brother was an easy-going, carefree sort, like the fighter pilot he was, so before long the party had regained its animation. The lieutenant drank with them for an hour.

"Well, please take good care of *sis*," he said to both Wada and Koji, using the English word. Then, waving the fan to signal his departure, he went back to his unit.

As for the decryption of Level-Oblique Secret, the increase in the number of known characters and the formulation of keys went ahead smoothly. Since Koji was to be transferred, the work was essentially given over to Shibasaki and Ensign Matsumoto, who was from the class behind Koji's. Koji would be going to either Shanghai or Hankow, depending on the needs of Special Services, but he would have to deal with the Chungking air force in either case, so every day he spread out a map of the Republic of China before him and, under the guidance of Lieutenant Shibasaki, endeavored to cram into his mind everything he could about the enemy's principal airbases. He found it very difficult, though, to detach himself from the military-attaché codes and ciphers that he had so long labored over.

Just before he was to leave Tokyo, a week before Wada's wedding, he went one night to the Kizu home to say his goodbyes. Dowry articles had been placed here and there about the house. He had earlier decided that word of his transfer should not go beyond his immediate circle of friends until he was about to leave, so the news came as a surprise to Blue.

"For all that, Lieutenant Obata, you're more timid than I'd thought, aren't you," she said with a smile. "The day I quit, when I went into C Section you left the room, didn't you. Wada's a cool one, though. There he was, so I greeted him as I had everyone else and said 'I've enjoyed working with you over the months.' He just said calmly, 'Oh, you're leaving us? We appreciate the work you've done. Take care.' I was dumbfounded."

When Koji left she saw him to the train station.

"But it's really a pity," she said, taking his arm as they walked. "I wish I'd asked Rear Admiral Kato not to send you off."

Koji had a seat on an August 17 China Theater Fleet flight. It was out of Fukuoka, so he took an express from Tokyo the night of the 14th. Well-wishers were not permitted on the departure platform at Tokyo Station, so Wada, Akie, and Tanii's mother and sister came to see him off from Shinagawa Station. Wada was in his summer whites and the three women were wearing light summer kimonos. Koji gazed at the gay figures with pleasure—and with sadness that he would be leaving them. This time he did not know when he would return to Tokyo again. He asked Wada to look after the Tanii women.

When the train's brief stop was over, the electric locomotive's languid whistle sounded and the train slowly began to move into the thin evening mist, richly tinted by the colors of the signal lights.

Koji was free for some 18 hours en route to Fukuoka, so he decided to get off the train at Hiroshima and stay overnight with his parents. He saw his father for the first time since he had fallen ill.

His father had a urine bottle at the side of the bed, and had a string tied to the foot of his paralyzed left leg, pulling it along after him so that he could crawl. Looking closely at his stricken father, he saw the deathly pale, puffed face of the stroke victim.

"You can see the shape I'm in," the old man said tearfully. "Come back home as soon as you can."

Koji felt that this would be the last time he would see his parents, but he was not sad.

After nightfall Koji visited Mr. Yashiro in town. His former teacher was happy for him that he was going to Shanghai. Intending to amuse, Koji related the Noriko Yano fiasco. Mr. Yashiro listened quietly.

"You've been to the Ibuki home today?"

Koji blushed.

"No, I haven't."

"I know bystanders ought not interfere," Mr. Yashiro began, "but the fact is I met Ibuki's younger sister some two months ago. I had the feeling she firmly believes there is some special relationship between the two of you. What are your thoughts? You don't think about her at all anymore, do you."

"I wouldn't say that, exactly," said Koji, attempting to justify himself, but not succeeding.

"This is a time when the destiny of the individual is being treated in a dreadfully offhand way, and I really can't tell you what to do, but in any event, I wonder if it might not be better to at least make your intentions clear."

Koji was not unmoved by Mr. Yashiro's words. That night, however, he forced such sentiments out of his mind.

Two days later just before noon the DC-3 with the China Theater Fleet landed at the airfield in Fukuoka. As Koji was waiting in the terminal with the other passengers, the pilot, wearing aviator boots, came in, dropped into the terminal mailbox a bundle of mail he had apparently been asked to bring from Shanghai, then lay down on a bench, pulled his cap over his face and proceeded to take a nap. There was no doubt that here was a man accustomed to going back and forth between China and Japan. It made Koji feel that the city of Shanghai was close indeed.

Koji exchanged his yen for military scrip at a currency exchange, getting a bundle of bills too thick to fit into his wallet. The pilot got to his feet after sleeping an hour. The DC-3 took off from Fukuoka at exactly one in the afternoon, and soon Koji could see the verdant terraced fields on islets near the coast gently passing beneath him; then the plane gradually gained altitude, and all he could see was the blue sea. He sat back in his seat by a window and opened the fresh air jet above him. Cold air hissed into the cabin. Cumulonimbus clouds rose like huge towers ahead of him, utterly immobile, shining with a fierce whiteness. After he had eaten the lunch he had brought from the airfield, he read for a while, but felt himself growing drowsy, perhaps because of the lower air pressure. He rested his sword on his lap and soon fell asleep, the air rushing in over him.

When he woke some two hours later, he saw wisps of clouds flying by under the starboard wing. The sea below was just then changing from a deep blue to a dirty, rusty red. He decided they must be near the mouth of the Yangtze River. He realized for the first time that the reddish-brown waters of the great river did not blend imperceptibly with the blue ocean; there was an abrupt change of color, a line drawn. He looked at his watch. It was a little after four.

Descending slowly, the plane passed over low-lying islands that stretched from the sea to the wetlands. Koji saw in the distance the Broadway Mansions building that he knew from photographs, and beneath him were the white walls and reflexed green roofs of a Chinese-style pagoda. As the plane banked, a new prospect rolled slowly into view. The plane glided smoothly along the ground. Tach'angchen Airfield. The big airfield was still; perhaps those in training were on break now. The air shimmered flame-like over the summer grasses.

Seven

It was now 1944, and the third and final autumn of the war that Japan had begun in the Pacific. Chungshan Park on the western outskirts of Hankow in China's Hupei Province, devastated and grimy, served as a billeting area for army units in transit. Mud-colored trucks were parked about helter-skelter, dampish tents had been thrown up, bridge supports lay destroyed, roads torn up, and amongst the trees in the park piles of mud and excreta lay upon decaying foliage. Standing there, Koji caught the odor of damp fallen leaves. Horse droppings dotted the road. The failing light of evening came streaming through tree branches that had yet to shed their yellowed leaves. He stood waiting at the crossroads in the park.

"Hut, two, hut, two."

He could hear a senior petty officer calling cadence as men in formation made a double-time circuit around the pond. The beardless young telegraphers passed at a fast scuffle in their clodhoppers, to be followed by the petty officers, older men, in columns of four, a phalanx of sullen faces. As one petty officer passed in front of him the man intentionally broke into a high stride. Koji was aware that most of the petty officers were unhappy with him.

"Hut, two, hut, two."

He fell in behind them and began running. The Naval Receiving Station he was attached to was across the road south of the park.

An hour later, after the evening meal, they would be free to leave base. They would go off looking for women and drink, the officers to the traditional Japanese restaurants, the enlisted men to the brothels. Unlike in Japan, there was no lack of food, drink, cigarettes, or women here. If he had been able to relax and look at all this with a more cosmopolitan, accepting eye, he, too, might have been able to throw himself into the fun and games and feel more at peace with himself.

The battle for Leyte was over. In the three-day sea battle off the Philippines and the fighting just before and after it, the battleships *Musashi*, *Fuso*, and *Yamashiro*, the aircraft carriers *Zuikaku*, *Zuiho*, *Chiyoda*, and *Chitose*, 10 cruisers, including the *Atago* and the *Mogami*, and 11 destroyers were sunk. From then until the end of November the battleship *Kongo*, the carriers *Shinyo* and *Shinano*, four more cruisers, and 11 more destroyers were sent to the bottom. The Combined Fleet, on which the Japanese had pinned their hopes for victory, was all but annihilated. And Koji was sure that Commander Ezaki, who had earlier been with Special Services, had, as Executive Officer of the carrier *Zuiho*, shared his ship's fate.

He did not know what to think of his own situation. His emotional state had, by degrees, turned wild and violent. He would not allow his men an inch of leeway. More than once he struck a petty officer who, having told the younger men not to say anything, would stay too long at some woman's place and fail to return to quarters by lights out.

He even slapped an ensign who smugly told him that their being posted to China was, in effect, a reward for their achievements, and that they should take it easy and enjoy life. At staff meetings he could only look with contempt at staff officers who gathered to debate for a good hour the decision of how to distribute bamboo brooms to each unit. On days when there was some sort of ceremony and each unit mustered at Headquarters, the other officers would cluster in groups of three or four in animated conversation, but he would usually stand apart, sword in hand. In sharp contrast with the boisterous camaraderie of four months before in Tokyo, he was now completely isolated. Life at the Naval General Staff had been an extension of his student days; all that had been required of him was that he work on the codes and ciphers that were his responsibility.

Now, however, he had 230 men under him, and he had to see that things proceeded smoothly. He was having trouble dealing with his own feelings and, at the same time, he was aware of how the old-hand petty officers felt, yet was not adept at dealing with them.

"Hut, two, hut, two."

The double-timing columns went out the Chungshan Park gate, cut across the road, and ran into the Receiving Station compound. Off-duty whistles began sounding in the unit.

That August, when he had arrived at his post, X Group, in Shanghai, District Fleet Staff had made the decision to send him on to Hankow the following week, and several days later he had set off by plane for his new assignment. Various navy units were scattered throughout the city of Hankow, from the Maritime Guards at the edge of the Japanese concession in the north to the Shore Guards near the airfield to the west, and including Base Forces Headquarters, a survey detachment, the Naval Attaché Office, munitions units, Land Guards, and anti-aircraft outfits. The Receiving Station that Koji was assigned to faced a broad country road that ran from the city to the airfield. It was officially known as the Eighth Detachment of the Yangtze River District Special Base Force, but in terms of its actual mission was called W Group and—together with Y Group on Hainan Island and X Group in Shanghai—was the China arm of the Naval General Staff's Special Services Group. The work assigned to W Group was the surveillance of the activities of Chungking China's and America's China-theater air forces. Lieutenant Commander Funaki, in charge of the Group, was also serving on the staff of Base Forces Headquarters, and, until the arrival of a replacement for the last detachment commander, a man from the first class of reservists who had recently gone back to Tokyo, Koji was appointed deputy detachment commander.

There was a brothel in town for the exclusive use of naval officers. It was named The Clear Stream, but of course everyone called it The Turbid Stream. A dozen or so women were employed there, birds of passage all. Staff and other officers spent night after night there drinking, singing, and wenching. Koji had also gone there several times since coming to Hankow, but shortly after the battles in Philippine waters ended, a civilian he had never seen before told him it was no wonder the navy had lost, if this was the way navy men spent their free time. Shamed, he abruptly stopped going to the club.

Autumn in Greater Wuhan was said to be a beautiful time. This year, however, the dreary rains had gone on and on. That day the long-absent sun had begun to shine weakly toward evening, so he decided to invite an ensign named Koizumi, who worked in the American section of his unit, to go with him for duck sukiyaki at the Officers' Club.

There was good food to be had in town. Standing and eating noodles on the broad boulevards and dipping cruller into the broth. Bread fuming in steamers in grimy storefront eateries. Potstickers. Dumplings. Or moon cakes. Pickled eggs, five-spice eggs. The Grand King, which offered soup buns made by wrapping pork and broth in thin casings made from flour and steaming them. All of these strange flavors of the everyday people were delicious. Mr. Chu had not been exaggerating when he spoke proudly of China and his Beijing. But with the free-fall month after month of the military scrip, a huge gap had developed between the money circulating on base and the money used in town, so that unless he sold his ration of cigarettes, the idea of sitting down to a meal in a regular Chinese restaurant was entirely out of the question. On his and his comrades' pay, even having noodles at a street stall was almost beyond reach. Given that he would berate his men for any breach of regulations, Koji had no desire to make money on the sly, and so he had no choice but to content himself every day with the humdrum Japanese fare at the Officers' Club.

Ensign Koizumi had been in the third class of student reservists and had come to Hankow a little before Koji. Koizumi was just about the only person to show friendliness toward Koji, who had gradually become more and more intolerant of his fellow officers. Koizumi had gone to college in America and had been repatriated on the first exchange ship of the war before joining the navy, so he was older than Koji. While he was quick to say that America was "a fine country," it was also obvious that he entertained considerable resentment against it from his experiences there.

They had eaten their duck at the Officers' Club and were walking back to their quarters.

"I think it would be a great mistake," said Koizumi, "to believe America will make any move toward compromise."

"Really? You know, I wonder now and again . . . ," Koji began. "Pretty soon they'll probably come looking for volunteers for the Special Attack Corps—the Kamikazes—from the ranks of us young, low-ranking officers. How about it? Could you go when the time came?"

"What about you?"

"Well, I don't know," Koji responded. "When the war began I thought I would be able to sacrifice myself, in this war at least. Even now in order to win—and even if we don't win—I want to work toward building Japan's future, but honestly, I really don't know if I would volunteer for the Special Attack Corps. I might even try to get out of it by thinking up some hypocritical pretext."

"Really? I'm sure I'd go. I could do it. I think America will come at us with every dirty trick in the book. If Japan is ever occupied by the U.S., I tell you it'll be picked clean. Couldn't you do it if you knew you were stopping that from happening?"

Koji said nothing, but remembered how the day they graduated from college Kurimura had told everyone never to volunteer for a suicide mission, that they must all come back alive.

"Ah, but when the time comes," said the slightly tipsy Koizumi with sudden fervor, "I've got to return to Tokyo and see my mom again!"

"You know," said Koji, "At this point I really wonder if work in communications intelligence can do any good at all."

Six years before, when Wuhan had fallen to Japanese forces and a local unit of Special Services Group was first established in Hankow, large numbers of naval attack bombers, 96s, were moved forward to the local air base. When the bombers went off in formations to bomb Chungking and Chengtu, this very same W Group, by breaking ciphers, provided vital and immediately useful intelligence on the deployment and movement of enemy aircraft. Thanks to this *sub rosa* support from W Group, the attack bombers were able to achieve considerable success in battle. Now, however, the situation had completely changed. The war with America and Great Britain was in its fourth year, and the navy's air units had long since withdrawn from Hankow. The communication intelligence struggle, likewise, was not directed against the Chungking government's air force, but against powerful American air transport units which, flying from India over high mountain ranges and into northern Burma, were landing or departing Kunming at a rate of one every 30 to 60 seconds, 24 hours a day; against swarms of B-29s steadily growing in number in Chengtu; and against China-theater American fighter and medium bomber units that were everywhere. In addition to Koji's current work on the codes of a network known as the Air Defense Intelligence Stations, W Group was trying its hand at every sort of interception, yet it had almost no noteworthy success to show for its efforts.

"I need something to clear out the cobwebs," Koizumi said.

"How about borrowing horses from the Land Guards this Sunday and going for a ride into the country?"

Koizumi thought that was a fine idea.

The two men returned to the Receiving Station late that night. All were asleep in the unit except for the men in Operations.

*   *   *

Sunday morning Koji asked Ensign Koizumi to wait for him in front of Headquarters while he took his report into the adjutant's office. It was an off-duty day, but he had to take care of some unit matters and a report on a POW interrogation he had conducted several days earlier.

Many small monitoring stations were scattered throughout the unoccupied areas of China, the original purpose of which undoubtedly had been to monitor the hostile actions of Japanese aircraft, but such activity had become quite slack recently since they almost never flew into the interior on raids. Curiously, these enemy monitoring stations had now begun tracking American aircraft and diligently telegraphing their reports to the subordinate Air Defense Intelligence Stations. A petty officer first class named Ono had stumbled across their frequency a while back and was monitoring it. If they could break the code they would know what the American planes were doing and would be able to turn the tables on the Americans and use the intelligence for their own air defense. The cryptograms, however, were only one-line numerical messages, so with little to work with they made practically no headway.

Several days before Koji had gotten permission from the army to go to a POW camp and interrogate an American airman they had in custody there. Koji had intended to draw information, however minor, out of the prisoner on the monitoring stations and the Air Defense Intelligence Stations. When Koji put his questions to the man through Koizumi, who was interpreting, the prisoner's expression was one of surprise.

"We have radar," he responded, "so our air units don't have to rely on old equipment like that."

"I'm not talking about America. I mean units of the Chinese air force."

"Don't know a thing about it."

"You never heard anyone talking about those things?"

"We don't have anything to do with Chinese pilots, so I haven't heard a thing."

He seemed to be telling the truth. The POW was a short, easygoing youth who had piloted a P-51 that was shot down on a bombing run over Wuch'ang. Getting nowhere, Koji relaxed the tone of the interrogation. The prisoner told him he was with a fighter squadron stationed at Chihjiang, that he had graduated from such-and-such college in the U.S., that he was a second lieutenant out of the ROTC, and that soccer was a popular off-duty pastime at his base. Koji sometimes thought he would not be surprised if Helmick, the American who had been studying Japanese literature at Tokyo Imperial University when he was there, was now at such a base working in intelligence, but he felt disinclined to pursue it. Koji asked the prisoner his opinion on the accuracy of anti-aircraft fire in the Wuhan area.

"Do you think," he answered, "that if Japanese anti-aircraft gunnery was accurate we would fly so low?"

And as to how the war would go, he was right to the point: "America will win in two or three years. And I want to return home as soon as we do."

Koji abandoned his questioning and at last the army man who was accompanying the prisoner asked him if there was anything he was dissatisfied about or wanted. The prisoner loosed a short burst of complaint, gibberish to Koji, then smacked his lips.

"He says he can't eat the food," interpreted Koizumi, laughing. "He wants food a bit more edible: steak, omelets, doughnuts. The food is unbearable."

The army man, nodding, also laughed.

The prisoner clicked his heels together, saluted properly, hand raised to his hatless, shaved head. A camp soldier took him toward the door, where he looked back, the expression on his face suggesting his loneliness, but he was taken away nonetheless. On the way out of the camp the army man stuck his head in the orderly room and told them it was just too hard on the American to expect him to eat what the Chinese POWs were eating, so they were to give a bit more thought to his food.

"Did you hear that guy?" Koji said when he was alone with Koizumi. "He was really solicitous, wasn't he."

Koji had been annoyed that what he had come for had eluded him. At the same time, however, it had struck him as almost bizarre that young men in precisely the same circumstances as himself and his comrades, young men who like doughnuts, should be flying those impudent, ominous P-51s that came in on their tree-top strafing attacks almost every day, their 13mm guns spitting fire.

He finished his business with the adjutant in ten minutes. The adjutant told him there would be a flight in from Shanghai that day. He came out and saw Ensign Koizumi, obviously cold, waiting for him, the reins of the horses in his hands.

"Sorry to keep you waiting. Let's go."

The water level of the Yangtze River was low, noticeably so. They could see wooden piers extending far out toward pontoons floating in the shallow water and strands of yellowed reeds here and there in the mud flats along the river.

Astride his mount, Koji loosened the reins and gave the horse a kick in the flank with the heel of his boot. The animal broke into a trot, the sound of its hooves quickening.

"Be careful on the asphalt!" Koizumi called out behind him. Koji ignored this and gave the horse's rump a good whack with the willow switch he was holding. They turned away from the Yangtze bank at the Officers' Club, passing through two or three narrow streets, which brought them to the northwest edge of the Japanese concession. A parched white road lay before them. The headquarters of the army's Luwu and Tung Groups came into view. Koji galloped on, head low, hips up off the saddle, looking back at the on-duty soldiers who were saluting them with automatic rifles raised to present arms. Scattered through a thicket of small trees he could see red-roofed houses that had been requisitioned by the army and were now serving as billets for high-ranking officers. Koji saw beneath him a creek, its water running along with his horse. He passed a two-wheeled cart pulled by a donkey, leaving it in his dust. The cart rattled along at a leisurely pace. An expressionless peasant in a blue tunic rode atop it, his arms folded, each hand in the opposite sleeve. Chickens, red and blue markings dabbed liberally on them to discourage theft, scattered squawking from under the horse's flying hooves to flee into nearby farm houses. He wanted to put to rout the melancholy that oppressed him. At last the city of Hankow had fallen behind him like a collage of shadow-lantern images, one upon the other.

He could feel his skin gradually warming, and his mount was sweating hard, the muscles in its neck rippling. Having driven the horse on furiously, he finally brought it down to a slow trot. When he came to a large pond he looked back and saw that Koizumi's horse had fallen far behind him on the arrow-straight road.

He turned the horse about and called out to his companion. Koizumi waved and said something, but Koji couldn't catch it. Koizumi's saddle girth had apparently loosened. He had dismounted and, pushing himself up against the animal, was cinching it up.

Koji dismounted too. His haunches smarted and he was hot all over. All was quiet about him. The pond was to the left of the road. In the middle of it floated four or five wild ducklings at play. A thin sheet of ice edged the pond.

Japan's dangerous, precarious position, and the hobgoblin of cipher numbers that now pursued him everywhere, suddenly rose to his consciousness, dark, depressing phantoms. The ducklings searched for prey beneath the water with nervous thrusts of their heads. Koji picked up a rock just the right size for throwing and threw it as hard as he could into the middle of the pond. The birds rose up as one and made their escape to another pond, their wings flapping ponderously in the air.

"I'm sorry," said Ensign Koizumi, leading his horse. "It came completely unfastened."

"Hold on, boy!" Koji's horse was about to munch on grass at the side of the road and he pulled the animal's head back. "There were some ducks here, but they all went off."

"Will the new C.O. be on the flight coming in today?"

"There's no telling when," Koji began. "He could be on it. He ought to be coming about now. It'll be someone I knew in Tokyo, at any rate. I hope he's a cheerful type."

The two men mounted their horses once again. A man selling roasted chestnuts approached, his wares balanced on a pole across his shoulders. He looked up at the horses and said something. They could smell the sweet aroma of roasted chestnuts. Both men were hungry, but when Koji asked in Chinese the price of a pound, he was surprised at the high price and started to trot off on his horse. The chestnut hawker came after him, saying that he was willing to drop his price, his gestures exaggerated. They still could not afford it, though, so they again set their horses to trotting, not looking back.

Urging their mounts on to the shore of the Han River, they rode southward through the western outskirts of Hankow and cut across a large piece of farmland, where they followed a road deeply rutted by truck wheels. As they stood atop the embankment which rose high above the river they could see that the water level was low. Junks that had come from the Yangtze were lazily making their way upriver, brailing up huge sails, the sort that were everywhere on the river. The sweat had gradually cooled on their skin.

They entered onto the chaotic People's Livelihood Road. A traffic circle with a bronze statue of Sun Yat-sen. A jumble of rickshaws waited cheek-by-jowl along the thoroughfare, shafts down. Their pullers, in padded clothes, sat cross-legged on the ground resting. Horse carts ran to and fro, bells clanging, and townspeople crossed just in front of the horses' muzzles, the picture of complete stolidity. A policeman, hat pushed back on his head, was bawling out orders left and right, but as soon as he saw the two horses, he stopped his shouting and saluted. Koji responded, saluting back at this alien policeman with utter indifference.

Taking in the grimy yet gaudy shop signs along the street that identified this shop and that restaurant, they rode over the crossing at Hsun-li-men Station and returned to their unit, guided by the antennae visible amidst a stand of trees.

An orderly came out to meet them, took their pistols for them, and told them the new detachment C.O. had arrived from Tokyo.

* * *

The two men left instructions for the care of the horses with the orderly and entered the wardroom. A lieutenant junior grade, wearing an overcoat, was hunched over a table, eating. Kihara from the first class!

Koji felt as though he had been punched in the stomach, but quickly regained his composure.

163

"Hey! Is that you, Kihara? Welcome aboard! How goes it?"

"Hey, Obata! How've you been? Put on weight, haven't you. Hear you've just been out for a ride."

Kihara, wiping his mouth, got up and approached the two men.

Koizumi had never met him before. He came to attention and bowed his head.

"Ensign Koizumi, sir."

Kihara's attitude was different toward Koizumi, and he brought himself erect. He spoke in the Osaka dialect, voice quavering.

"You're Koizumi, eh? I've heard the name. Lieutenant Junior Grade Kihara, now taking my post as Commanding Officer of Detachment 8, Yangtze Base."

"Have you met the Group Commander, sir?"

"No. Lieutenant Commander Funaki's out, I'm told. We left Shanghai at 7 this morning. Mean air pockets over Mt. Tapieh. Got a Three Castles on you? Really sorry to trouble you. You got some of the good stuff here, right? Let me have some. It's awful in Tokyo now. Food, drink, whatever, there's nothin'. Oh yeah, they gave me a bunch of letters to bring. I'll give 'em to you later."

Kihara rattled on, smiles creasing his acne-scarred face, its ruddiness betraying his fondness for drink. Both Koji and Koizumi were interested in the situation in Tokyo, and peppered him with questions.

An orderly brought in the two men's lunches in a tote box, the kind restaurants use. Moments later Kihara, luggage in hand, set off for his quarters at the heels of a sailor showing him the way.

"Is he from Osaka?" asked Koizumi. "He seems to be an interesting, down-to-earth man."

"'Down-to-earth'? I hadn't thought of him quite like that."

Koji's mind was elsewhere as he joylessly stuffed his mouth with his meal of now-cold white radish and boiled meat. He kept thinking about that uproar a year ago, back in Special Services in Tokyo, over a series of thefts, including the taking of Kuki's alligator belt and Wada's raincoat. The incidents were hushed up at the time, but later they'd all agreed that Kihara had been the perpetrator. He was a terribly violent drinker, and a story had made the rounds that when he and Captain Morii had been down at a communications unit in Kaohsiung in Taiwan, he had gone out of control and struck the captain. The captain, furious, drew his sword and chased Kihara, coming within a hair of cutting him down.

Koji finished his meal, lit a cigarette, and moved to the sofa with the broken spring. Of all the possible candidates for detachment C.O. they had really drawn a lemon. He was terribly depressed. With Kihara as his superior officer he could easily imagine what his life here would become.

Koizumi finished his lunch and went upstairs. A little later Koji stood up and himself went upstairs to Operations on the second floor, a glum expression on his face.

The room where the decrypting and routine clerical work was done was flanked by A Section and C Section radio intercept rooms, where mixed in with the howls and whines of the air waves could be heard the loud voices of U.S. military transmissions.

"Able Fox, over."

At a desk beneath a military telephone Chief Petty Officer Kumai, stroking his abbreviated black moustache, was diagramming enemy aircraft sorties ascertained that day. The lines he had painstakingly drawn in with colored pencils formed countless chromatic threads between the various bases.

"This is supposed to be Sunday, but there sure is a lot going on."

"It looks like Hankow gets a reprieve today. There're an awful lot of transports moving between Kunming and Chengtu. That's certainly suspicious."

"Maybe B-29s are heading for Manchuria again."

"It kind of looks that way," Kumai responded. "I've already issued an alert."

A sizable force of B-29s were stationed at air bases in the Chengtu area in Szechuan Province, and they had already bombed northern Kyushu, Taiwan, and Manchuria any number of times. And whenever air transports loaded with stores of aviation fuel were coming into Kunming in Yunnan Province from India 24 hours a day, and transport activity was lively between Kunming and Cheng-tu, it meant that gasoline stockpiled in Kunming was being supplied to Chengtu. This also meant, at the least, that there was a strong possibility the B-29s at the Chengtu bases would be going on bombing missions. When he flipped through the file of messages he saw that an alert based on W Group's intelligence had been dispatched to Kyushu, Canton, Taiwan, and Manchuria while he had been out on his horse.

"By the way, Lieutenant Obata, I understand the new detachment C.O. has reported in."

"Uh-huh."

"If there's no alert," Kumai said, stroking his moustache and apparently relishing the idea of some saké, "we'll have a welcoming party, maybe tonight?"

"I expect so," Koji answered, leafing through the small stack of Air Defense Intelligence Station messages that had accumulated on his desk. Even though Koji was no longer able to feel—as he had when he was in Tokyo—that his decrypting work was of great import, he still remained scrupulous in its execution. But today he wanted to quit early; Kihara had said he'd been entrusted with letters for Koji. He asked Kumai to cover for him in the afternoon as well, took a quick look into A Section, and went down the stairs.

When he returned to his room he could hear Kihara stowing away his gear in the C.O.'s room diagonally across the hall from him. If the rumor had been true, Koji thought as he took off his shoes, that damned Kihara might well have relaxed his defenses because he was going overseas and brought along the articles he stole from Kuki and Wada. If he had, then Koji could start putting the pressure on Kihara bit by bit. He then noticed a packet of letters by the door that Kihara no doubt had had an orderly bring to his room. He closed his door, lay down on the bed, and with indescribable pleasure set about opening the fat bundle of half a dozen sealed envelopes as though they were the most valuable of treasures. As he read the letters from Wada, Tsutsumi, Hirokawa, and the others, his gaze fastened itself upon phrases out of his Tokyo past like "Yotsuya Mitsuke," "the

Yamanote line," or "a maid at the Officers' Club" as though to extract the last drop of nostalgic meaning from them. Among the letters was one sent in care of Special Services Group from Tanii on Shumushu Island. The postmark was fairly old.

I got both your July and August 10 letters yesterday. You're a real bastard. I split my sides laughing, the first time in a long while. If I had stayed in Tokyo Wada and I would have crossed swords. But I can't believe that you found out Yano was a dunce, and that Wada married Blue. I wrote Wada a letter congratulating him.

I heard you were going to China. Don't know if you're in Shanghai or where, since you didn't give a return address, so I'll send this to the General Staff. If you're in China I'll bet you lack for nothing and that there're plenty of women. You must be up to your ears in good times, which I'm sure you dearly appreciate. Here we're already getting ready for the wintering-in. It's been four months since I was assigned here and I've got used to the place and have come to be something of a Kuriles bum, so called. My beard grows and grows and all I've gotten better at is fighting and drinking. You could never appreciate how awful a Kuriles bum is. Last night, for example, I got into an argument with the detachment C.O. while we were drinking together. I've no recollection of it, but I punched him out, then barged into a play the men were putting on, earning an ovation to rend the heavens—can't remember how to write the last character in "ovation" . . . happens a lot these days—in a rendition of who knows what. That's all I remember, but when I woke up it was morning and I was in the men's barracks. I had thrown up and I was sleeping, arms entwined, with one of the men. I had apparently sprained my wrists, and they hurt like hell. And a few nights before that I got drunk and very deliberately ruined the engine of the C.O.'s car. Thereafter I have enjoyed his immense good favor. I don't give a damn about anything anymore.

There's a grog shop called The Station Inn (even here at the end of the earth) catering to people with Russo-Japan Fisheries, and a woman there in her thirties, Hokkaido-born, has taken a fancy to me, offering her selfless devotion. Thus it is my good fortune to be unburdened of washing and mending. I seem to have been born—as I suspected—with the power over women that Prince Genji had. You, I think, will always be his faithful vassal Koremitsu. I'm wondering if I should take up skiing or something this winter. My joy now is *sashimi* made from king crab, and to savor raw sea urchin you've just cracked open is really something else. It would seem our good foes have seen the folly of landing in the Kuriles. That's just fine by me.

The mail boat for Ominato leaves in 30 minutes and if I miss it I don't know when there'll be another one, so I'll stop here. A stiff upper lip and the best to you. If you weren't so far away I'd send some sea urchins.

It amused Koji to see the pale, timid, foppish Tanii displaying his awfulness in all its glory.

He now felt the fatigue of his ride, and when he had finished reading the letters he pulled his blankets over himself and in a short while had dropped off to sleep. He woke up an hour or so later at the sound of knocking. He answered and got up. CPO Kumai's face was peering in at him.

"We just had a phone call from the group C.O., sir, and he says we are to have a reception tonight for the new detachment C.O. after all. How about boiled chicken or something at the Officers' Club at six. You don't mind if I take care of it, do you? The group C.O. said he would be going there directly from off-base."

"Fine. Please do."

Koji put on his cap and left the room. The sun hung low in the west. The land the base was on had once belonged to the China Aeronautical Committee. There were meadows, swampland, and woods on the spacious site and they would often catch sight of creatures such as pheasant, rabbits, weasels and raccoon dogs. He cut through the woods and walked toward the volleyball court at the edge of the base. He could hear the cheers of the players.

*   *   *

The next morning Koji awoke early, but it was too early to get up and too cold, so he drew his head back under the covers and thought about his codes and ciphers. He had drunk only moderately at the reception the night before, so the alcohol was out of his system and his mind was clear.

Ever since it had achieved spectacular results against the Chungking government's air force some years before, the post of group C.O. had traditionally been occupied by an officer from C Section, and even now, when the object of the unit's work had become the powerful U.S. air forces in China, priority in the allocation of receivers and intercept operators still remained with C Section. It was not unexpected, then, that A Section, seeing its chance, would attempt to switch the focus to itself, that C Section would resist this, and that bizarre skirmishes over turf would break out again and again in the unit. To Koji this was folly. The group C.O., Lieutenant Commander Funaki, was from C Section, while the new detachment C.O., Lieutenant Kihara, and Ensign Koizumi were A Section men and Koji himself was the senior officer in C Section. The intercept operators under him would come by from time to time to complain.

"With our good receivers being moved to A Section one after the other, we cannot fulfill our intercept mission as directed. You've agreed to this situation, sir? If so, there's no longer any point in sitting there through the night with our earphones on. Will this not be to the detriment of our country?"

He wished he could tell them they were right.

Whenever Koji received a request from A Section for men and material—for example, that they wanted to monitor a certain frequency in a certain band and could they have an RCA receiver and one petty officer sent over?—and it happened again and again, he always had to consider his men's feelings, even though he believed the requests to be entirely justified. And if he sensed that the veteran A Section petty officer who came to make the request was implying that C Section couldn't expect any results worthy of the name in their work anymore, there was a good chance he would take it as a personal affront and this would affect his own attitude negatively. The reality was, however, that since they were dealing with the weakened Chungking air force, their work amounted to little, even if they were to put into place a perfect array of intercept stations and knew every tactical move the Chinese forces were to make. Any real effort put into it would be, in the end, merely tilting at windmills. But as for this near-obsession with the Air Defense Intelligence Station codes over the last month, he wanted to make a breakthrough somehow, to do a job that would convince both himself and his men that they had accomplished something worthwhile.

He lay in his bed constructing number groups and taking them apart in his head, when suddenly and quite fortuitously a thought came to him. Inspiration; a possible breakthrough! He jumped out of bed and, skipping breakfast, ran up to the second floor and sat down at his desk.

He looked at an Air Defense Intelligence Station message: XGN 0022 1350 7568 0903. He and his men had already determined that the XGN at the beginning was the callsign of the sender, the second group indicated the location, the third the time, the fourth the type of plane and number, the fifth the direction the aircraft were to fly: their departure, arrival, and flight legs. As for the numbers indicating the time, this was cleartext, pure and simple. If it said 1350, it meant 1350 hours, though this was Chungking time, which was only one hour earlier than Hankow, on Japan time. And in the case of the last group of numbers, referring to departure, arrival and route, for the routing, at least, Koji knew that the Chinese were using the clock face to indicate direction, so that 0903 meant from 9 o'clock to 3 o'clock, which is to say, from west to east. Transmitter callsigns alternated: one sign on odd-numbered days, another on even-numbered. Chungking's odd-numbered day callsign XGN changed to WFA on even-numbered days. Most of these callsigns were known and since most of the transit points were not far from the transmitting stations, Koji had little trouble with these either. It was the four digits of the fourth group indicating the type and number of planes that baffled him, and it would not be terribly meaningful intelligence to say that unspecified aircraft would transit such-and-such a place at a particular time in a certain direction, since American aircraft were flying all over China day and night.

The idea that had come to him as he lay in bed was that if the first two digits of the four identified the kind of aircraft and the last two the number, he should separate out the aircraft-type digits on an even/odd-day basis and see if they also alternated like the callsigns. Until now he had been utterly stumped by this number group. Small-scale air raids were flown against Hankow every day and on the basis of the information he had gathered Koji would decide the next one was sure to be B-25 bombers, for example, only to have a single P-51 fighter come along.

He selected two dozen or so old messages he thought relevant, sorting them according to his hypothesis, and compared them with reports he had collected of raids they had actually had. Although there were some inexplicable anomalies, he was gradually able to make sense of things. On odd-numbered days, for example, 75 was consistent with the dispatch of B-29s and on even-numbered days it changed to P-51s. Numbers 80 and 91 were B-29s on even days, but on odd days 80 meant a C-47, a cargo plane, and 91 had been a P-38 fighter. The rules were simple. He was excited now. On even-numbered days 20 meant B-24, on odd days 46 meant B-25, and 16 on odd days apparently was the Japanese Army's Type-4 fighter. As he worked on it for some two hours he was able little by little to figure out the differences.

Petty Officer First Class Ono, whose job it was to look for these messages, emerged from C Section's radio room, pencil in mouth, and dropped a message on Koji's desk.

"We've got one, sir."

JRD 3041 1015 8095 0902.

Koji knew the sender. It was a station in the town of Ch'angte on the western edge of Lake Tungt'ing, right on the Japanese Army's front line. Today was December 18, an even-numbered day, and when Koji applied his newly-derived formula to the message, the solution told him that the first part of the fourth group meant B-29, the 1015, figuring the time difference, was 11:15, and that a number of B-29s had approached Ch'angte from the west and left heading east-northeast.

He looked at the clock above Chief Petty Officer Kumai's head. The time was 11:20. Something struck him as exceedingly odd. He knew even without touching a map that the route would take the planes right over Wuhan. Not once had B-29s from Chengtu bombed cities on the Chinese mainland; Hankow was almost due east of the Chengtu base. If the B-29s were really heading this way now via Ch'angte, it meant they had swung south first, a very round-about course to take, whatever the reason. Koji felt that the solution he thought he had discovered might well be wrong. Nonetheless he shouted angrily into the radio room.

"Petty Officer Ono! Haven't you got the next one? There's something queer about this. Make sure you get it right!"

He was now feeling a curious sense of anticipation. He carefully checked the time, then went downstairs to Lieutenant Commander Funaki's quarters, briefly explained the situation as he believed he had just unravelled it, and showed him the Ch'angte message.

"B-29s?" said Funaki. "That's certainly odd."

In fact no one in Hankow had ever seen one of the renowned bombers.

"Well, I'll be right up."

Koji went back to Operations.

"We've got one, sir." Petty Officer Ono, proud that his work was now of some importance, brought Koji another message, his expression intense, almost a scowl.

WFQ 3950 1020 8080 0802

WFQ was the even-number day callsign of a station in the town of Tz'uli, northwest of Ch'angte. This meant that at 11:20 B-29s had passed over, flying from the southwest to the northeast. The heading was the same as before, and would lead directly to Hankow.

"Have someone else bring the messages. You man the receiver."

Koji turned to Lieutenant Commander Funaki, who had just come up the stairs.

"This next one is the same. I believe Hankow is the target. We have 20 to 30 minutes." He desperately wanted the air raid to happen.

"Looks like it might be, doesn't it," Funaki responded, still not entirely convinced. "Perhaps we should let Headquarters and the anti-aircraft batteries know, just to be on the safe side."

The order was given and CPO Kumai stood up to ring the field telephone bell, at which instant the phone rang.

"Hello, Receiving Station here. 1135 hours," repeated Kumai, "Wuhan area on alert, Roger."

All of Operations was suddenly tense. Instantaneously, sirens in the city began to wail. The lookouts were ordered to their stations.

Koizumi and Kihara came over from A Section.

"Chengtu has been requesting a homing beacon this morning," said Koizumi.."It seemed a bit suspicious."

"I'm not surprised," Koji said, feeling both excitement and a kind of unease. "B-29s are on their way. I'm sure they're coming."

Messages sent by Air Defense Intelligence Stations continued to come in. Some were unrelated messages from north China, but others reported B-29s (or so Koji hoped) transiting Tz'uli in a northeasterly direction. Intelligence from army radar began coming in on the direct phone line to the army. CPO Kumai was busily juggling two telephone receivers and a Group memo pad.

"Yes. Yochou Special Lookout, target number one. 1128 hours, west, formation small."

The clock on the wall said 11:38.

"Explosions Hsienning, direction east."

"Correction of direction. Present time, Hsienning, formation of large aircraft, direction north."

"Yochou Special Lookout, target number two. 1136 hours, southwest, on fixed course."

The order to assume air battle stations was issued. Koji went out on the second floor balcony and could see men running in all directions from the barracks, carrying gas masks, steel helmets, and rifles, and scattering every which way. In the Receiving Station everyone but the radiomen on duty and the spotters fled to safety. Three hundred meters in front of him, however, at the navy's air defense unit, four anti-aircraft guns raised their muzzles and slowly pivoted around like living creatures.

Koji restlessly paced back and forth between his desk and the balcony. He hoped that the attacking planes would be B-29s, even if the whole of Hankow went up in flames.

Again the city's sirens, giving warning of the imminent raid, began sounding in short, intermittent bursts.

* * *

Suddenly Koji saw an orange flash of light. The glass doors rattled and there was a deafening roar that shook him to the core. The anti-aircraft guns next to Special Services were spewing fire.

"Oh!" shouted the teenage radioman who was acting as spotter, "I've found them, sir!"

Everyone in the room came out onto the balcony.

"Where?"

All they could hear was a faint metallic drone. The A-A guns again belched fire. Moments later puffs of smoke roiled black in the sky.

"To the right of the smoke . . . left of the antennas. Two fingers away. What a beautiful sight!"

"Idiot!" CPO Kumai bellowed. "What the hell is beautiful about it? What's your name, sailor?"

"There they are!" shouted Koji and Koizumi simultaneously. The planes were at about 7,000 meters, the sun behind them, in a formation shaped like an umbrella, in groups of three. The formation advanced slowly, glinting fitfully in the sun like slivers of metal foil. The huge wingspan and the single gigantic tail: B-29s!

"Spotter! How many planes?"

"Three, three, three . . . fifteen."

"No, you're wrong. Fourteen planes."

"It's fourteen, sir."

Fourteen? An idea abruptly broke through the tension Koji felt and presented itself to him. He scurried ferret-like back to his desk and grabbed the first Ch'angte message Petty Officer Ono had intercepted that morning: JRD 3041 1015 8095 0902.

As one, the 14 B-29s broadcast countless black specks from their bellies. These broke up in mid-air, emitting an intense ivory-colored light and sounding like a handful of beans thrown on a tin roof as they fell through the air over Hankow proper. Black smoke immediately billowed up from that direction. Koji subtracted 81, the reverse of today's date of the 18th, from the number 95, the last half of the fourth group in the message he held tightly in his hand: 95 minus 81 equals 14. The number 14.

I've broken it!

Holding tight to the balcony railing, Koji suppressed the urge to dance with joy. The message was now crumpled in his hand. Tongues of fire rose up from the direction the incendiaries had been broadcast.

He went back to his desk again and applied the same process to the day's second message, the one reporting the overflight of planes at Tz'uli. He subtracted the number 81 from 80 non-arithmetically—digit by digit (for example, 00-99=11)—and the answer was 9. Koji received a stream of messages from Petty Officer Ono reporting the transit of B-29s over Ch'angte and Tz'uli, suggesting a really massive raid. In his excitement he held tightly to his pencil, moist now from his sweaty palms.

"Next formation spotted!" a spotter shouted. The anti-aircraft guns once again spewed fire in unison.

"There're nine planes. Am I right?"

"They're glinting in the sun. Ah, yes. Nine planes, sir."

He was right. He had solved two problems at a stroke, and everything he had calculated had been correct. He struggled to keep his happiness from betraying the serious expression on his face.

The second wave of nine planes, shimmering beautifully in the stratosphere, dropped clusters of incendiaries from their bellies. The anti-aircraft fire was scoring no effective hits at all. Black puffs of flak dotted the sky, only to disappear futilely. Here and there they would see a tiny army fighter fly up gnat-like, but not make the slightest suggestion of attack, apparently because it couldn't gain sufficient altitude.

"You can do better than that!" blurted Lieutenant Commander Funaki in frustration as he watched from the balcony. Black smoke rose anew from the streets of the city. The nine-plane formation changed course slightly and flew out of sight.

The receivers in the intercept room abruptly fell silent. The electricity had gone off.

"Damn! Switch over to batteries!"

Petty Officer Ono and several men ran out and into the storage battery room, their faces flushed. Koji was searching for the third message to determine the number of planes in the third wave.

"Third formation spotted," a spotter called out. "Ten aircraft. They are coming directly over us."

Ten B-29s in tight formation, seemingly from out of nowhere, advanced directly toward the air space above the Receiving Station. Koji held up his fingers to judge their course and saw absolutely no deviation. He felt stifled, as though a heavy weight were pushing down on him.

"Withdraw!" ordered Lieutenant Commander Funaki, staring through his binoculars. "All personnel are to evacuate immediately!"

Koji hooked his chin strap.

Petty Officer Ono, who had quickly switched the power over to batteries, now had on his headset, his eyes flashing with determination.

"I can't leave here now. No way will the Receiving Station be bombed." His fighting spirit had been aroused. The men under him, poised for flight, now didn't know what to do. Koji was also at a loss for an instant, but when he saw Chief Petty Officer Kumai swiftly and silently stuffing classified documents into a canvas bag, he knew what to do.

"All right, Ono, get the men out! That's an order. Monitor again when the raid is over!"

That was the signal for all hands. The 20-odd petty officers immediately threw down their headsets and turned their receivers off. They fled down the stairs and, simian-like, down a rope ladder from the balcony. Kumai, Koizumi, Lieutenant Commander Funaki, Kihara, and Koji also dashed out, first grabbing as many documents as they could carry. Kihara, experiencing a massive air raid fast on the heels of his arrival at his new assignment, appeared dumbfounded.

A good many foxholes had been dug in the corner of the adjoining meadow and near some pigsties. These were their only shelters. The drone of the planes sounded directly overhead. The ack-ack guns were firing furiously, barrels high. Several of the younger sailors, apparently near breaking, had run over to a pigsty and were hiding under its eaves.

"Hey you guys!" a petty officer shouted in a rustic Kyushu dialect, "you sure ain't no better off in a pigsty."

Everyone chuckled at this.

Black grains beyond number poured out of the bellies of the ten bombers. Koji watched them until they burst in midair, emitting a brilliant light, apparently magnesium, and then he crept into the closest foxhole and hugged the earth. Eyes closed, he counted the seconds. The suspense made his skin crawl.

Suddenly he heard the sound of things giving way, in the midst of which a clatter like tumbling buckets filled the air. Something, a tremor of the earth, shook him. He restrained himself for several moments, then raised his head. Koizumi was likewise lifting his head in the foxhole in front of him. The two men grinned at each other. The danger had passed.

The incendiaries had fallen into a slum district some 500 meters further along the path of the bombers, and an impenetrable wall of yellowish smoke rose from the area. The fires seemed to spread unhindered through the shacks, and red pillars of flame began to flare up everywhere. Koji could now hear a furious crackling, like the roar of a bonfire.

Bombing run completed, the formation of planes disappeared. The fourth wave now made its appearance in the skies over the city. More than once the aircraft were visible, only to be lost in the smoke from the fires.

"Lieutenant Obata!" called out Petty Officer Ono, standing up in his foxhole. "May we go back to our posts?"

"Hold on! No heroics!"

Ono was keyed up like a horse at the starting gate.

The fourth wave of B-29s in formation was followed by a fifth and a sixth, at intervals of five or ten minutes. They were dropping their bombs far away now.

Koji went out the compound gate. The sky over the Japanese concession was totally obscured by billowing black smoke. Masses of impoverished Chinese, burned out in the raid, fled in an almost constant flow along the road to the airfield carrying furniture, bedding, bundles, and their injured. They chanted rhythmically to themselves as they carried their burdens. Every single soul was filthy, and their faces were expressionless, as though they had absentmindedly left behind their suffering and their anger. Across the road at the entrance to Chungshan Park, an army guard, his bayoneted weapon at the ready, stood and watched the refugees go past. A saddleless horse, bucking and galloping, ran by.

A little while later a large formation of B-24s came into view and seemed to be heading directly toward the Receiving Station, but swung northward before it got there and dropped its bombs on the airfield. That was apparently the last of it, and the skies were silent at last. The all-clear did not sound, but in the compound the order to return to duty stations was issued. Ono was the first to run back to his post. The thundering of what were probably gasoline stores exploding could be heard over and over again from the direction of the airfield.

The second floor was milling chaos. It didn't look as though power would be restored anytime soon. Fewer than half of the receivers were making their dit-dot sounds on the batteries. The phone rang again.

"Present time. Wuch'ang Special Lookout. Target number four. Northwest 40 kilometers. Small formation. Gradually leaving area."

"1340. Explosions heard at Hsiaokan, westerly direction."

The officers went out onto the balcony and brought over the rattan chairs that had been set off to the side. They were excited, their conversation animated.

"Yesterday's Kunming-Chengtu transports, they were the key after all. But I never thought the bombers would come to Hankow."

"I'll bet they were supplying them with gasoline."

"Ferrying the gas a planeload at a time over India? That must have cost the Americans a fortune."

Koji was also in very high spirits. Surviving the peril of the raids and breaking the code had flushed away the gloom that had dogged him for so long. Preoccupied with his triumph, he scarcely thought about whether the citizens of Hankow who had been burned out of their homes might be suffering.

A cook's mate carried in rice balls made with precious white rice, pickled radish, more mutilated than sliced, and hot tea, all in generous portions. To parched throats the coarse tea was delicious and the white balls of rice seemed to taste extraordinarily good. The men on duty bit into the rice balls without even removing their headsets.

"How's Headquarters?"

"I've had no luck getting them on the phone, sir," CPO Kumai responded, "but they seem to have been spared. It would appear the Japanese concession in the city's been badly hit."

"The Land Guards and the Officers' Club, that area's probably a total loss," Lieutenant Commander Funaki said, then turned to Kihara. "You did your first and last drinking there last night," he laughed.

The conflagration from the slum district had come closer, but a large field stood between it and the base, and the day was windless, so there was no danger the fire would spread to the compound. Only the guards stood confronting the fire.

Petty Officer Ono again began getting Air Defense Intelligence Station messages and bringing them to Koji, who worked on them at

179

his desk. They were all about B-29s returning to base. Using the method he had worked out, Koji was able to decipher all fourth-group numbers, aircraft type and number, with almost no anomalies. According to reports from the army, it was apparent that the B-29s had taken a southerly course, swung north in a wide arc, and attacked Hankow from the east. They were now moving due west, heading for Chengtu, following the northern bank of the Yangtze River.

"That code business," Lieutenant Commander Funaki said, "turned out to be a pleasant surprise."

"Yes sir." Koji was grinning. Kihara and Koizumi were still drinking their tea on the balcony.

Suddenly, in the distance, they heard the drone of engines. The four ack-ack guns next to them abruptly began firing.

"Hey, what the hell! They've come back again?"

They went out onto the balcony and looked up into the sky. Over the river a dozen or so enemy fighter planes—they looked like P-51s—were eagerly attacking something, diving one after the other, in a crescendo of roaring engines. Now they could see their fighters determinedly setting upon the American planes. But every time a pursuer closed in on a P-51, the latter would break away in a graceful swoop, putting a healthy distance between itself and the Japanese plane in the twinkling of an eye.

"What a miserable showing!"

"What's the matter with them?! Damn! They're going around in circles."

Two of the small planes described circles in the sky, round and round, as though the encounter were just a jolly lark.

"They've got one! They've got one! He's falling into the river."

One of the fighters suddenly lost speed and, now all too quickly, dropped like a leaf fluttering down from a tree. Moments later a column of smoke rose high into the air.

"Look! Another one's going down!"

A number of the fighters, small as black beans, fell to earth, but they couldn't tell for sure whether these were Japanese or the enemy's.

Toward dusk the skies over Wuhan were finally free of enemy aircraft. After the all-clear sounded, the army sent word that almost all the planes shot down had been Japanese fighters.

Night fell, but the lights did not come on. The fire in the slum district was petering out, but from the direction of the city itself the sky glowed crimson. The whole city looked like it was still ablaze. The stream of refugees carrying their personal belongings, chanting under their burdens, still flowed on.

Koji went downstairs to take a bath. The fires raging in the city reflected red on the windows of the *furo*. As he soaked his chilled body in the hot water, he felt his sense of imminent exhaustion gradually dissolve within. This was a mellow delight. He stretched out his arms and legs in the water and sat for a long while with his eyes closed.

Returning from the bath, Koji passed by the senior petty officers' quarters. The door was ajar. He could see Detachment C. O. Kihara *tête-à-tête* with a senior petty officer; they were drinking saké from water glasses, a half-gallon jug before them. The faces of the two men were gargoyle-red and grotesque in the candle light. Kihara called out to him.

"Well, come on in! You broke some real good messages today, huh?"

"Yes, things went well," Koji answered politely, though not without a sense of pride.

"How 'bout a drink?"

"Fine." He hesitated, then took the glass from Kihara.

Eight

The Officers' Club had been gutted and was padlocked. No longer able to enjoy duck sukiyaki, Koji experienced his first New Year's in Hankow without cheer. He wrote New Year's postcards to his family and to Mr. Yashiro, but couldn't be sure they would get them.

Most of the damage from the raids was restricted to the Japanese concession, which was burned out completely; it was the only total loss. The French concession, just across the road, was largely spared—almost surgically—from the flames. The navy's Land Guards building, the Commandant's official residence, and the Officers' Club had been burned down. When Koji went over the morning after the raids to see what had happened, many corpses were still lying by the side of the road. They were stiff as boards, their hands clutching the empty air. He saw a human arm atop an unburned section of roof at the Land Guards building. All the dead were Chinese civilians.

One day toward year's end Chief Petty Officer Kumai returned from town to say that he had seen prisoners being paraded through the streets. Two American POWs said to be crewmen from a downed B-29 had been led blindfolded through the streets of Hankow, an MP at each arm. There was much fanfare and many banners flying condemning the Yankee devils and calling for the defeat of England and America. Kumai told how Chinese, outraged over the air raid, would run out from the side of the street one after the other and spit at the prisoners or pummel them. Their faces covered with blood and spirits broken, the men went by half-dragged, half-walking.

"It was really awful," Kumai said. "I couldn't bring myself to watch."

It had been a political sideshow put together by the army, which was responsible for the defense of the Wuhan area and had lost face because of the bombing. The truth was that not a single B-29 had been shot down. The army had spirited the American prisoners from a POW camp in Nanking to Hankow by plane and passed them off as crewmen of a raiding B-29. Koji wondered for a moment if they had used the young, easy-going prisoner he had earlier interrogated. He did not, however, give it that much thought. Not that he didn't consider going to see if it was him, but he probably couldn't have found anything out at that late date, and anyway, he decided against doing anything. He sensed that on the whole he was gradually becoming desensitized to this sort of thing, that feelings of compassion and goodness were deserting him bit by bit.

Lieutenant Kihara was having no luck whatsoever with the foot-loose women of The Clear Stream and because of that, or simply from exoticism, he began frequenting the Korean brothels set aside for the enlisted men, and on base he drank on the sly with them. It was apparently nothing for him to polish off a large bottle of saké, and whenever he met Koji in the hall on the way to the bathroom, a grin would crease his beet-red face.

"Sorry, sorry," he would say in his Osaka dialect with an obsequious bow of the head. The older petty officers had become quite thick with Kihara, as though as to get back at the demanding Koji. Koji couldn't abide him. He even felt a physical aversion to the man: the coarse, boozy-red face, his stoop-shouldered, bouncy gait, the way he talked in that broad Osaka dialect that stuck to you like glue. Whatever the man did disgusted him beyond measure, even his yawn.

A few days into the new year, when Koji went to take his evening bath, he found that Kihara was already in the *furo* and he could hear the sound of water splashing on the other side of the frosted glass door. Kihara's clothes were folded up in a dressing room cubbyhole. Koji suddenly had the urge to get to the bottom of something that had been nagging at him for some time. Looking furtively about, he noiselessly withdrew Kihara's trousers from the clothes bin, and was astonished to find there exactly what he was looking for. It was more than he could have hoped: Kihara had been wearing the alligator belt stolen from Kuki in Tokyo. It was a buckleless belt. Kuki had boasted about it at Special Services and Koji had a sure recollection of it, reinforced now that Kuki was dead. He quickly put the trousers back into the cubbyhole, took off his clothes, and opened the glass door, his face innocence itself.

Koji could see in the billowing clouds of steam the naked Kihara working up a lather on his head with a bar of soap.

"Who is it?" Kihara called out jauntily, his eyes closed. "Lieutenant Obata?"

"Hello," Koji responded. He doused himself with hot water, got into the large tub, and, as he roiled the incoming hot water with his hands at the underwater inlet, watched Kihara's back with indescribable distaste while the latter vigorously washed his head. Kihara rinsed his hair, then, bucket in hand, came over to Koji.

"Ya know, Koji," he said in his broad Osaka accent, speaking *sotto voce* for reasons not entirely clear to Koji, "I got a feeling Japan may be getting the wrong end of the stick before long. I can't depend on the others, ya know, so you and me, let's do our damndest for the outfit."

Koji was at a loss for an answer.

Several days later Kihara called him to his quarters, saying there was something he wanted to talk about. The detachment C.O. was sitting in his rattan chair, an uncommonly severe expression on his face.

"Come in."

"I'm getting a lot of messages and I'm really busy. What's this about?" Koji made no effort to hide his hostility.

"Forget that. I wanna ask you something. A while back you entered my quarters looking for something, didn't you. What were you up to?"

Koji was taken aback. He didn't know what Kihara was referring to, but he immediately sensed that the miscalculating Kihara was terrified. Groping for a way to take advantage of this, he retorted in as malicious a tone as possible:

"You say I was looking for something in your quarters? I don't appreciate being treated like some thief. You've lost something?"

"You don't just go wandering into a man's quarters. Don't think you can play games with me."

"What are you talking about, Detachment Commander?" Koji persisted. "Have you lost something?"

"I haven't lost anything, but—"

"I'm not trying to play games, nothing of the sort. This is the first time I've been in here since the going-away party for the last detachment C.O."

Kihara was momentarily lost in thought, his face clouded.

"All right, I'll ask you something else. You touched my clothes the other day when I was in the bath, didn't you."

"Yes, I did," Koji responded, somewhat discomfited.

"What were you up to?"

Now Koji had his back against the wall. His gaze fixed on Kihara's face, he wondered if it would be better to screw up his courage and come out with it. But his only evidence was the belt and the story that had been making the rounds in Tokyo. The odds were not in his favor. Suddenly, he had an inspiration.

"That . . . your . . . as I was getting ready to go into the bath I noticed the very fine belt on your trousers and wanted to take a quick look at it. I did touch your things. Sorry."

"I make a habit of folding my clothes neatly." Kihara nodded at each of his words, as though he were delivering a monologue. "When I got out it was obvious someone had been rummaging through 'em."

"Oh? Then I apologize. But that's a fine belt now, isn't it. Where did you buy it, sir?"

"It was given to me by an uncle who'd been to Singapore."

Liar. Koji, suppressing his loathing for the man, was as ironic as he could possibly be.

"Anyway, it's certainly uncommonly fine alligator skin."

"Well," said Kihara with some relief, "there's no problem if that's all it was." He picked up a Ruby Queen cigarette from his desk and lighted it.

185

"You say there's no problem, but what about this business of someone entering your quarters and rummaging about? I don't like the sound of it. Shouldn't we look into it?"

They soon discovered what had actually happened. When Kihara summoned his orderly and questioned him, the orderly replied that he had gone into Kihara's quarters to make the bed precisely during the time Kihara was referring to.

"Well then," said Koji, "I'm afraid I've work to do."

He returned to Operations fully satisfied that he had struck home—cantankerously so—with his secret weapon. But he would not be able, he thought, to breathe a word of this business to anyone.

* * *

American forces had begun their invasion of the Lingayen Gulf in the Philippines. *Eight hundred and fifty ships* of the 7th Fleet under the command of Vice Admiral Kincaid—the figure astounded and depressed Koji. It was announced in February that the Americans had marched into Manila, and this was soon followed by their invasion of Iwo Jima. Koji's hopes and sanguine expectations for Japan's victory were now shattered for good. The wardroom radio still provided broadcasts from Tokyo of the heroic *Dreadnought March* followed by announcements of great victories, but Koji had now lost confidence in the pronouncements of Imperial Headquarters. Even if they weren't outright lies, he could still sense that American naval forces were steadily advancing, right on schedule, essentially turning all "victories" into defeats.

His work in cryptanalysis and intelligence was his only source of strength. Doing his job right, convinced he was doing a good job, this gave him solace of sorts. He had heard that during a battle at sea, men with the paymaster, who had no battle stations to go to, inevitably spurred by extremes of impatience and unease, would volunteer to carry ammunition to allay their anxiety. It occurred to Koji that his own emotional state was now not much different.

Ever since he had broken the Air Defense Intelligence Station code, the mood of C Section intercept operators had cheered visibly. They were happy to take on extra duty time. Since the code was broken, the direction taken by the sorties of B-29s out of the Chengtu base was immediately obvious. Soon, however, the messages began to lose relevance. The B-29s, their principal adversaries, were no longer flying out of Chengtu. The men in A and C Sections, Lieutenant Commander Funaki included, kept telling each other this was all very strange. They traded conjectures: Do you suppose the weather's been bad? Do the Americans have something new up their sleeve? They soon received intelligence from Tokyo that a number of B-29s with ID numbers belonging to planes that should have been in Chengtu had turned up at the base on Saipan. Unknown to Koji and his comrades, the mass of Superfortresses formerly stationed at Chengtu had been shifted to the western Pacific. And then came the great Tokyo air raid of March 10th. Of course, they had no idea of the scope of that raid.

The discord between Koji and Kihara gradually worsened. Koji was now convinced Kihara had stolen things at Special Services in Tokyo. One evening there was an uproar when Kihara was going off base and had the truck wait for him because he couldn't find his raincoat. Quite by accident Koji found it hanging in the senior petty officer's quarters. As he was taking it to Kihara, he discovered that the name that had been sewn into the back of the collar had been torn out, making him even more certain that the man was a thief. And when Kihara put it on it didn't fit at all. It was absurdly short for him and tight in the shoulders. Aware of Koji's scrutiny, his response was offhand.

"When we went through they just threw it together—didn't even take our measurements—so it doesn't fit me. A real disaster. Well, hold down the fort."

He ran off to the waiting truck.

There were still no real shortages when Kihara's class was commissioned, so to say that officers' raincoats had been "thrown together" without tailoring was to tell a boldfaced lie. What really infuriated Koji beyond words was that his own superior officer had turned up wearing things stolen from his very best friends, Wada and Kuki.

One day in February after some snow had fallen, the men in the unit had a snowball fight in the field and Koji and Kihara joined in the melee. Koji could see that Kihara, who was coatless, was still wearing the alligator belt. Throughout the mock battle the outraged Koji's eyes were fixed on it. Kihara stopped wearing it after that.

Koji had heard from someone that the word among the C.O. of the Land Guards and the staff officers and their adjutants at Headquarters, men supposedly responsible for the spiritual training of the young officers, was that Obata, the lieutenant junior grade at the Receiving Station, was a cocky bastard who opposed his detachment C.O. at every turn and was raising hell with unit morale. For his part, Koji realized that it must certainly be a disaster for Kihara to go overseas only to bump into someone who knew his secret. Koji was sure that Kihara hated him, regardless of his casual front. When he went off base there was no telling what nonsense he was spreading around. And Koji could feel not the slightest respect or affection for the incompetents at Headquarters, who appeared incapable of showing any enthusiasm for anything, aside from their squabbling over women. No wonder everyone said that the Yangtze Base staff was third-rate, that Hankow was the navy's dumping ground. Here in Hankow, for example, illegal diversion of rock-salt or collusion with civilian traders raised not an eyebrow. A bizarre rumor would fade away unexamined, to be routinely replaced by the next bizarre rumor.

When Koji was in college the words "career naval officer" meant to him, in his naiveté, rigorous precepts and an assemblage of superior individuals who had dedicated themselves wholeheartedly and selflessly to their cause. Now his disillusionment made it utterly impossible to ignore the truth. He wanted to be sent back to Tokyo, if at all possible. He had no idea how bad the food shortage might be, but how wonderful it would be if he could chat with all his good friends every day—Wada, now married to Blue; Hirokawa, married to Chizuko Kayama; Tsutsumi; and Ono—to be able to talk openly about things that outraged him. But travel to Japan proper kept getting ever more difficult. B-24 bombers, which came like clockwork every night, were laying mines in the Yangtze, and Hankow and Shanghai were linked only by shallow-draft motor-sailers that traveled only at night in an attempt to evade detection by P-51 fighters. And hearsay even had it that passage on flights between Shanghai and Japan was now essentially restricted to flag rank officers. The likelihood of a transfer to Tokyo was quite slim.

What great guys Hirokawa and Wada were! I don't know when I'll be able to see them again. This extravagant nostalgia only intensified his hatred and contempt for Kihara.

Spring was now in all its glory. When work was slack he would go to the pigsty and play with the pig. In the marsh, rank with water-oat, Koji could see carp and snakeheads moving about in the warming waters. The plum trees were in blossom and beautiful young leaves were sprouting on the willows around the pigsty. The only pig there, a huge jet-black sow, likely a Berkshire, was pregnant. Koji would take a bamboo broom with him and scratch the sow's big belly as she stuck her snout into a slop pail. The pig snorted continuously, apparently enjoying the scratching, and soon rolled her massive bulk belly-up in the mud to encourage yet more scratching. She would lie absolutely still as Koji scraped the mud caked on her skin with the tip of the broom. It must be true, Koji mused, that pigs are fastidious creatures. During the winter they had paid a neighboring farmer a 1000-yen stud fee to bring a boar over to mount the sow. Koji had promised the men that if they waited until the piglets were born and got big enough, there would be plenty of pork cutlets to eat. They were planning to supply their own provisions, so they were also raising a lot of ducklings and chicks. Sometimes Koji wondered how the war would be going by the time the men ate their cutlets. He certainly could not foresee what would happen a month later in Okinawa.

Nine

I n May of 1945, roughly a month after the Americans began
their landing operations on Okinawa, W Group received word
that Naha, its capital, had been occupied. At about the same
time the courier returned from the military post office with an
unusually full sack of mail from Japan proper. Koji received a regis-
tered letter from his father in Hiroshima and, out of the blue, two
letters from Chieko. Her first letter began:

> I simply did not have the courage to go over to your mother in
> Hakushima and ask her how you are faring, so I brazenly
> imposed on Mr. Yashiro and was at last able to get your address.
> I worry that a letter from a woman to a navy man may cause him
> trouble, but I write because my feelings would not let me do oth-
> erwise. I took to my bed for a spell because I had damaged my
> health, but I finally recovered this year and now I am reporting
> to work every day at my old job at the Clothing Depot. Yukio
> was at the naval hospital in Sasebo, but recently left for the
> south once again. I think he has probably gone to Taiwan.
> Things here at home have gradually gotten more difficult for us
> as we enter a time of straitened circumstances. My spirits revive,
> however, when I think of Yukio and you.

In her second letter she wrote:

> Ikuko has married a lieutenant in the navy named Shiro Ando.

Shiro pilots a fighter plane, but he is a shy and playful fellow and will be turning me into an aunt this June. Ikuko eagerly awaits your return home.

This last sentiment, the "eagerly awaiting," ran through Chieko's letter like an endless thread, but did Chieko really believe he would be coming back to Hiroshima any time soon? Should Okinawa fall, they could expect the Americans' next landing to be either on the Chinese mainland or directly on Japan itself, and in either case, he concluded, he had now pretty much lost any chance of returning home alive. Koji did not answer her letters.

His father had included a Japanese 1000-yen money order in his letter, the latter brush-written in his unsteady, palsied hand. One thousand yen might still be a lot of money in Japan, but at the official rate of exchange for military scrip it amounted to only 18,000 *yuan*. In Hankow it was doubtful you could buy a pair of shoes with that. Koji was touched, though, when he thought of his parents' intentions.

"That's the kind of mail I like!" Ensign Koizumi was eyeing Koji's desk.

"Got some money from my father. How about going out on the town tonight? I have to get some stuff done for the afternoon courier."

"You can tell me the truth," teased Koizumi, laughing. He knew about the letters from Chieko.

Koji ignored this and again invited Koizumi to go out with him.

"The detachment C.O. has ordered me to do some work. Listen, I'm supposed to compare the requests for a homing beacon and aircraft departures, and get it done tonight."

"Forget that. Let's go!"

Koji refused to take no for an answer from the wavering Koizumi, so that evening they rode the truck into town. The two men hadn't strolled through the streets of the town for some time. They visited squalid eateries here and there and made the rounds of the taverns.

In a large grog shop with shelves and a dirt floor lined with jugs and jars of all sorts and sizes, the two men made small talk with the proprietor, a huge, grossly fat man, as they sampled liquor from the jars, ladling it out with a bamboo dipper. The shop offered all sorts of spirits: a fermented sorghum brew from Shansi, spicy *wuchia* liquor, Shaohsing wine, exotic varieties of every imaginable hue.

The men made their way through the town first eating at one place, then another, putting away potstickers, steamed bread, cheap sweets, and whatnot, as the spirit moved them. The 18,000 *yuan* went far enough at this level of diversion.

The calls of hawkers selling their wares on the streets of the city aroused a feeling of kinship in Koji.

"Wow, I really enjoyed that! Thanks," Koizumi said. "Maybe we should bring something back for the detachment C.O. and Chief Petty Officer Kumai."

"Yeah, let's."

They bought steamed pork bread and potstickers in a bustling stone-paved alleyway called Floral Mansion Street, had them wrapped in large green lotus leaves, and late in the evening headed back to the base, their hands sticky with cooking oil. Kumai, still at work in Operations, was soon happily munching away.

Lieutenant Kihara was the duty officer for the day. His quarters were already dark, however. Koizumi called to him several times, but got no response.

"Well," said Koji, "we can give it to him tomorrow."

"Right. Goodnight, then."

Each man returned to his quarters.

It was a warm night. Koji changed into his nightclothes, got into bed, and began reading an adventure story from the Steel Library series. He could hear a mouse gnawing on wood inside his closet and saw another one scurrying from place to place behind the curtains, unfazed by the light in the room. Eyes glued to his book, Koji imitated a cat meowing under the blanket. The gnawing mouse abruptly stopped gnawing. Amused, Koji meowed again, but when he stopped the mouse began chewing again. An hour later Koji became sleepy. He turned off the light and was beginning to drift off when suddenly he heard shouting. Jolted awake, he sat up in bed. The light was on in Koizumi's quarters across the hall and on the window glass he could see the shadows of two men struggling.

"Lieutenant Obata!" Koizumi shouted. "Come here, please!"

"I'll be right there!" he yelled back, pulling his raincoat on over his nightclothes and dashing from his room.

A beet-faced Kihara, his breath reeking of alcohol, had entered Koizumi's room in his street shoes and, without allowing Koizumi, still in his nightclothes, to get up, was slapping him across the face with a grimy slipper.

"You bastard! You call yourself an military man!? You think you can fuck with the detachment C.O.!?" Kihara had pushed Koizumi, who was trying to evade his blows, back onto the bed and was hitting him furiously.

"I'm sorry," said Koizumi. "I'll be careful from now on." His face pale with fear, he turned to Koji imploringly. "Lieutenant Obata!"

"You'll be careful? And just how'll you be careful? Listen, you've been playin' me for a fool! Am I right? Spit it out! How'll you be careful!?"

Kihara was in an insane rage, his head cocked to one side in disbelief. He set upon Koizumi yet again.

"Just hold it a minute, sir," Koji said putting himself between the two men. Kihara turned to Koji.

"Obata? You get back to your quarters! What're you doing here? This doesn't concern you!"

When Koji saw his face, the raging eyes, the dirty shoes, the spittle at the corners of the man's mouth, he too felt fear.

"Please wait, if you don't mind. They can hear you in the men's quarters. Please tell me what the problem is."

Koizumi quickly slipped off the bed and out of Kihara's reach.

"Tell you what the problem is? You two are in cahoots and playing games with me!" At the words "in cahoots" he shook his head back and forth violently, as though the words themselves were intolerable. "You still think you can keep order in the unit?" He poked Koji hard in the chest, pushing him off balance.

"You're going to hit me?" Koji demanded. He was defiant now. Kihara did not strike him.

Gradually they were able to make sense out of what had happened. It seemed that whenever Koji and Koizumi went off-base together, Kihara would take it as a personal affront, and tonight was no exception. He had been pretending to be asleep when his light was out. As Kihara, his brain befuddled by drink, mulled over Koizumi's setting aside work he had assigned him for a night on the town, his anger grew into an intolerable rage. The chore of duty officer rotated amongst the three men, so whenever one man was on duty, the other two could go off base. From day one Koji had had no desire to go out with Kihara when he was off-duty, and lately Koizumi had been just as reluctant and had rebuffed him. This had apparently rankled Kihara more and more as the days passed.

They heard someone in the hallway.

"Who's there?!" Koji called out sharply. The intruder fled, his feet sounding as he ran.

"Son of a bitch! I'll cut 'im down!" Kihara, sword in hand, burst out of the room in pursuit of the eavesdropper.

"I'm afraid now's not the time to try to talk to him," Koji said quickly. "Let's let him talk himself out, then we'll put him to bed. He's gone crazy. I'll explain everything to him tomorrow."

Koizumi was bleeding from the mouth. Kihara soon returned, his breathing labored. He was no longer violent, but now he began to lecture the two men at great length with what to Koji was typical Osaka obstinacy: the detachment C.O. is the father of the unit; everyone must suppress their egos and, in concert and high concord, work together with the detachment C.O. to harmonize the unit as a whole. Marveling at Kihara's ability to fashion a solemn lecture out of such drivel, despite the fact that he surely realized Koji knew his secret, Koji sat there with Koizumi and listened docilely to Kihara's sermon.

It was around two o'clock when Koji finally got back to his quarters. He went to bed, then first thing the next morning he asked Koizumi to come to his quarters. Koji told him everything he knew about Kihara's drunken rampages and his light-fingeredness.

"The fact is, I should have told you earlier."

"Well, wouldn't it be best to report it immediately to the group commander, sir?" Koizumi said with some rancor. "I tell you, at this rate we don't know what he'll do to us next."

"But you know," Koji began, "I've seen nothing of the belt recently. We don't have any proof, and it would be meaningless to bring up the matter and then make a mess of it. Lieutenant Commander Funaki and Headquarters apparently think I'm a troublemaker who opposes his detachment C.O. at every turn, so let's wait a while longer. Besides, I have something in mind."

Several days earlier he had seen a message from Special Services Group in Tokyo advising that a lieutenant junior grade would be assigned to W Group in the near future to bring it up to strength. Koji doubted the need for this at this late date, but it occurred to him that there was the distinct possibility one of his former classmates might be sent and if that were the case, the problem of Kihara would then be much easier to deal with.

A little while later, Koji ran into Kihara in front of the wardroom, now full with the morning sun.

"Well, morning," said Kihara with seeming openness. "I'm sorry I got so drunk last night. Don't hold it against me."

Koji turned away without answering.

*　　*　　*

Thereafter the days passed with nothing unusual happening, on the surface at least. A short time later, however, the regular promotion roster was published. Kihara had been made full lieutenant and Koizumi was now able to pin the rank of lieutenant, junior grade, on his collar. Clearly aware that he was now a rank above Koji, Kihara began to adopt an overbearing attitude toward him. Both Koji and Koizumi talked with their detachment C.O. no more than was absolutely necessary. The response of the men reflected this and the unit's sense of unity was lost completely; some took the detachment C.O.'s side, others tried to get closer to Koji and Koizumi, and still others adeptly flattered both sides. On top of this, one heard contemptuous comments in the ranks of the petty officers about all three because they had been student reservists.

Even outsiders commented on the problem. A young lieutenant junior grade, who occasionally dropped by to visit from the anti-aircraft unit next to them, asked Koji one day, "What's happened? The Receiving Station is in something of a mess these days, wouldn't you say?"

In the midst of all this, Kihara summoned Koji once again.

"You intend to hold a grudge against me forever because of what I did that night?"

"I do," Koji replied, his expression sullen.

"If you two can't bring yourselves to change your quarantine-flag attitude toward me, I've got some ideas as to what might be done."

"Go right ahead," Koji said. "That you have 'some ideas' doesn't necessarily mean that I am without 'some ideas' of my own, does it."

Not surprisingly, Koji's reply seemed to have an effect on Kihara. He made no effort to strike Koji, but through the scuttlebutt of the orderlies word soon got around that Kihara was sleeping with a sword in his bed. Koji then decided to sleep with a American-made 5-shot pistol under his pillow. It was loaded and had no safety.

Day followed depressing day. Of the lieutenant junior grade who was to come from Tokyo there was not a word. Perhaps the order to send him had been postponed. Spring seemed to abruptly turn into summer; muggy days followed one after the other. Koji passed the time playing with the sow, which had dropped nine piglets, and going to shoot pigeons in Chungshan Park with Petty Officer Ono, loading their rifles with lead pellets.

As for work, it was largely abandoned. Given the disparity that had now developed between the strengths of the American and Japanese fighting forces, Koji could only regard communications intelligence work as basically meaningless. Still, he would sometimes find himself in the grip of a kind of zeal, as though his early earnestness had returned, and spasmodically seize upon a message, trying one solution, then another, in almost feverish experimentation.

The price of commodities in the area of China under the control of the Chungking government turned up in crudely enciphered messages about payrolls. He would tabulate this and make tables, all the while taunting himself: why are you working on this when Japan's area of control is on the verge of disintegration? He could hear petty officers talking in an adjoining room.

"What're you guys working on?"

"Nowadays Lieutenant Obata is gathering stuff on Chungking's rice market." The work he was ordering his men to do could only make him blush in embarrassment.

Then came the incident of the maneuvers. It happened when he was watch officer. In the afternoon he heard the horn of what had to be an expensive foreign car from the compound gate. A guard ran in, breathless, pursued by the deep, gruff voice of the senior staff officer from Headquarters.

"Where's the watch officer? Watch officer!"

Koji rushed out and saluted the officer, who was sticking his head out the window of a black Cadillac with a red, three-cornered pennon on the fender.

"Listen now! We're having maneuvers! Assume that at 1400 approximately 500 U.S. airborne troops dropped on the Hankow airfield. They are now attacking, heading for the heart of the city. The Receiving Station, acting independently, will defend itself, ambushing the enemy in the streets, overwhelming and annihilating them. Where has your detachment C.O. gone? Get him at once!"

Lieutenant Commander Funaki was also present in his capacity as second in command. These were surprise maneuvers. Kihara, as was his custom, had apparently been drinking since midday in the men's quarters, and now came flying out, red-faced in his drunkenness and astonishment.

"What the hell!" the senior staff officer barked. "Are you drunk?"

Unsteady on his feet, the utterly abashed Kihara, head bobbing obsequiously, could only respond with a string of yessirs.

Koji summoned a runner and had all hands off duty ordered to battle stations. He unsheathed his saber and laid it on his shoulder.

"Get a move on! Hurry up!" he shouted at the men who came running out of their quarters and the galley, rifle in one hand and helmet in the other, whereupon Kihara likewise began shouting at the men to hurry.

The orders to fall in were hastily given. Part of the unit was to stay behind to guard the compound, and Koizumi was put in command of them. Koji ran out into the street fronting the compound at the head of the rest of the men. Several Chinese farmers gazed blankly at them as they went by.

The exercise went well enough. Kihara, however, bereft of the command of his men, went through the maneuvers at the heels of the senior staff officer, the man's reproaches constantly in his ears. This, of course, delighted Koji. It was decided that the American paratroopers were, in the end, soundly defeated. An hour later Koji brought his mud-caked men back into the compound.

"The actions taken by Lieutenant Obata as leader of his men were quite satisfactory."

The senior staff officer, as he reviewed the exercise, could not criticize Kihara in front of the men, but seemed to do so obliquely by praising Koji and Koizumi to the skies. And he told them they could expect frequent maneuvers like this in the future, that machine guns would also be allotted to the Receiving Station, and that he intended to conduct exercises on close-quarter attacks against the M1 tank soon. He then got into his Cadillac and left.

Kihara was beside himself that night. He dragged Koji and Koizumi into the wardroom to resume drinking where he had left off. He forced saké on them, closed the door, and finally sent his orderly from the room. Whenever the two men made a move to get away, he would shout at them.

"Don't get up! That's an order!"

When they heard the phrase "that's an order" they absurdly faltered, no matter that the saké made them queasy. Kihara had gotten a pistol from somewhere and placed it under the table. Suddenly he invented a ludicrous pretext for beating Koji and Koizumi. Koji sensed real danger. He couldn't get away and he couldn't hit back, nor could Koizumi. The two men were unarmed. Ashamed, they were unable to shout for help, and let the berserk Kihara, shrieking gibberish and laying into them, have at them as he wished. Koji felt the shame of the spineless weakling, as he had when bullied as a student. But even as this thought was going through Koji's mind, Kihara had begun to slap him roundly about the head and cheeks as he ranted.

"Here's the compassion of your detachment C.O.! Accept it, if you will!"

Koji's cheeks were swollen and burning, his ears ringing, his mouth bleeding. Koizumi crouched under the desk to escape Kihara's blows.

"Don't try to get away!" Kihara shouted. "Straighten up! You won't straighten up?!" He kicked Koizumi in his rump. Koizumi staggered to his feet, groaning, only to be hit again.

There was the sound of men jumping up in the senior petty officers' quarters in front of the wardroom and Koji sensed that several men were looking in to see what was happening, but no one came to the doorway. Spewing incoherent babble, Kihara continued to hit away, dividing his blows between the two men on either side of him, every ounce of his long-smoldering resentment concentrated in the flat of his hand. Koji no longer felt any desire to resist. To the contrary, he felt a sense of exhilaration as Kihara worked his will on him. He was numb in both body and spirit, and somewhere in the back of his mind he thought vaguely that Kihara's hand must be hemorrhaging internally, that it must be hurting him.

"I'm gonna go file a charge with the group commander," Kihara finally said. Bellowing brutishly, he kicked open the door and left.

The wardroom was suddenly quiet. Koji and Koizumi exchanged indescribably dispirited glances. Chief Petty Officer Kumai came in from the next room.

"What happened, sir?" he asked, pausing, then: "There's no damn way you can resist a superior officer. Both of you certainly showed self-control in not responding. That one's real wild. You couldn't have asked anyone to intercede for you."

Koji tossed Kihara's damnable pistol on the table. Koizumi held his hand against his cheek as though to cool it. He took out a sheet of tissue paper, wiped the blood off his lips, and spit into the paper.

"The senior staff officer's review of maneuvers did him no good," Kumai observed.

"When things get this bad," said Koji, turning to Koizumi, "there's no need to remain silent anymore."

Koizumi nodded wordlessly.

"You oughta explain everything to the group commander, sir," Kumai said, a change in his tone.

Kihara had run into Lieutenant Commander Funaki's quarters and ranted on for some time. The superior officer calmed him down, and he apparently had passed out and was sleeping it off there. The two young officers went back to their quarters. The next day Koji and Koizumi went together to see Lieutenant Commander Funaki and at last related everything, beginning with the night before, going on to the incident at Kaohsiung with Captain Morii and the matter of the alligator belt and the raincoat. The lieutenant commander, arms crossed, listened to Koji's story, a perplexed, melancholy expression on his face.

"I'll look into it and take the appropriate measures," the senior officer said dully, and the meeting was over.

*　　*　　*

Some days later, in mid-June, they received a message from X Group in Shanghai: *Lieutenant Shinkichi Tsutsumi, to be attached to W Group, is scheduled at the first available opportunity to proceed to duty station.*

A few days later Tsutsumi suddenly called from the airfield to tell Koji he had arrived. Koji went out to the compound gate to nervously wait for the car from the airfield to show up, feeling almost as though he were meeting a girlfriend. He was absolutely delighted that the new man was Tsutsumi. At last he caught sight of a beat-up old truck loaded with people coming down the arrow-straight road, and when it came to a halt at the compound gate, Tsutsumi, his face now almost canine in its gauntness, hopped down from the bed. He carried only his saber and a dirty-looking basket.

"Yo!" he exclaimed.

"What happened to you? You're all skin and bones!" Koji stared in wonder at the bedraggled Tsutsumi, who looked, head to toe, the personification of Tokyo itself. Tsutsumi had wrapped gaiters above a pair of shoes that had seen better days, and he wore a khaki uniform made of a cheap synthetic fabric that had an unpleasant sheen to it. He looked like nothing so much as a sanitation worker.

"First things first. Give me something to eat. Have you an officers' club here?"

"It burned down, but we're starting it up again. We'll get you whatever you like. Get a grip on your appetite," Koji put an arm around Tsutsumi's shoulder and took him into the wardroom.

"'Get a grip on your appetite,' you say? How can I help but be famished? Listen, the situation in Tokyo is terrible!"

Tsutsumi hurriedly tended to the formalities of officially reporting for duty to the group commander and Kihara, then sat down at the table and, like a man on the verge of starvation, began putting away the insipid food brought to him by an orderly. After his fifth bowl of rice even the orderly serving him was grinning.

"Didn't you make up for lost nourishment in Shanghai?" Koji asked, smoking a cigarette.

"Couldn't do it, no way!" laughed Tsutsumi, having apparently eaten his fill at last. "The food went into me like water into parched earth."

They then went up to the veranda on the second floor. Kihara and Koizumi, along with Chief Petty Officer Kumai, were sitting together in the rattan chairs.

"Hi," said Tsutsumi, meeting Koizumi and Kumai for the first time: "Hi, how are you."

He told them he had brought a lot of mail for them from Tokyo, but then immediately began relating how he had been burned out of his quarters in an air raid one night just before he was to leave the city.

"'The heat! The heat! I can't stand the heat!' I was screaming and digging at the ground," Tsutsumi told them, clawing at the air.

"I realized the next morning I was lucky to be alive. You know, I had scratched out a hole in the ground with my fingernails and stuck my nose in it to breathe. I could hear my hair sizzle as it was being singed. It was a sea of flame all around me and I couldn't get away. I really thought I was a goner. That night the Yamanote district was leveled, all in one night. Tokyo is now a vast plain of ashes. And as for food, forget it. Our one miserable helping of boiled barley and rice became the object of the censure and envy of the citizens of Tokyo. Imagine my surprise, gentlemen, when I arrived in Shanghai. On my way to Fleet Headquarters to pay my courtesy visit I passed through town by car and saw bread in the bakeries, hams hanging from racks, chocolate, cigarettes aplenty, mountains of shoes in the shoe stores—with all this how can you know how things are back in Japan?—and I wondered if I'd arrived in the land of make-believe. Of course, later when I went out myself and took a look at the prices, I got another surprise. The bunch at Headquarters talk loftily of stemming the tide of our misfortune with the will of a hundred-million-man suicide corps, then spend their days chasing skirts. Sure, I did some playing around while I was in Yokosuka, but I was outraged. I can't believe middle-aged guys can be so hungry for women."

"Whoa! Whoa! Don't talk about such painful subjects," Kihara interrupted, laughing. "One of these days after you've settled in I'll show you some places that might interest you."

"Really? But the first thing has to be food. I want to fill my belly with honest-to-god food at least once before I die. I want to sleep soundly through at least one night without an air raid. This is what the citizens of Tokyo want now, I tell you. Nobody thinks for a minute we can win. A guy in my class who's been assigned to the Suicide Corps at Kawatana told me he's almost hoping Japan will be defeated before he's sent out. Everyone feels that way."

"Maybe so," Koji muttered. He remembered at some point discussing with Koizumi whether they would go if the call came for volunteers for the Suicide Corps, and now he was relieved to hear this. To Koji and Koizumi, who had left Tokyo close to a year ago, before the air raids had begun, the city that Tsutsumi was now describing sounded like some strange, exotic place.

"Let's say you're on the Chuo line downtown," Tsutsumi went on. "There's nothing for miles, nothing 'til you get out to Asagaya! There's a sign at the Koenji station telling you it's Koenji, otherwise you'd never know it."

"You were lucky to be transferred here now, I'd say," Koji volunteered. "That's even worse than we imagined. Is it really that bad? You're sure you're not exaggerating a little bit?"

"Hell no, I'm not exaggerating! It's just that you guys don't understand. Well, of course you don't understand. It's too unbelievable. But we're thoroughly beaten! If you think we have a chance . . . ," Tsutsumi began, then: "Hey! Take me to the Officers' Club tonight!"

There were not enough rooms, so they decided to put another bed in Koji's quarters. Koji promised to take him to the club, then the two of them returned to Koji's quarters to rearrange the room.

"Kihara's been a real problem," Koji began, filling his friend in on what had happened recently.

"I suspected as much. The Thieving Lieutenant. The word in Tokyo was that you just might be up against it. But I'm surprised you kept quiet all this time. You should've reported him to wherever you report that sort of thing and gotten rid of him."

"Listen, it's not that simple. Besides," Koji said, forcing a smile, "I don't know if my body could stand up to it, even though my fighting spirit is at its peak."

"Let's watch him a little longer, and then I'll make a statement. We ought to take that raincoat from him and send it back to Wada."

"He knew it was risky to keep it, so he sold it off in town. I'm sure of that."

"Oh yeah, let me tell you about Wada," Tsutsumi began. When the Shitaya area burned during an air raid, Tsutsumi said, Wada and his wife Akie worked heroically to keep their house from burning and were finally able to save the old place.

Tsutsumi continued to display an insatiable appetite, both in the unit and at the Officers' Club, for whatever he could get his hands on: meat, eggs, fried noodles, rice, bean-meal gruel. When it came to food, he was by turns wheedling and demanding of the orderlies and the petty officer in charge of the canteen, until it struck Koji that his friend's personality might even have changed a bit. But when Tsutsumi's body was finally able to accept the fact that there was absolutely no shortage of things to eat and had lost the need to consume everything in sight, he managed to develop dengue fever complicated by a virulent intestinal catarrh called Yangtze Diarrhea, and had to be hospitalized.

Meanwhile, Lieutenant Commander Funaki had quietly concluded his investigation of Kihara. He had received an opinion from the legal officer that the man could be imprisoned for what he had done, but it was Funaki's judgment that Kihara should be reassigned and that would be the end of the matter. He queried Shanghai in writing, and soon received a reply stating that X Group could not be expected to accept such an officer. The request was sent on to Special Services Group in Tokyo and they were now waiting for Tokyo to recall him. Lieutenant Commander Funaki said that would take a few days.

It struck Koji as odd that Kihara's miserable behavior would actually allow him to return to Japan. But in any case he was delighted that Kihara would be leaving, and thus waited, together with Koizumi, for that day to come, absolutely determined not to rock the boat in the meantime.

The piglets, ducks, and chicks grew bigger with each passing day. Summer came to Hankow, said to be the third hottest place on earth, and intolerable nights followed one after the other, when one's sweat left a body-sized stain on the bed. Tsutsumi came back to the outfit after some 20 days in the hospital.

One morning in early August, Koji was startled to see on the front page of the *Continental News*, a Japanese-language newspaper published in Hankow, an article headlined *Atomic Bombing of Hiroshima*. Hiroshima had not experienced any air raids worthy of the name, and he had not been worried about his family, but the communique said that "extensive damage has been inflicted." This time, he thought, there was a chance his parents might have been in danger.

They learned more details on the extent of the damage from a top secret message from Imperial Headquarters, almost the same time they got word that the Soviet Union had begun its invasion of Manchuria.

There was a petty officer from Mukden who was always proclaiming excitedly: "Manchuria will be okay, no matter what!" His fervor no doubt came from the religious faith the Japanese in Manchuria had in the very name of the Kwantung Army. If you had a map before you as you listened to the news, however, it was obvious that Soviet troops were advancing with unexpected speed and had swiftly penetrated unexpectedly deep into the colony.

And everyone in Hiroshima must be dead. Koji felt no surge of melancholy or anger, only the sense that what was to happen had happened. His senses were now completely dulled. In fact, the only thing that still worried him was the chance that under the circumstances Kihara's transfer might be cancelled.

The anti-aircraft unit visible to the west of the veranda had recently begun practicing horizontal firing with their four ack-ack guns, notorious for their inaccuracy, so that they could function as anti-tank weapons should the need arise. Things had sunk to depths that would have been unimaginable just a few months ago. Now Koji felt he had to be ready for the worst, and he glumly considered the possibility of dying soon, all too soon, his cheap, store-bought Japanese sword in hand, in the cow pasture that lay under the guns, now lowered to zero angle and shooting off rounds so ineptly.

They had an exercise the night of August 10—they had had several in the past—defending the Receiving Station. Koji was in charge of the defense, Koizumi the offense, and Group Commander Funaki, Kihara, and the recuperating Tsutsumi were the judges. The exercise began at eight and the defenders under Koji, two-thirds of the men off duty, were thoroughly routed. Koizumi had surprised Koji by massing his attacking force at the lotus pond behind the athletic field, a point ten yards across that Koji had left lightly defended, fording across, going under the barbed wire and quickly breaking through the defense. The attackers were covered with mud, hips to shoes.

Their only weapons had been rifles, Japanese swords and one machine gun. Koji doubted the usefulness of this sort of war game in preparing them for the real thing and could not help feeling they were simply playing soldier. Yet when the judges declared the exercise over and the two sides came back together, everyone was in a surprising state of excitement, and after they had bathed together, washing off the mud and sweat, and gathered in the wardroom, they talked loudly of the exercise.

"Boy! We really took a beating!"

"I never thought you'd come from that direction!"

The clock showed it was a little after ten. They were pushing their chopsticks into a nighttime snack of buckwheat noodles when a Nisei—an America-born Japanese—radio-telephone intercept operator came down from the second floor, bowed, and handed a small piece of paper to Koizumi, who was still on duty.

Koizumi stopped eating and silently read it. There was something odd about the expression on his face as he asked the operator something quietly, nodding several times as he listened to the response.

"Sir!" He called out to Lieutenant Commander Funaki and held out the scrap of paper to him. Funaki read it without saying a word. The piece of paper went to Kihara, and from Kihara to Koji.

"Who is this an exchange between?" Funaki asked.

"We don't know, sir," answered the Nisei intercept operator. "It's not an official communication."

Scrawled in pencil were two sentences in English. *Don't get excited. Japan has agreed to an unconditional surrender.*

Koji quietly asked Koizumi what the term "unconditional surrender" meant in Japanese. Koizumi looked quickly in Funaki's direction, then curtly explained. Koji was startled, but this was immediately followed by a profound sense of relief. He was afraid this might show in his face and quickly affected a somber expression. Everyone was silent for a while, each staring into his bowl of noodles.

The intercept operator was told to tell absolutely no one about this and ordered to continue intercepting. As he was going back upstairs another operator, also a Nisei, passed him on the way down, another piece of paper in his hand. Its import was the same. It was apparently a private conversation between soldiers at two American airfields over their radio-telephones.

Hold on to your hat! Japan has agreed to an unconditional surrender. The war is over! If you don't believe me, listen to the 11 o'clock broadcast from San Francisco tonight.

Lieutenant Commander Funaki suddenly turned and faced his men.

"All right, dammit, if this is true we're going off into the hills of China to raise hell as bandits!" He exploded into raucous laughter, but no one said anything in reply.

Lieutenant Koizumi stood up as though he had just remembered something. Then Tsutsumi, Kihara, and CPO Kumai got up. There was no longer any interest in rehashing the exercise or eating noodles. Everyone divided up into their respective units, relieved the men on duty, and took over at the receivers, tuning them to the frequency of what they called the American rumor-mill broadcasts.

As he turned the dial back and forth, the buzzing and squawking and static eventually gave way to crisp Japanese, and over his headset Koji could hear a shortwave broadcast from Hawaii that was being beamed to Japan.

"This is the Voice of America. This is the Voice of America. Ladies and Gentlemen, Japan . . ."

The intonation was curious. Over and over again it informed its listeners that Japan, through the Allied Powers, had made a declaration of intent directed at America which expressed "a willingness to accept the terms of the Potsdam Proclamation." The speaker's pitch-accent when he said "a willingness" struck Koji as singularly odd and he could not get it out of his head. The broadcast abruptly changed to English, reporting that the station was KRHO and that it was broadcasting on 16.5 megacycles. This was followed by a triumphant, heroic-sounding march and the fading in and out peculiar to overseas broadcasts.

Koji tossed aside the headset, passed through the blackout curtains and went out onto the balcony. Tsutsumi stood with his arms folded in the darkness. He rested his hand lightly on Koji's shoulder. He spoke in a whisper, but with conviction.

"Koizumi just told me America will not be easy to deal with, not easy to deal with at all. He was all excited. He's probably right, but when they hear this in Tokyo you can bet everyone will be relieved. 'Just think,' they'll say, 'as of tomorrow no more air raids.' I know exactly how they'll feel. And we'll be able to go home."

Looking toward the barracks, Koji caught sight of a faint glimmer of light whenever the breeze moved the blackout curtains. The men off duty were apparently all asleep. From time to time a frog would croak in the pond. Koji's feelings were mixed and he was not able to respond to what Tsutsumi said.

A charcoal-burning car started up in the garage. Lieutenant Commander Funaki was taking the information to Headquarters.

Ten

Four days earlier and 1800 kilometers away in the city of Hiroshima something extraordinary and incomprehensible had occurred.

Mr. Yashiro, who taught at Hiroshima Senior High School, had been living with his wife in a house in town, having sent his two children to safety in the country. That morning he was scheduled to go to the school at ten, but left home earlier than usual so that he would have time to get a haircut and stop by the bank to renew his certificate of deposit.

The neighborhood shop that he regularly patronized was not open for business and there was a sign on the door which said they faced compulsory evacuation in the near future, so Mr. Yashiro retraced his steps partway and went to a barbershop on a backstreet in the Kamiya District. There were no other customers and the barber was sweeping the floor in his undershirt, but as soon as the teacher entered he took up his clippers and started to work. In thirty minutes Mr. Yashiro had his haircut and a shave as well. He put his military-style fatigue cap on his trim, close-cropped head, put on his glasses, picked up his briefcase and left the shop. He looked at his wristwatch. He still had some time. It would be almost an hour until the bank opened at nine. He had nowhere else to go, so he decided to walk along at a leisurely gait, taking care not to work up a sweat.

The sun this August morning was already casting its harsh rays on the city. There had been an air-raid alert some time earlier, but it had just been cancelled. He could hear, however, the drone of an airplane somewhere high above him. He looked up at the sky, but could see no hint of a plane. In the city everyone calmly walked and worked, and Mr. Yashiro, little concerned about any aircraft, strolled eastward as slowly as possible to kill time—away from what would become the blast epicenter.

He went—describing his route in terms of the streetcar stops—from Aioi Bridge-Gokoku Shrine, the site later determined to be the epicenter, eastward past the main intersection in the Kamiya District, where he had gotten his hair cut, to the Hatcho-bori intersection. The bank was four more stops down the line.

It happened as he was approaching Hatcho-bori, the Fukuya department store building on the corner before him as he walked. He suddenly saw a vivid red barrel-shaped fireball, above him and slightly to his right, descend upon him. A shout of astonishment escaped him and he broke into a run, but instantly something struck him hard on the back and knocked him to the ground.

When he regained consciousness he was, inexplicably, in pitch darkness, imprisoned in something vault-like. Groping in the blackness, he felt all around himself. He was surrounded by rough walls of concrete. He writhed like a worm on a griddle and shouted for help. No matter how loudly he shouted, however, there was no response, none. Was there no one around? Perhaps sounds could not get through to the outside. It seemed to him there was dead silence outside.

He did not know what had happened, but he guessed that he alone had met with a dreadful disaster of some sort. He yelled out dozens of times before finally giving it up as pointless. He hoped that someone would fortuitously dig where he was, but he was fairly certain no one had seen him struck down. That was the problem. If he simply waited he would gradually starve, the air would turn foul, and he would weaken and die. He was overwhelmed with a sense of having left so very many tasks undone: the book he was writing on ancient Japanese prosody, things he must do for his students, the school's Patriotic Corps. But his two children were bigger now, and no doubt his wife could get by somehow. Anyway, there was nothing he could do, he thought, and resigned himself to accepting death where he lay. It was an exceedingly unremarkable feeling, not the least bit colored by a sense of the heroic. After he had made his decision, he was able to relax. He stopped moving about and assumed a comfortable face-down position, letting the strength drain from his body.

He could not see his watch in the total darkness. Ten, maybe twenty minutes passed. Suddenly, listening carefully, he could hear something that sounded like the muted roar of the sea. Mr. Yashiro recalled the great red ball of fire he had seen just before he had been struck down and suspected that a fire had started. The sound seemed both quite distant, somehow obstructed, then, indeed, roaring close by. Would he be roasted alive, the fat dripping from his body? He imagined this with a chill of horror and was now desperate to get free, once again shouting out and contorting his body. Yet with each movement his elbows, shoulders and head thumped futilely against the walls of concrete. He shouted for a while, then quietly lay flat on his stomach again. He now resigned himself to being burned alive and lay, eyes tightly closed, in the darkness.

Yet as he lay face down waiting, absolutely nothing happened. He knew he was gradually losing heart and could only too sharply sense that he was, in fact, conscious, that he apparently still had time, and he began to feel it would be a dreadful waste to simply lie there. Three times his spirits rallied, and he resolved to try to break free as long as he had a breath of life in him.

Mr. Yashiro felt something wedged between himself and the concrete at hip level. He reached down and realized it was his leather briefcase. Groping in the dark, he opened it and took out one by one his savings passbook, his official seal, a notebook, his lunch box, and his pocket knife, all articles familiar to his touch even if he could not see them. He grabbed the knife and threw everything else aside.

He edged forward, crawling on his stomach military-style, calling from time to time for help. He finally managed to move forward two feet or so and stretched out his hand to the wall directly in front of him and felt about. One spot was soft and damp. Earth. He felt a quick thrill of hope.

The earth crumbled as he cut into it with his knife. He thrust his hand into it and much more fell away. After he had hollowed out a hole some five inches deep he saw a tiny white speck. He could not be sure whether it was a patch of white sand or a point of light leaking in, but hope suddenly welled within him. He dug away at the earth furiously, his eyes riveted on the white speck. Dirt filled his mouth, his nose, his ears, and his tongue was coated with grit. He dug his way along doggedly, a handful at a time, throwing the loosened earth back over his shoulder. As he dug on and the hole got bigger, he realized the white speck was definitely a light hole. Very soon a dim, dusk-like light was shining in through it upon him. Mr. Yashiro threw himself into widening the hole in the earth so that he could push himself through it.

By turns he pushed with his hands and gouged out earth with the knife. Finally two boards scissored open before him, and in that instant the bright light of day dazzled his eyes. Mr. Yashiro, mole-like, stuck his face up against the opening. He could not get his head through. He pulled his head back, dug away more earth and was at last able to stick his head through the hole. Now it was his shoulders that were blocked and holding him in. Suddenly, the incredible, pent-up brute force of a creature restrained surged through him. Board, clod, and rock gave way, to be thrust aside by the strength of his arms and shoulders. The momentum of the rush of adrenaline pitched his body out into the open. He pulled his legs out of the hole and stood up. For the first time he felt he was not going to die.

But he was not prepared for the indescribably grotesque scene around him. Every single house within sight had been flattened. A thick, dust-like haze enveloped everything, and the sun shone dully like a red moon. There was nothing moving anywhere. It seemed as though every living thing had been exterminated. The streets were buried under collapsed buildings and rubble, completely confounding his sense of direction. Smoke rose from countless fires, both nearby and in the distance.

As he stared dumbly at the spectacle before him he noticed a man some 20 or 30 meters in front of him shakily get to his feet.

"Hey!" Mr. Yashiro called out, "Which way is east?"

"That way, that way," the man answered. He walked toward Mr. Yashiro, staggering like someone who had had too much to drink.

"What in the world's happened to you?" the teacher asked in astonishment. The man's face was charcoal black and from his naked torso his skin hung down over his hips like a shirt in shreds.

"Damned if I know," the man answered.

"Nobody else around? Your family was able to get away okay?"

"What are you talking about?" he replied. "They're all dead."

Mr. Yashiro could see nothing around them that looked like bodies.

"I can't get my bearings. Which way is east?"

"That way, that way." The man answered without pointing, his arms hanging limply before him like a ghost from an old Japanese play. Then he staggered off.

Mr. Yashiro felt lucky that he was in better shape. Looking up, he saw that the windows of the large department store building directly in front of him had become as dark as caves. He remembered how things had been before when he was walking back from the barber's and was able to regain a general sense of direction.

He realized now that what had happened was in no way his own personal disaster. He knew that first of all he had to return home to see if his wife was safe, then decide whether to go to his school or leave town. As he began walking he suddenly felt cramp-like pains in his back and legs. He reached around and touched his back. His palm came away wet, coated with blood and dirt. His wristwatch crystal was shattered and blood had trickled onto the dial. The hands were stopped at 8:15. He put the watch to his ear and shook it. The hands fluttered to the ground, their job somehow done.

Mr. Yashiro headed in the direction of his house, but when he turned off the main street with the car lines toward where he guessed his house might be, he saw that before him on both sides of the road—if it was the road—fires were burning furiously. He realized there was no way to get through.

He and his wife had earlier decided that in case of an emergency they would take refuge at the home of a colleague, Professor Mori, an English professor who lived at the north end of the city in the Ushita district. Mr. Yashiro knew that if all had gone well she would already have arrived there safely, so he decided he would also go there.

He knew that in fleeing the city he would have to avoid getting downwind of the fires, so he stopped for a moment to determine the direction the wind was blowing. When he ascertained that the wind was coming more or less out of the north and that he was downwind, he started doubling back to return again to the intersection where he had been injured. For the first time he noticed all the charred corpses lying under the rubble around him and at the side of the road.

In front of the old Fukuya building an army officer lay dead, his body riddled with countless shards of glass. He was coatless and wore a pair of brand-new custom-made boots which he had obviously put on for the first time that day. The body of a woman lay close by. She was naked. Her face was a dark red and badly mangled, so it was impossible to guess her age. She had apparently been in her last month of pregnancy, but her baby had prolapsed and lay dead between her thighs.

A huge fire raged to the north where, he guessed, the tax office had stood, and smoke rose high into the sky. He wanted to avoid that street and make his way to Professor Mori's house by cutting across the middle of the Western Drill Grounds, so he circled back behind the collapsed houses. The canal that ran behind the street was full of people packed like sardines in the water they had sought refuge in; some had their heads thrown back, others drooped forward. Their hair was singed to a frizzle and most were dead, though every 20 or 30 feet there would be someone still alive, and—as if by mutual agreement—he or she wordlessly faced Mr. Yashiro, eyes turned up into their sockets. The teacher fled in blind horror, stepping barefoot on roof tiles and boards as he ran. He had lost his hat, shoes and glasses, and had thrown away his briefcase, but, curiously, still clutched his inexpensive knife tightly in his hand.

He found even more bodies when he got to the Western Drill Grounds. They were apparently men from the Second Division, Western Japan. Every single one of them was naked to the waist, his exposed torso blackened. They were shoeless, with only leggings wound round their legs, their burned bodies heaped here and there about the grounds, and in trenches and air-raid shelters as well. From time to time Mr. Yashiro's bare feet would strike a body as he ran.

He cut across the drill grounds and came to the Combined Area Headquarters on the road that led to Hakushima. There were long columns of refugees on the road, an endless flood of people fleeing the city. Some walked along with half-burned shirts hanging in tatters, but worse, women with huge blackened breasts exposed, naked men, nothing covering their loins; the skin of every person in this mass of humanity was the somber red of rotting sausage.

One woman hurried along in the procession, fully clothed in a kimono. A soldier, shirtless, called her to a halt.

"You! Take off those clothes!"

He made her parcel out her kimono and underthings to the naked around her.

"All of you, look sharp!" he shouted, his task completed. He broke into a run in pursuit of the columns of people as though charging the enemy.

Mr. Yashiro joined the procession and began walking. Most of the people let both arms hang limply in front of them. The teacher saw the way they held themselves and the color of their burned, blistered bodies, and knew this was nothing less than a progress of the walking dead.

Near the Hakushima terminus a streetcar stood demolished on the tracks. A man who had apparently been the motorman lay dead on the pavement in front of the car. He appeared to have died in intense pain; the buttons on his fly were undone and the fly was open.

The buildings on the narrow road running from the end of the streetcar line to Tokiwa Bridge were beginning to burn, so the column broke up into scatters of refugees as people ran through the tunnel of flames. It then re-formed as two columns, some evacuees going up the Hakushima levee that lay ahead and others crossing the bridge and heading for the Nigitsu Shrine. Mr. Yashiro hesitated for a moment. He knew that if he got up the embankment and found that the Kanda Bridge beyond it was down, he would not be able to get to Ushita, so he decided the best thing to do was to go over the Tokiwa Bridge, which was still standing. The bridge railing on the north side had been knocked over and into the river and the entire length of the south railing had collapsed onto the bridge.

A middle-aged man of around fifty came scurrying across the bridge from the other side. One of his eyes had been injured and he had obviously taken leave of his senses. Whenever he saw a woman in the column of people coming toward him he would go over to her, joyfully take her by the arm and run his hands over her body.

"Yoshiko! It's you! You made it back all right!"

The woman would be horrified.

"No! Get away!" she would scream, shaking free and running off. For a moment the man would stand there, an expression of disbelief on his face, and then immediately run up to the next woman and give a shout of ineffable joy, as much a sob as a shout: "Yoshiko! It's you!"

His shirt had narrow vertical blue stripes and these were burned through, shredding the shirt into fine strips of cloth. The skin beneath it was likewise scorched in a striped pattern.

In the river, people with burns and other injuries soaked themselves in the water, splashing water on each other's wounds like children at play.

The procession moved eastward over the Tokiwa Bridge to the Sanyo line overpass. A string of black freight cars which had come to a standstill atop the railway embankment had begun smoldering car by car. Going to the right would take Mr. Yashiro to Hiroshima Station and if he went left and passed below Nigitsu Shrine, he would arrive in Ushita. Hordes of survivors, naked and half-naked, poured toward him from the direction of the station. Three buildings in the shrine compound were afire and some of the big pine trees were also burning. Mr. Yashiro tore off a pine branch that had been broken and was hanging from the trunk, and used it as an umbrella to protect himself from firebrands. He quickly passed along the road below the shrine.

He could see a large number of evacuees on the opposite riverbank.

Fires had broken out throughout the Ushita area as well. As the teacher crossed the Futamata levee and advanced along the road which followed the river, he sensed that the severity of the damage was at last lessening somewhat. All the houses had heeled over as though there had been a severe earthquake, and household belongings and roof tiles were strewn everywhere. But in this area, all the houses were at least partially intact.

The teacher went along a street that sloped down from the approach to Kanda Bridge, finally arriving at Professor Mori's home.

There was no sign of anyone in the house. Thinking that his wife might be lying down somewhere, Mr. Yashiro went into the garden and around to the side door and peered into the house. Furniture and fixtures were scattered all about, but there was no one home. From the looks of it, it was not possible to set foot inside the house. The *tatami* mats had been blown up off the floorboards, and desks and cabinets and a great many books had been thrown together in a jumble and he could see dark holes where the floor had been ripped up off the framing.

The teacher came back to the entryway and squatted under a fig tree, his energy drained.

There were rice paddies across the road from the front gate. In the lush, green, bountiful fields the rice plants had been scorched unevenly, forming a pattern of many long stripes, like the rays of the rising sun flag. It struck him as bizarre. He had absolutely no idea what in the world could have caused such a thing. His throat was parched and he wanted water, but once he squatted down numbness infused his body and he lost the energy to get up and go look for it. Dazed, he simply stayed in his crouch.

*　*　*

About the time Mr. Yashiro had been running below Nigitsu Shrine with the pine branch umbrella, the broad white riverbed across the river from him was filling with people. Koji's parents were in that group, watching entranced as the flames burned their way through the houses on the levee. Koji's mother and father knew many of the people on the riverbank by sight, those from the neighborhood, but an unending stream of people they had never seen before, people horribly injured, had made its way down from the levee road to the dry riverbed: beggar-like soldiers in ragged uniforms, students, their whole bodies seared and mangled, mincemeat monstrosities, a blood-drenched woman with red gashes harrowed across her chest. When they found a spot on the riverbed, they would sit down or throw themselves on the ground, saying nothing to those around them; it was as though they were in another world. Only those with the severest wounds made any sound, a continuous moan.

That morning Koji's father, paralyzed on his left side, had, as usual, dragged himself out from the living room to use the chamber pot that had been put out on the veranda. He had clung with his right hand to a rope suspended from the lintel, and, half-squatting, strained.

Koji's mother, waiting for him to finish, was looking at the morning paper. She had on the eyeglasses, as thick as magnifying lenses, that she had been using ever since her operation for cataracts, and was facing the south windows.

An eerie blue-white flash suddenly enveloped the house.

"Oh dear!" She started to get up, but at that instant a typhoon-like wind began blowing through the house. The structure shook and, with the sound of things falling about her in her ears, she was blown to the floor and her glasses were sent flying.

She shouted out to her husband as she lay on the floor: "Father! Father!"

"I'm over here! Over here!" she heard him calling from somewhere.

The wind stopped blowing. Groping, she stood up. Her glasses were gone and her vision was a murky blur. The black summer work smock she had on began smoldering in the sleeves and at the knees. Frantic, she ripped away the burning fabric.

"Father! Father!" she called again, "Where are you?"

"I'm here! I'm over here!"

It was then that she saw him. He had tumbled off the veranda and lay in the garden, unable to get up. The hem of his kimono was still up over his buttocks and he was rolled into a ball like a *daruma* doll.

"Wait. I can't help you by myself. I'll go out front and get someone."

Mrs. Obata took off her burned smock and went to the front of the house in her underwear. A full-length mirror stood in the small six-mat room.

Well, she thought, *the dressing mirror's still standing.* The tea cupboard and tables and shoji doors had been knocked over and there was glass everywhere.

She had been painfully burned at the two places where her dress had smoldered. She didn't understand why the dress had started to burn when she had felt no heat. She daubed spit on the burns.

Out on the road in the front of the house, she saw that houses all over had collapsed, both those on top of the levee and those at the bottom.

Looks like this whole area has been very heavily bombed. The long-pampered terrier of the childless couple next door was barking wildly in its excitement.

Small groups of neighborhood people had come out onto the street. All were suffering from injuries of one kind or another, but when Koji's mother asked for help, several people came into the house, improvised a stretcher from a storm shutter and without a moment's delay carried Koji's father from the garden to the dry riverbed in back of the house.

Koji's father had apparently struck the top of his head when he fell from the veranda. Blood streaked his bald head, but he appeared to be unhurt otherwise, almost lively.

"What the devil was it?" he asked his neighbors as they carried him along on the door.

"Seems like they dropped a bomb close by," responded the man who ran the pawnshop two doors away, "but it looks like the worst is over."

A woman who had come to help brought out one of the wicker baskets that had been stacked on the veranda into the garden and kicked it over the edge of the embankment, safe from the flames.

Koji's parents had stubbornly resisted urgings that they evacuate the city, and they hadn't even sent any of their belongings out of harm's way in the countryside. The old folks firmly believed that one should never hoard anything and that Hiroshima would not come under attack.

"This area is especially safe. If this place should ever burn in an air raid, Japan will be finished anyway."

Beginning this spring, however, it appeared that Japan's medium-sized cities were also being destroyed one by one in fire-raids, and the Obatas had also heard wretched stories of people being burned out of their homes. Finally, several days before, they had decided to gather together some of their clothes and send them for safe-keeping to a farming family outside of town on the next wagon run out. Four or five of these packed baskets and trunks had been stacked up in a corner of the hallway awaiting shipment.

When they got out on the river bed, Mrs. Obata knew that the clothes her husband was wearing, the urine bottle and umbrella she had brought out of the house in the excitement, and the wicker basket lying at the foot of the bank were now all their worldly possessions, but fear thoroughly stifled any desire to go back into the house again to get the other trunks and baskets.

At last the flames reached the woods and buildings on the Shinto shrine grounds on the other side of the river, the freight train immobile on the Sanyo line trestle, and the houses on the levee.

Below the Nigitsu Shrine visible on the opposite shore they could see the procession of blackened humans, naked, their arms hanging limply before them as they made their escape toward Ushita. A huge cloud of smoke rose high above the city, its ineffable menace intensifying slowly, yet relentlessly.

Koji's mother sat motionless on the sand at her husband's side as he lay blankly staring, wide-eyed, into space.

The flames, which had engulfed the homes along the street atop the levee house by house, took an hour to envelop the house Koji was born in. His mother turned her eyes to the river to spare herself the sight.

*   *   *

Chieko's health had worsened again with the onset of the rainy season that year and it had been agreed that she would temporarily be excused from her work at the clothing depot. On the morning of the sixth she left home before eight to submit a doctor's statement to the depot and, at the same time, pay a courtesy call on the officer in charge.

In exchange for slightly exaggerating the seriousness of her chest problem in his written statement, the doctor, a friend of her father who had examined her before, had made her promise that this time she would follow a strict regimen of rest and quiet until she was completely recovered.

Chieko and her parents were all that remained of the Ibuki family in Hiroshima. Her brother Yukio had been transferred from the hospital in Sasebo to Kaohsiung in Taiwan and her younger sister Ikuko had already had a child, and was living in Yokohama.

Chieko also wanted to visit her best friend to tell her that she would not be able to go out for some time. To get to the army's branch clothing depot she would have to take the Ujina line from Hiroshima Station. She knew her friend Tanaka brought her girls'-school students to the Eastern Drill Grounds behind the station every day for labor service. When she got to the station, Chieko checked the train schedule for the time of the next train, then headed toward the drill grounds.

The air-raid siren had sounded an alert as she left the house, but this was a daily occurrence, so she walked along unconcerned, and when she got to the entrance to the Eastern Drill Grounds, the all-clear sounded.

Just as I thought.

Chieko headed for the area below the Toshogu Shrine over at the drill ground's north corner—a good distance—where she expected her friend Tanaka and her troop of schoolgirls to be. She gave a wide berth to a rail siding several tracks wide that the military used. Here and there she could see soldiers on work details of some sort. Atop a hillock at the foot of Toshogu Shrine she could make out the small figures of schoolgirls practicing semaphore signaling in their baggy *mompe* trousers.

The all-clear notwithstanding, a lone B-29 bomber flew westward past clouds high up and directly overhead, the metallic roar of its engines trailing behind it. As she walked along she would now and again look up, head back, and watch it. Suddenly three small parachutes were floating in the sky. That struck her as curious. At that moment there was an urgent change in the sound of the plane's engines. The aircraft sped quickly out of sight, a thin vapor trail following behind it. Then all at once a flash like arcing electric current flared across the sky.

Startled, Chieko dashed toward a large boulder for cover. She heard a dull sound of things giving way and in the same instant was lifted up and slammed down on the huge rock, and her face and arms and legs were peppered all over with something hot and stinging like burning sand.

It was suddenly pitch black all around her and deathly quiet, as though movie film had abruptly broken in its projector. Her baggy black *mompe* had burst into flames at the knees. She immediately ripped them off as she lay there, leaving only her white bloomers. But now she was paralyzed with embarrassment at the thought of being so exposed.

Suddenly she heard a girl wailing nearby. As the darkness around her gradually lifted, visions presented themselves to her: a school girl, her face deathly white and her eyebrows burned away; a soldier, the skin of his face peeling off and dangling in the air like a dust mop turned on end; a woman, her face scorched charcoal black, vomiting blood.

Looking towards the city through the abating darkness, she could see an indistinct column of smoke rising into the air. It quickly swelled into the shape of a gigantic question mark, the middle of which was a vivid crimson, and as this thunderhead-like column billowed upward through the sky, she could see a red ball of fire at its core. The earth below was enshrouded in a sheet of fire, a dust storm, a chaotic commingling of red, ocher and brown.

She could make out individual shouts.

"Help! Help me!"

"Men of squad one! Are you alive? Fall in!"

Nearby she heard a soldier call out absurdly: "Son of a bitch! Those bastards must have figured out we have troops here."

Chieko got to her feet gingerly, testing her footing as she rose.

I must get home immediately.

Her shoes were gone, blown off her feet. Her white blouse was torn, but as she looked at those around her she realized she was in relatively good shape. Her embarrassment vanished when she saw that everyone else was naked.

The dead and dying lay everywhere. One man lay dead in a pool of blood, his eyeballs, blown from their sockets, hanging at least five inches down his face, each the thickness of a thumb. He had bled profusely from the nose and mouth.

As she went on, walking over bodies, she accidentally stepped on a man's leg. He suddenly regained consciousness and called out for help, then without warning grabbed hold of her leg.

"Let go! Let go of me!" she screamed. She shook off his hand and ran on.

Gasoline that had been stockpiled on a platform at the military siding was burning furiously, pouring black smoke high into the sky. The track ties had been lifted up off the ground and were afire, and freight cars were derailed and overturned and enveloped in flames.

As she stood there by tracks twisted like licorice sticks, anxiously looking for an escape route, a man wearing leggings, his face burned, ran under the ties from the other side. He was apparently a soldier.

"Hey! You! What're you doing?" he demanded roughly. "Where're you going? There's no way you can get downtown. Hiroshima's gotta be blown off the map. There's no one to issue orders—nothing. I'm the only one to make it out from Second Division. Just about every-one from the Second to the Western Drill Grounds is dead. Go that way. Over there."

He spread his arms out to turn her back.

Chieko had absolutely no idea what had happened. She obedi-ently did as the soldier told her and began to retrace her steps across the drill grounds, once again working her way through the mass of corpses. She decided if it were not possible to get back home she would look for her friend below Toshogu Shrine and join the people from her school.

The huge mushroom cloud that stood high over the city was gradually changing shape, swelling and growing as it vigorously sucked up smoke from below.

As she walked along, Chieko could not fathom why everyone should be naked, yet there was no doubt that almost all these people running about in confusion had no clothes. While some people had quickly had their wounds treated and bandaged, Chieko saw others whose peeling skin was hanging in shreds all over their bodies, peo-ple injured so badly you could not tell the front of their bodies from the back. It was the bodies of the dead that still wore their scorched clothing.

When she arrived at the area beneath the Toshogu Shrine, she found that some of the injured had gathered to rest on the grassy field and under the trees. She stopped a student and asked her where her friend Tanaka was.

"Miss Tanaka is leading a group of wounded students through the hills to safety in Ushita. She left a little while ago."

Her heart sank. When she told the schoolgirl she was a friend of Miss Tanaka, the girl told her they were about to leave with a teach-er and urged her to evacuate with them. The girl watched Chieko's face as she talked, concern in her eyes.

Chieko, who was standing, felt something warm dripping on her instep. She realized for the first time that she was bleeding.

I must have bruises, burns, and cuts all over me, on my legs, my neck, my face.

Suddenly she felt pain throughout her body. She put her hand to her forehead. Her palm came away sticky with blood.

"My face is injured, isn't it."

"Yes, it's bad," the girl replied, then immediately averted her eyes as though she had said something rude.

Chieko felt the blood drain from her head. She dropped weakly to her knees, then fell to the ground.

Startled, the girl shouted for her teacher to come: "Mr. Kimura! Mr. Kimura! A friend of Miss Tanaka's is here and she's badly hurt!"

The instructor named Kimura came over. The other students gathered around the fallen Chieko, each urging her to flee to safety with the group, but Chieko suddenly felt she had lost both the energy and the will to do so. She forced herself to raise her head in response several times simply because they were obviously concerned about her. She was certainly not capable of keeping pace with anyone who was uninjured.

"I'll stay here," she said softly. "Please go on without me. The fire will not come this far, so I'll be all right. If you see Miss Tanaka in Ushita, please tell her about me. I'm Chieko Ibuki of Kamiyanagi-cho."

They were clearly anxious to be on their way to safety, yet they continued their entreaties, but now Chieko could not even answer. She lay face down on the grass and said nothing. They soon abandoned their attempt to take her with them and, with their teacher in the lead, the group left for the road that would take them through the hills.

Beyond the drill grounds Hiroshima Station burned a bright red. The cloud looming up to the right of the station had grown thinner at its base, and, assuming yet another shape, now had several layers of gigantic mushroom caps slowly boiling out of its peak.

Signs of life, any movement, gradually disappeared from the drill grounds, leaving behind only the bodies of the dead.

Hours passed. As evening drew near the force of the fires in the city seemed, little by little, to spend itself at last. Chieko tossed and turned on the grass, her mind intent on her parents: were they safe? But there was nothing she could do.

She spent the night there on the grass. A dozen or so people who had been unable to flee had somehow drawn together, and now lay next to one another.

On the drill grounds Chieko could see soldiers who had survived pouring gasoline on the corpses that had been brought in and collected in great heaps, a hundred here, two hundred there, in half a dozen places, and setting fire to them. Eventually the stench of the burning flesh was carried by the breeze to where Chieko and the others lay.

An old man, his head shiny bald, lay to her left. They exchanged glances.

"Dreadful!" the man said. "What an atrocity!" Then muttering as though talking to himself: "We must be grateful for having survived." He prayed, invoking the Buddha's name over and over again.

Chieko's sleep that night was fitful and her dreams grotesque. She awoke in the middle of the night and could see large blue fireballs in the direction where the bodies were burning.

*   *   *

Mr. Yashiro had squatted down at the entranceway to Professor Mori's house for a long while. Two hours later the Professor and his wife returned home. The two of them had just finished working in a rescue party directed by a local woman doctor. They were surprised to see Mr. Yashiro waiting for them and immediately set to washing with salt water the wounds that covered his body. They carried a desk out into the street, spread a *futon* over it, and laid Mr. Yashiro on it. Mrs. Mori left again to do more rescue work. Professor Mori went into the house and began putting things back in order so that they could at least get around inside the house.

Toward evening he carried Mr. Yashiro inside. They shared experiences, Mr. Yashiro telling the professor and his wife how he had made his way to the house after he had been injured, and they telling him in turn of the bombing victims in the city they had observed as they worked in the rescue party, and of the schoolgirls

226

who had made their escape through the hills from the Eastern Drill Grounds.

"There's not a scratch on us," said Mrs. Mori, "so even though we do our best to help, I still can't help feeling a little guilty somehow."

The three of them came to the conclusion that the Americans had obviously used a new secret weapon of some sort.

"Some are even saying it's a death ray," said Professor Mori. "There's a blue stain now on the wall of my study from the ink bottle that was on my desk in the opposite corner of the room!"

Mrs. Mori cooked some of the rice she had earlier set aside for special occasions and made salted sesame seed rice balls, putting some of the precious meal aside for Mr. Yashiro's wife, but she did not appear, even after nightfall. They put up the customary mosquito net and the three of them squeezed under it to sleep, but there were practically no mosquitoes flying about that night; perhaps they had been killed off too.

The next day Mr. Yashiro thanked the Moris for their kindness and set off to look for what was left of his own house, forcing himself along, weak from his injuries and fever. When he came to the Hakushima embankment and looked south toward the heart of the city, he was confronted with a burned-out wasteland extending as far as the eye could see. All the trees left standing had been turned to charcoal, bodies lay all about, and those who had survived moved about with animal dullness on the slopes and in holes along the river banks. As he moved closer to the center of the city his nostrils were assailed by the stench of the dead and the oppressive smell of burned-out ruins.

Only steel-reinforced buildings had survived, standing here and there like ancient ruins abandoned in the desert. As he was walking along Mr. Yashiro picked up a hoe that had lost its handle. He estimated the location of his house and began looking for his wife's remains. Everything made of wood had been turned to ash. Rice bowls and glass bottles had melted and fused together into lumps like jelly candy. As he dug about he discovered in one place and another shards of roof tile and the remains of what he recognized as his radio, the sewing machine, and pots and pans. But he found no bone fragments.

As he was searching he heard a woman call to him. Without his noticing it, the housewife from what had been the house next door had come and was standing by him.

"Mr. Yashiro, it's you!" she said, and immediately burst into tears, as though she had been waiting for this moment to cry. She was barefoot and her hair disheveled like a madwoman's. She went on at some length to tell him how her husband was missing and that her five-year-old son had been crushed under falling bricks and when she finally was able to dig him out, the boy—his belly split open and his intestines exposed—had run unsteadily 30 or so feet, then fallen dead.

A bit later she spoke again, suddenly recalling something.

"I met your wife yesterday as she was going out. She said she was going to the neighborhood association for some rations."

Mr. Yashiro threw down his hoe when he heard this, thanked the woman and set off to look for his wife along the streets she always did her shopping on, beginning at the neighborhood association. He then spent a good deal of time searching the area from the high school to the Ujina district, but he found nothing, and returned to the Mori home that evening.

*　*　*

The same morning, on the grass below the Toshogu Shrine, Chieko awoke to the cries of a man asking for water. In the first light of dawn she could see that half of the people who had lain down around her were dead, still, and cold, including the old man who had been saying his prayers the night before.

"Water! Give me water!" pleaded a middle-aged man, his eyes shut tight against the pain. Another middle-aged man, his companion perhaps, stood up unsteadily and went off somewhere, returning with his battered briefcase full of water and dripping as he walked. He gave the groaning man a drink from it.

"Thanks. Thanks." He expressed his gratitude again and again. He quieted down at last after he had finished drinking, and a short while later he died.

The sun rose, and the mountains of white bones where the bodies had been burned the night before looked like fish bones heaped high, yet even from a distance Chieko could see heads and arms and legs the fire had not consumed lying strewn around the mounds.

Chieko's body was racked with pain and she felt an intense lassitude that robbed her of the will to stand, so she stayed where she lay. From time to time someone looking for a relative would peer into her face, then move on. Each time this happened she would try to cover her naked breasts, her hands moving wearily. All was still, as though everything had been exterminated; no insects moved in the grass.

Some time had passed since daybreak. Chieko was wondering if it might not be around noon, when she realized that someone was calling her name.

"Chieko Ibuki! Is Chieko Ibuki here?"

She raised herself up and saw her father shouting out her name as he walked in a half stoop along the road that wandered gently down from where she was lying. She tried to cry out to him, but her voice was too weak. She raised her hand and waved, and this he saw. He came running up the slope.

"Chieko? Are you Chieko?"

In the space of a day her face had darkened and swelled to melon size and her lips were swollen and puffy. Only her eyes and nose were normal, almost lost in the middle of this polished round face of ebony.

"I can't believe you survived!" her father exclaimed. "Well, let's go. We'll evacuate to Kinu's place in Shinjo."

"What about Mother?"

"Your mother is dead."

Her father told her what had happened. Her mother had been pinned under a collapsing lintel, her pelvis and legs crushed, and the flames had reached the house before he could pull her free. Half-mad, he had tried to cut off her legs to get her out, but Mrs. Ibuki urged her husband to flee alone to the village of Shinjo outside the city, to the home of a former maid. He plucked some hair from her head, held her hand for the last time, then made his escape.

As Mr. Yashiro was digging about in the ruins of his house with the handleless hoe, Chieko's father was carrying her to Shinjo. And there on his back she let the tears stream down her blackened cheeks.

Her father, out of breath, had to set her down and rest many times along the way. Each time he would tell her a little more of what had happened since the previous day and ask her questions in turn. A bag filled with bones hung from his waist. Early that morning he had gone to where their house had been and dug out his wife's bones from the burned-out ruins. He had not known what had become of Chieko, and walked about searching for her, asking friends he happened on.

Someone had told him he had just seen Chieko in front of the Red Cross Hospital. That seemed unlikely, but his informant was quite sure it was she, so Mr. Ibuki looked all around the hospital, but to no avail. He then walked over to the clothing depot, where another acquaintance told him he had seen Chieko.

"I saw her yesterday getting on a streetcar at Hatcho-bori."

Mr. Ibuki then realized that his informants were not intentionally talking nonsense, but were obviously confused, and telling him of things they had seen days or weeks before. Taking a dreadfully roundabout way, he at last retraced the route Chieko should have taken, coming to look for her at the Eastern Drill Grounds.

The dead still lay along the roadside, in ditches, everywhere. Chieko and her father saw hunks of flesh, roasted charcoal-black like sides of beef, just torsos, the arms, legs, and heads missing. In the river blistered corpses, bloated as cows, were tied together in rafts of ten or twenty, tethered to the river bank lest they float away.

They went westward over the Tokiwa Bridge. Here and there where the wall along the roadway was still standing, people had written messages to notify family and friends of their fate or where they were intending to seek refuge. In one place the sentence "Haruo and Jiro have moved to Ushita" had been crossed out and another added: "Haruo dead."

Late in the afternoon the two of them at last arrived at the maid Kinu's house in Shinjo. Kinu's family were farmers. The main house, the pigsties, and the chicken coops had all been badly damaged by the force of the blast, but they had been able to get things back into a decent state of repair, and several injured who had come to them for help—relatives perhaps—lay in one room. The leaves on the stand of bamboo at the back of the house were scorched where they faced south.

It was decided that for the time being that the Ibukis, father and daughter, would live with Kinu's family. Chieko complained of pain the first night and did not sleep well, and the next day her suffering was much worse. The oil and mercurochrome applied to her wounds appeared to have no effect and she continued to run a temperature between 102 and 104 degrees. They could see clearly that she was beginning to weaken. Her father brought in his doctor friend, who had been evacuated to the countryside, yet it was obvious that even this doctor, who had come five miles on foot to make the examination, could do little for her. Her father and Kinu nursed her, and were constantly at her bedside, but her condition deteriorated with each passing day. All the symptoms of what would later be called the atomic disease began to manifest themselves: she developed spots over her body, her face didn't regain its normal shape, and she immediately vomited whatever she ate.

A week after the holocaust, when the doctor friend came again to examine her, Chieko's father called him into another room.

"I'm sure absolutely nothing can be done to save her, but what do *you* think, frankly speaking?"

"The nature of this condition differs from that of ordinary burns and external injuries," the doctor began. "This is the first time we've seen anything like it, and diagnosis is difficult. But to be completely honest with you, whatever its nature, Chieko has only a day or two to live. Even if she were to survive longer than that, recovery—barring some kind of miracle—would be out of the question. That's my opinion."

Her father was silent, his arms folded, briefly lost in thought. Then he spoke.

"Well, if she's going to die no matter what is done—I can't stand to see her suffer. I'd like to make it easy for her. I don't suppose I could get an anesthetic from you."

"I've got it ready," the doctor said, choosing his words carefully, "but—and you may think this cowardly of me—it's not possible for me, as a doctor, to inject it and euthanatize your daughter."

"It's all right if I do it, isn't it?"

The doctor did not answer.

Chieko's father, his face ashen, wordlessly drew his friend's satchel to him and took out the syringe and narcotic. His hands were shaking.

When the first injection took effect Chieko's pain-contorted face became tranquil and she fell into a peaceful sleep.

She slept soundly until evening, then suddenly opened her eyes languorously, like a child after a good night's sleep.

"I had a good sleep," she said, seeing her father by her side. Moments later she spoke again. "How odd. Has Koji come home?"

"You want to see Koji?" her father asked, bending over her. Chieko turned her face away from him and nodded.

"Don't worry. Koji will be here soon. So will your brother and Ikuko."

Chieko accepted this and closed her eyes.

"You're not in any pain, are you?" her father asked. She shook her head and opened her eyes.

"Water, please."

Kinu immediately drew some cool water from the well and brought it to her. Kinu was weeping.

Chieko drank half a glass of water.

"It tastes so good," she said, and closed her eyes once more.

Shortly afterward, her father gave her another injection, a large dose. She died.

Two days later the war ended. The news of surrender did not immediately reach everyone in Hiroshima.

*   *   *

Mr. Yashiro also died.

At first the burns over his body simply swelled up, but from about the time he returned home after searching for his wife's remains they began gradually into break down into a mushy ooze, and the next day they were even worse, exhibiting a state of decomposition like a peach that has begun to rot, and they were itchy and painful. Flies would not leave him alone, constantly alighting on his wounds. First-aid stations had been set up in the city, but rumor had it that they had run out of medicine and were daubing red ink on people's wounds instead of mercurochrome.

His hair began to fall out about the time they heard in Hiroshima that the war was over, and his hair loss worsened with each passing day. Two weeks later his hair was coming out in handfuls. And just as he was wondering if he had fallen victim to mere baldness, his gums began to hemorrhage, his upper lip split in the middle, he bled at the back of his throat, and he was afflicted with a persistent, if painless, diarrhea. There was blood in the watery stool.

Mr. Yashiro was nursed by his two children, who had returned from their refuge in the country, Professor Mori, and a cousin from his home village. He died toward the end of September in a hospital on the outskirts of Hiroshima. The doctors said his death was probably due to his having returned to the still-radioactive city on the day after the bombing and walked around all day in his injured state, and not due simply to the injuries themselves. His wife was never found.

Flies plagued the city after the bombing. When the body of one of Koji's cousins was cremated on a river bed—Koji's mother was also there—one of the children suddenly screamed.

"Look! Sister's alive!"

What had actually happened was that the sharp-eyed child had

233

detected masses of maggots squirming deep within the decomposed flesh as they tried to escape the heat of the fire.

If you were injured and walking downtown, the flies would fasten themselves onto you to feed and would relentlessly follow you home, even if you brushed them away or slapped at them.

Koji's mother was also tormented by flies after her burns began to fester. His father had become extremely forgetful. He suffered once more from a small amount of internal bleeding early in the fall, after which he became utterly senile and unable even to pull himself along on his knees.

At the time, the two of them had moved to Ushita and were renting a house that had somehow survived the conflagration. There were holes in the roof and when it rained Mrs. Obata prepared meals with an umbrella in one hand.

When Mrs. Obata was working in the kitchen her husband would often call out loudly for Koji, as though he wanted to talk to his son about something.

"Koji! Koji!"

"Dear," his wife would explain, "Koji went to China and hasn't come back yet. The war is over and demobilization has started, so he'll be home any day now. Let's be patient a little while longer, all right?"

"Of course!" the old man would say, smiling broadly, "it's just like I've been saying. You mustn't worry."

Before long he would call out again.

"Koji! Koji!"

His appetite made an extraordinary recovery, though, and for this reason he was constantly soiling himself. The ailing old man would then weep with his wife as she cleaned him.

"Please," he would say, crying unashamedly like a child, "please put me out of my misery!" His jaw, false teeth gone, quivered uncontrollably.

Koji's mother also worried about getting enough rice.

"Shall I let you in on a big, big secret?" he asked, staring at her with vacant goggle eyes. He told her that five casks of rice were buried amongst the roots of the pine by the back gate. He was furious when she didn't take him seriously. The "back gate" was the gate facing the river bed of the house on the levee they had been burned out of. In his mind, he had never left the old house.

Late one night toward the end of February the following year Koji's father started snoring, a loud, singular snore. Mrs. Obata awoke and turned on the light. When she took his hand in hers he suddenly stopped snoring, tensed his body into an L shape, and breathed deeply, twice. Those were his last breaths.

His body, in a light cotton jacket patched and tattered like something a stage beggar might wear, was placed in a pine coffin.

The hearse, which Mrs. Obata had secured only after considerable effort, was a taxi with its back knocked out, jury-rigged so that a coffin could be slid inside. The wooden coffin, hanging halfway out the back of the taxi, jolted violently as it began its journey to the crematorium: a bitter, nightmarish end to 77 years of life.

Eleven

I t would soon be the second anniversary of the deaths of the Hiroshima bombing victims.

The little suburban trolley taking Koji along the edge of Hiroshima Bay shook impatiently as it ran toward Miyajima at dusk. A year and a half had passed since his demobilization, and it was the second summer since Japan's defeat.

June 17 under the old lunar calendar was the Festival of Court Music at the Itsukushima Shrine outside of Hiroshima and its observance was being revived spectacularly this year. Today, August 3, was the festival day according to the modern calendar. Koji had set off on this outing after he and his friend Ishikawa had decided it would be a fine idea. Ishikawa had had some business in Otake and should be waiting for him on the Miyajima dock.

From the trolley window he could see countless fishing boats, awnings up against the sun, floating sleepily between the shore and the island of Miyajima. He could also see on the bay several freighters riding high in the water, their dirty red-painted bellies exposed.

The summer sun was setting, and in the distance the Ujina breakwater and the shipyard buildings glowed indistinctly through the haze. The islands floating upon the serene blue sea displayed in vivid patterns their red-earth folds and, in outline, their terraced hillside fields, as though each isle had been individually sculpted. A small steamer plying its way to the island, its white hull reflected in its wake, ran on a parallel course with the trolley. The boisterous babble of chatting passengers filled the car. The immediate pain of the atomic bombing was at last beginning to be forgotten, and yet its scars were obvious: the clothes too drab for a gaudy festival, the glassless, boarded-over windows of the houses that flowed past the windows of the trolley, the disfigured faces of several people he could see simply from where he sat.

He gazed at the bay and the stunning light of the sun, dropping through the sky as they went along, and leaned back in his seat, lost in solitary recollection.

*   *   *

He could still hear the sound of the RCA receivers, after having been battered with sledge hammers, being thrown into the turbid, swirling waters of the Yangtze River. On August 15, two years before, all hands had mustered in front of a radio to hear the Emperor's broadcast, delivered in a curious inflection, which came to them through pulsing static, and the officers had explained the meaning of the speech—its import abundantly obvious to Koji almost immediately—to their men, after which the unit was thrown into a panic when they heard that those in communications intelligence, lower ranks included, would be punished as war criminals. All intercept operations were terminated, the antenna masts cut down, and in accordance with a message that came from Headquarters—which they were to "incinerate after receipt"—piles of classified documents burned fiercely in the yard for two days. Half of the receiving equipment was smashed with sledges and thrown into the Yangtze before they eventually realized the war criminal rumor had no basis in reality. Koji fell sick with dengue fever and was in the hospital for some time, and then he was sent to the former Maritime Guards base which had been appropriated for use as a prison camp. When the dust had finally settled after the confusing mechanics of bringing the war to an end, it was the middle of October. The first time he had seen American troops in town he felt an instinctive aversion to their ham-colored skin, and, on the other hand, entertained a good deal of affection for the Chinese soldiers, dressed like beggars, who rode into town wearing straw sandals and carrying old-fashioned oilskin umbrellas. There was no denying he was somehow moved by President Chiang Kai-shek's exhortation to his people to avenge outrages with virtue, not rancor from the past. But what a long conflict it had been.

"*We* didn't lose the war!" wept an army trooper returned from the front, planting himself on the ground in front of the T'aichihwen train station. One day an American soldier shouting "Get off! Get off!" knocked Koji off his bicycle, then robbed him of his belongings at knifepoint. And there was the German couple, exporters, whom he encountered walking along the banks of the Yangtze. Their eyes shone as the man spoke with absolute confidence:

"Germany lost, and now Japan has gone down to defeat. But Germany will rise again. England and America will meet their inevitable downfall!"

The waters of the Yangtze had begun to fall, as they did with the onset of winter, making it difficult for the repatriation ships to navigate upriver; nonetheless the prospect of returning to Japan did not seem quite so far off. In sharp contrast to the year before, the weather all through autumn had been superb, and Koji felt like a man waking from a long dream. The day when he would be freed of all his burdens was fast approaching, and he was struck again and again with the sense that a broad vista of fresh hope lay open before him.

It turned out that he did, after all, find himself with Kihara again, in captivity this time. The staff officers who had called on their men to go *en masse* to a glorious death now dispelled their despair with games of mahjong. The older Special Services officers threw themselves single-mindedly into the pursuit of clothing to have something to take back home in the way of souvenirs. He fell into bleak depression when he looked at the photographs in *Life* magazine and thought of his parents in Hiroshima, sure that not a soul had survived. He tried to transcend this by thinking instead about the mountain of tasks that awaited him when he returned to Japan. Now was certainly the time for him to go back once again to the literary career he had dreamed of ever since his student days.

The defeat confronting him was real enough, yet his heart was filled with a hope which grew, then grew again, expanding almost infinitely within the quotidian fantasies of his restricted life as a POW.

"When I get back to Japan," he once told Tsutsumi and Koizumi, only half in jest, "I'm going to marry a woman of scientific genius, father a son, and have him study nuclear physics."

He was thinking of Chieko when he said this, but he was almost certain Chieko, too, was dead.

In February of the following year he and 800 other naval officers and men left Hankow, part of the first repatriation unit. As the coal scow they had boarded pulled away from the dock, they had a sweeping view of the familiar stone buildings along the riverbank glowing in the morning sun. During the one-week voyage they briefly dropped anchor at Shihhuiyao, stopped at Chiujiang and passed by Anching, Wuhu, and Nanking. They arrived in Shanghai just as Koji's father was breathing his last.

The willow trees along the river had come into leaf and were reflected in the water, which glistened with oil. The Whangpoo river was literally covered with double rows of American LSTs and warships that extended without break to the horizon. Radar antennae rose high above each vessel and the Stars and Stripes flew high. At the upper reaches of the river, where the Cathay Hotel stood, a newly-painted heavy cruiser was calling to a sister ship, its bluish signal light flashing. Popular tunes poured forth in an endless stream from the ship's P.A. system and sailors, their white hats at a jaunty angle, coiled cable at an easygoing pace.

*   *   *

The little trolley glided into the station at Miyajima. The passengers hurriedly surged toward the gate for the ferry and Koji could see the tall Ishikawa in the crowd of people who were waiting.

"Just got here on a Hiroshima-bound train," he said.

"There'll be a boat soon?"

A small ferry operated by a private company was also having a banner day carrying people to the island and had come alongside a jetty next to the railway dock, its engines chugging and its white-painted hull throbbing. A boatman assiduously solicited customers. Gentle waves quietly lapped against the jetty, wetting it only inches above the waterline.

"They've started boarding."

Jostling began in the crowd. The two men were pushed through the ticket gate and out onto the long pier. The sun was starting to set and a cool, soft breeze blew across their faces.

"Wow! Some crowd, eh? Which reminds me, I bet the Ginza and the other places are totally rebuilt by now."

As happens with people who have left Tokyo and settled down in the provinces, Ishikawa had quickly worked the city into the conversation.

Ishikawa had been able to evade military service for years, working in his father's clinic in Hiroshima. In April of the last year of the war, however, he had finally been called up, made a cadet in the medical corps and sent off to the south coast of Shikoku. Ironically, the posting had saved his life, and now he had returned to Hiroshima to begin his own practice. He had lost his wife, whom he had married during the war, his father and mother, and two younger brothers in the bombing. He had always been something of a cynic, but these days he was even more likely to display a cynical condescension toward everything.

When the ferry, jammed with sightseers, left the pier, the two of them went up on deck and sat down on a bench. Ishikawa began telling Koji again about one of his perverse sallies against the career officers in Shikoku who had graduated from the military academy. Ishikawa had been shielded from harm by his status as the sole medical officer in the unit.

"I've already heard that story," protested a laughing Koji, but to no avail.

Ishikawa had pressed Headquarters for maps.

"Since, however, my sole concern is to flee to safety," he had told them, "I'll only need maps of the rear areas."

This, of course, earned him the wrath of the combat officers, but he had a retort for them.

"Perhaps you should consider who will be treating the wounded when the Americans invade."

It was his favorite story. Koji wondered whether such rash talk—it couldn't be called anything else—was commonplace then in units back in Japan proper as well. It also amused him to think that if he and Ishikawa had been in the same unit and not been friends, they might well have fallen to arguing.

The shrine's big red gate looked as though it were floating in the shallow water offshore.

"Have you been to the War Crimes trial in Tokyo?" Ishikawa asked.

"No. I haven't."

"Why not? You've got connections, haven't you? If you ask me, it's absurd that they're not putting the Emperor on trial. But setting that aside, if you went you'd be able to say you'd observed the process that led to the hanging of that bunch, wouldn't you."

"Somehow it depresses me," Koji responded. Digesting what he had read in the newspapers, he couldn't bring himself to accept at face value America's exhortations to "Democracy," the lessons it drew from the war, the War Crimes trials, nor the wholehearted hosannas of support for these things to be found in Japan's press. Even so, he wasn't sure what position he should take.

"It's nothing to me if a guy like Tojo is hanged," he went on. "In fact, we could almost do it ourselves. He should have killed himself when he resigned as Premier. But when you read the accounts of the trials, they make it sound like it was only Japan that did anything wrong. Was it really that simple?"

"Listen, Koji, there's no way around it. It was an awful war. Japan did a lot of incredibly stupid things."

"I guess you're right," Koji conceded. "And we got carried away and became willing accomplices. But Japan's call—however specious —to put an end to America and England's history of aggression in the East, to return Asia to the Asians, was that wrong too? For hundreds of years Western nations have used their guns and ships and sense of racial superiority just to fill their coffers. Did they care that what they were doing was evil? All Japan did was get a late start in the game and make a spectacular mess of it, copying the Western countries, and doing it badly. If imitation is to be put on trial, what about the masters of evil who taught us how to do it? When I was in Hankow, a fellow officer named Koizumi who'd studied in America was forever telling us that America wouldn't be benevolent, that if Japan were occupied it would be picked clean. They talk about atrocities! What do you suppose was the most despicable atrocity of the war?"

Ishikawa laughed. "You haven't changed! You're still working yourself into a sweat about that sort of thing, aren't you. What's the point? The answer is obvious enough, isn't it? We lost. That's all."

They could see silvery fish, pursued by the ferry, flee through the water, their tapered bodies flitting in one direction, then another.

"Then what're we supposed to do?"

"Well, the wise thing, I suppose, is for everyone to get enough to eat. This is the sort of age we live in. You probably think that's mere pragmatism or some such thing. You say you're going to write, but can you do it on an empty stomach? It was okay while your father was alive and you had money coming from Manchuria. Now, if you'll excuse my bluntness, you haven't got a yen to your name."

"Right you are."

"Nothing bothers you, does it," laughed Ishikawa. "You know, it should have sent you reeling. Are you planning to go back to Tokyo?"

"Yeah. In the fall."

The ferry slowly approached the Itsukushima pier, its wake churning. They could see the shrine's great gate in the shallow water to starboard. The passengers had gathered at the gangway exit, giving the boat a slight list.

The ferry came to a stop and the two men left the lighted dock and headed for a narrow street flanked by souvenir shops alive with people.

Koji had ruined his health in Tokyo with his less-than-healthy cooking habits and had returned to Hiroshima in the spring to convalesce for a short while. In a city favored by a warm sun and gentle breezes and fresh fish and vegetables—much cheaper than Tokyo's—he found himself gradually regaining his former vigor. All around him he was also hearing about the experiences people had had in the bombing and he wanted to somehow bring it all together in a reasonably coherent form before he went back to Tokyo again in the fall.

"Of course," Koji said as they walked along, "I understand that it'll probably be difficult to get it published right away if I describe the hideousness of the bombing in too much detail."

"You mean there's no money in it?" answered Ishikawa. "For the life of me, I can't fathom thinking like that. I mean, the bombing is fine enough as a subject, but what's the point of writing if you won't get paid for it? Someone like Ibuki can go back to Osaka and do what he's doing, but that's because, at the very least, the university is guaranteeing his living expenses. You've got nothing like that to back you up, do you? Maybe it's not my place to say you're taking too rosy a view, but if you nonchalantly return to Tokyo thinking like that, your health, which after considerable care is just starting to mend, will break down again in no time. I can still hear something on the right side of your chest, you know. Anyway, my thinking is crystal clear. Money and power. It may not be the very best way to look at it, but, well, just wait a few years. I'll see to it that the three of us, you, me and Ibuki, go skiing again. Listen, if a doctor decides he wants to make money, there's little to stop him. He's like a robber: with people's lives in his hands the money'll come in. And these days there're an awful lot of guys out there who don't care in the least if someone socks it to them. Sometimes it disgusts me, but I've decided not to lose any sleep over it. To use an English word one hears a lot nowadays," Ishikawa concluded with a cheerful laugh, "taking money under the guise of *humanism* is not to be confused with robbery, is it?"

When they came to the end of the street with the souvenir

shops, they turned and took a road lined on one side with stone lanterns which skirted the sea, and walked toward the vermillion-lacquered main shrine building. There was a light in each of the iron lanterns suspended along the galleries between the shrine buildings, and the day's flood tide was so high that the long walkways, with their bends and corners, appeared to be floating in the bay. The pilings supporting the galleries were submerged, and it looked as though the sea might well lap at the walkways, which simply sat, unbolted, on the galleries they linked. The light from the lanterns fell on the water.

The two men were not sure where the festival would begin. They went inside the shrine, but the closeness of the crowd oppressed them, so they went outside again and strolled toward Omoto Park.

A full moon was rising through the branches of the pine grove at another shrine building up on a bluff. A *yashi*, a fly-by-night pitch-man *cum* entertainer, had attracted a crowd with his feats of psychoenergetics. He was bending a fire tong with his thumbs, accompanying himself with rhythmic shouts and much sweating.

Koji and his friend entered a stall selling shaved ice and had some, looking back at the showman from time to time to see what he was up to. Finally it appeared as though something was about to start and people began hurrying over to the main shrine building, so the two men followed the crowd over there.

They took off their shoes, stepped into a corridor and little by little threaded their way through the crowd, getting almost as far as the shrine office. As they were waiting they suddenly heard from the mass of people a flurry of clapping, the sort one hears from supplicants at a shrine. A roofed shrine barge with musicians had apparently arrived in front of the main shrine building, but the crowd blocked their view of this. The galleries in front of them surrounded a square patch of bay, and soon a boat of rowers, chanting lustily, came gliding into the square. The boat was a traditional Japanese-style craft, long and narrow, equipped with seven oars on each side. White paper lanterns with the crest of the Itsukushima Shrine dyed into them had been hoisted high. The young men fell like wheat before a scythe as they threw themselves into each stroke. A bronzed man stood at the stern, legs apart, a baton clenched in his hands, and as he waved it about, the oarsmen, chanting as one, their oarwork crisp, brought the boat smartly around within the square patch of water with ferocious energy. They executed three turns, then rowed the boat over to the gallery to their right. On command, the youths, dressed in white costumes with red sashes, gathered together in the middle of the boat and abruptly fell silent.

*   *   *

He recalled how he had come out on deck after his travel orders had been processed and discovered that the turbidity of the Yangtze was far behind them, and that large blue swells, a sight he had not seen for a year and a half, undulated abeam of the scow.

Japan and its islands were the color of spring. The surrounding waters were a rich dark blue and the crests of the waves white with foam. He gazed intently at the pines that stood along the dark shores of the Goto chain of islands. They landed at Hakata and he immediately returned to the gutted city of Hiroshima. He found to his astonishment that his mother was still alive. And he heard of the horrible deaths of so many people; yet, curiously, he felt no sense of shock. As for Chieko's death, he told himself more than once he had to bear at least some responsibility, but that was only on an intellectual level. It was not actually a great emotional blow to him.

That at least one person, his mother, had survived with only minor burns, and that wheat was starting to shoot skyward, spikes and all, covering every single empty field, on land they said no man could live on for 75 years, these were joys that more than made up for everything else. The aspirations that had seethed within him during his time in the prison camp had not subsided in the least. By the time his elder brother and his wife returned home—they had had the good fortune to be transferred from Hiroshima to Beijing two months before the war ended—Koji had taken care of the returns that had to be filed, estate taxes, overseas assets, and such bothersome and almost endless tasks. He was now able to leave for Tokyo.

When he would go downtown on these business errands he would always go through the charred ruins of Hakushima and take the road that ran along the moat behind Hiroshima Castle. The citadel, which had been called the Carp Castle, had been obliterated. All the ancient structures, the tower, the gates, the keep, were gone without a trace. Only the old stepped stone wall rose in outline against the unavailing sky. Lotuses grew lush in the moat before it, covering the entire surface of the water, and when there was a breeze, the huge, broad leaves rustled and glistened in the sun. He liked, these spring days, to pass along the road by the castle ruins, ruins for which the ancient Chinese phrase 'deserted castle' was inadequate. These ruins were infinitely more bleak.

Before long Koji had entrusted his mother to the care of his elder brother and his wife, who had returned to Japan with a single rucksack between them, and left for Tokyo. Yet even as he looked out from the night train to Tokyo at the fluorescent moth lamps dotting the rice paddies, he was thinking, Japan is going to become a fine country, and he knew he would go back to his work.

When he arrived at Tokyo Station, the very first place he went to was the University of Tokyo to look for Wada in the classrooms. As he climbed to the third floor of Physical Science Building Two, his own footsteps echoed with disagreeable loudness in his ears. Totem poles, primitive pestles, weapons, and all sorts of devices of unfathomable usage festooned the stairway walls in no particular order. A slip of paper on which was written "Human trap, New Guinea" hung from a bizarre contraption that looked like a huge tennis racket minus its strings. An awl protruded from its center.

Pretty damned weird!

Inexplicably happy, Koji knocked on the door.

"Mr. Wada is apparently ill," responded a young man who was rooting about in a box of dust-covered human bones. "Let's see now—his house did survive the fire-bombing."

Koji passed through the campus, encountering a scattering of scruffy, seedy-looking students. He himself shuffled along in filthy, mud-caked shoes. He went to Wada's house in Shitaya, not far away.

Blue undid the latch.

"Good heavens!" she said, recognizing Koji. She ran to him and put an arm around his shoulders.

"How are you? When did you get back?"

"I understand Wada is sick."

"Yes, he is."

"What in the world's wrong with him?"

"Well, he's in the University hospital. It looks like typhus."

"You're kidding! You mean, from lice?"

"You're dreadful! Not so loud. Anyway, come in for a bit."

Koji accepted the invitation and went into the house. He asked if he could wash up and changed out of the now-soiled shirt he had worn on the train. He heard a baby crying. Blue's cheeks flushed lightly.

"You didn't hear about it, did you. I had a baby in December of last year." She brought the warmly bundled infant out from a back room.

"I'd like to see Wada today, if possible," said Koji. "Would that be all right?"

"It should be okay, as long as you yourself are up to it. I'm going to the hospital right now."

Koji left with Blue, who was carrying a basket of food, and returned once again to the campus.

"What's this?" said Wada, looking up from his bed, "You've come back?" His cheeks were hollow and he had a black stubble of a beard. "How was it?" he asked. "Was it rough? How did you get back? I've got the stuff you left with me and letters to give you."

"Don't worry," Koji responded. "That can wait until you get better. What happened? You're okay?"

"Yeah, though at one point I thought I was going to die."

A nurse came in. She handed Wada a thermometer, asked him to take his temperature, and went out again.

247

"We've been through a lot and look where it's got us," said Wada, the thermometer under his arm.

"You don't know what happened to Tanii?"

"We've no way of knowing what the situation in North Korea or the Kuriles is. Tanii's mother used to be youthful and quite pretty, but her hair's all white now."

Blue now came over to the bed, re-arranged the bed covers and began pounding his neck and shoulders lightly with her fists to loosen his muscles.

"Tsutsumi went straight back home, right? Hirokawa is with the Ministry of Education. Ono works at the Japan Travel Bureau. Lieutenant Nakada has got himself a good deal with the Foreign Office—no, I don't think it's the Foreign Office, it's War Crimes Investigations. What gall," laughed Wada weakly, "he was a war criminal if there ever was one!" He seemed exhausted and immediately closed his eyes.

The nurse came in again, took the thermometer and held it up to look at it.

"Your temperature is up a bit," she said, looking at Koji with a hint of reproach in her face.

Koji got up. "I think I've been here long enough today."

His friend nodded from his bed. Through the window they could see that a strong wind was blowing. Blue saw him to the front entrance and he went out into the burned-out streets of Tokyo.

*　　*　　*

The sound of ancient reed pipes and a Shinto flute drifted across the circumscribed square of water. The shrine barge with its complement of stringed instruments, bedecked with lights, was being quietly rowed into the square. It was a ponderously large vessel made of three new, natural-finish traditional Japanese boats assembled side by side in one unit, and had four stands of large paper lanterns, the design of which was a red hexagonal crest dyed onto a white background. A large number of lanterns with the crest of the shrine hung from the gunwales as well. Koji could see in the dim light within the cabin atop the boat the aqua *hakama* and black ceremonial caps of the white-robed Shinto priests as they played their instruments. Steersmen stood at the bow and stern noiselessly dipping their poles into the water.

"The piece they are now playing is *Gakkan'en*," someone from the shrine office announced to the crowd of sightseers.

"I'm not sure I follow this," said Ishikawa, clearly bored. "You want to watch it some more?"

"Don't you think it's pretty? Let's stay a while longer."

On the bow of the music barge, fires burned in iron caldrons suspended over the water on both sides and the steersmen from time to time would scoop up sea water and sprinkle it on the gunwales, apparently to keep the boat from scorching. As the fire died down, more wood would be thrown on it, showering sparks over the water. The wood smoldered for a while, giving off white smoke, but soon burst into flames, casting a red glow on everything around it.

The music barge, as had the boat of rowers before it, made three circuits, albeit leisurely ones, of the square of water, to the accompaniment of Shinto dancing and music. Then, bringing the bow around, the steersmen began to ease the barge out into deep water. A flurry of prayer claps erupted again in the crowd. The commotion created faint stripe patterns on the surface of the water, and these, in turn, slowly turned into broad ripples which spread out in pursuit of the music barge as it headed out toward the offing.

*   *   *

Yi's house had been a god-awful shack.

Koji had begun his new life in Tokyo, getting a small, four-and-a-half mat room in the house for very little rent from Yi, a Korean who had graduated from Waseda University twenty plus years before and had remained in Japan—he was now head of a small, struggling company—on the condition that he, Koji, leave when Yi's wife and children returned from where they had been evacuated to during the war. Strings of shriveled red peppers, used facial tissue, and chipped rice bowls darkly encrusted with uneaten rice lay all about the house. Yi hardly ever went near the place except to sleep, and it seemed to Koji more a lair for wild animals than humans. It was so filthy that when he took a duster to the shoji screens with their torn rice paper and the half-inch rolls of dust on their frames, the paper on every piece of framing he touched gave way, wraith-like, under the duster. Before winter arrived he was forced to paper over the shoji with newspapers as a stratagem to keep out the wind.

It gradually dawned on Koji what it meant for Japan to have lost the war and for him to have been deprived of the wealth of his family at a single stroke. Since Yi tended never to be around, Koji was able to sleep and write whenever he wanted, yet in spite of his considerable effort, the novel simply did not come together as he intended it should. If he pumped the rusted, creaking well pump handle thirty or forty times, he would be rewarded with a dribble of orange water. He had cooked his meals in that water, using a navy mess kit. He was always hungry and thought of nothing but food. He gradually found he no longer knew whether he lived for his work, or if it had become more important to get food in the house and a little money, and thereby be able to eat two meals a day.

*   *   *

Suddenly the young men, now wearing *happi* coat-like costumes with a red design on the back, once again moved the rowing boat away from the gallery. They rowed the short distance between the square patch of water where the music barge had been to the gallery on the opposite side, where they left the boat *en masse* and headed for the main shrine building. A little while later they came roaring out of the shrine, shouting and weaving wildly, a huge sacred *sakaki* tree on their shoulders, tramping noisily across a walkway. The youths then jumped into the rowing boat with the big *sakaki* tree, cascading into the vessel like a human avalanche.

"Hey! We did it! We did it!" they shouted happily to one another.

Taking up their positions in the boat once again, the youths, attired in black leggings and white *tabi* socks, chanted in unison as they headed the boat out into the deeper water off shore.

The hour was quite late now and the festival appeared to be winding down. The crowd was beginning to disperse, but Koji and Ishikawa also encountered people who were staking out places in the galleries, preparing to spend the night there. The tide was ebbing gradually, and the foundation pilings could be seen above the water. The two men, with a shared sense of melancholy, began walking along the gallery toward the exit. The music barge once more came into the square body of water. This time, however, no music was to be heard. There was no one inside the cabin, and the fire in the caldrons had almost died out. The only sound was the near-silent punting of the steersmen as they pushed their poles into the water.

They decided to wait for daybreak stretched out on the red blankets of a nearby tea stall. Koji remembered how many years before his father had brought him to see this same festival. He had completely forgotten this until just now, when he had seen people sprawled out on the galleries, and it had suddenly come back to him. He had been in the third or fourth grade, and he recalled that on the way home his father had bought him a tangram in the shape of an airplane in a souvenir shop. It must have been the following year that the Manchurian Incident took place.

"Really, when you think about it," he said absently, "I grew up in the midst of war—it's been going on ever since I was a kid."

Ishikawa was exhausted, his eyelids heavy with fatigue.

"Huh? Oh, yeah," he answered half-heartedly. He stretched out on the blanket-covered bench and before long had drifted off to sleep and was snoring.

*   *   *

A half year of cooking for himself in Tokyo had completely shaken his self-confidence. His 150-pound body had begun to waste away before his eyes, and when he caught cold it would worsen and he would get feverish. No matter how gently he spread out the *futon* in the confined 4-and-1/2-mat room, clouds of dust would billow up to irritate his throat. Little by little, both his will and the sense of self-worth that he had harbored when he was repatriated from China had been eroded away, leaving him despairing at his faintheartedness.

His friend Ibuki, who had returned to his old job at the Institute of Microbiological Research in Osaka when he had been repatriated, came to Tokyo to attend a conference in February. Koji had begun to be troubled by coughing and a fever a month earlier. It had been almost five years since they had seen each other. Ibuki took one look at Koji and immediately took him, willy-nilly, to the Tokyo University hospital to see an acquaintance in internal medicine. After X-raying his chest and asking him about his lifestyle, the doctor gave him his prognosis.

"Can you go back home and do nothing but rest for the next six months or so? If you don't, you'll only get worse, living like you do. It looks like pulmonary infiltration in its earliest stage. You're young, and if you live a normal, well-ordered life for a while, you'll mend right away. If you have an appetite, you don't need any medicine or special treatment. And if you decide to have your portrait taken, forget your face. Have them take an X-ray of your chest instead. And butter, milk, eggs, fresh vegetables, clean air. That's what it amounts to."

The doctor spun his swivel chair back to his desk and, ignoring Koji, began writing something.

Koji wondered how he was going to get hold of butter, milk, and eggs. He wordlessly bowed his farewell.

They left the hospital. As they walked along Ibuki repeatedly assured Koji he had nothing to worry about, and urged him to return to Hiroshima. Neither of them said anything about Chieko. Instead, Ibuki earnestly attempted to explain the research he was currently doing.

"You know," he said, "you need beef and sugar to cultivate bacteria. In the lab, at least, germs are eating much better fare than people these days."

Most of his talk about biochemistry was lost on Koji, but he felt a twinge of envy as he listened to his self-absorbed friend talk of his work with such zeal.

After he and Ibuki parted company, Koji resolved to once again recover his health and spirits. Several days later he packed his things and went back to his mother's home in Hiroshima.

*   *   *

Yet recovering the spirit, just how does one go about doing that? Over the half year he had regained his health, but what had he done in terms of his emotions? Had he been able to prepare himself mentally to go back to Tokyo in the fall, taking with him what he had written, which, as Ishikawa had pointed out, would earn him nothing? Their efforts in the war, were they, all of them, simply criminal blunders? If despicable things had really been done, what were they?

Only one thing finally was beginning to make itself apparent to Koji: a feeling of indignation against what appeared to be several ill-defined forces attempting to quietly change the explosion of the bomb—a bomb that had killed Mr. Yashiro and killed Chieko and slaughtered a quarter million people—into a gay, festive occasion, a godsend that had brought peace.

Koji thought a long while about this as he lay next to Ishikawa, who had dropped off to sleep, but soon he, too, began to doze off, the tormenting mosquitoes notwithstanding. And when he awoke, the early summer morning was beginning to dawn.

Ishikawa was also awake. Both men were exhausted, their bodies leaden, no doubt because they had been exposed to the dew of the night. They stood up, their faces listless, and, having decided to take the first ferry, began walking slowly toward the wharf. In the early light they caught clear glimpses of dirty tea stalls, empty soda bottles lying all about, discarded paper, and the figures of people still asleep on the ground.

The channel, too, was still asleep, wrapped in the morning mist. Lights which had survived the dawn along the shore and in moored boats began to go out. Wholesalers carrying canned goods, middle-school students on their way to school in Hiroshima, and a small number of people returning home from the festival came aboard with Koji and Ishikawa. Neither man said much now, but the students were bursting with energy and scampered about the deck like puppies.

The two men crossed the channel, over which lay a faint haze, waited briefly at Miyajimaguchi station, and returned to Hiroshima on the train.

Hatsukaichi, Itsukaichi, Kai. They could see farmers already at work in the rice paddies.

Two days later, August 6, would be the second anniversary of the atomic bombing. This year the city and the newspapers were sponsoring various events in commemoration, so when Koji and his friend arrived at the train station and went out front, they found workmen in the square putting the finishing touches on a large arch decorated with cryptomeria leaves. Written in bold strokes on the supporting pillars of the arch were the words *Festival in Celebration of Peace.*

Festival in Celebration of Peace. He turned the phrase over and over again in his mind.

Ibuki would be coming down from Osaka on the 13th, the anniversary of Chieko's death. Koji promised Ishikawa the three of them would get together then, and the two men parted in front of the arch.

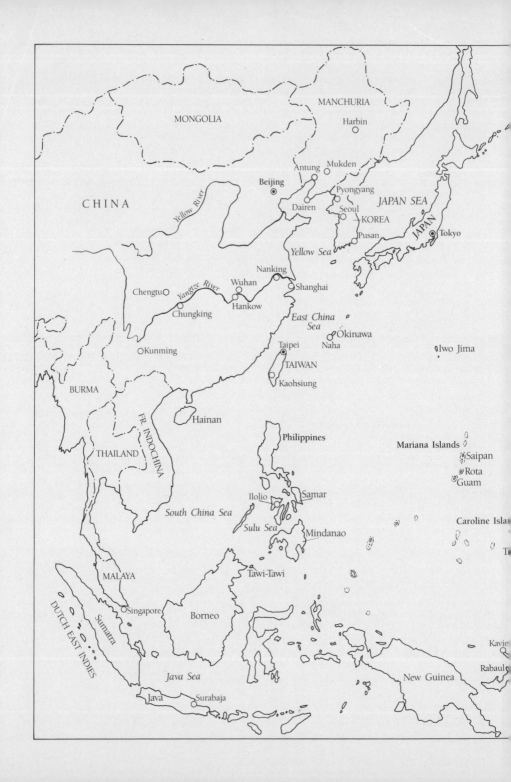